Hello Dear Reader,
   Get ready: the book
   is about to begin...

So who is Robin Cooper?

Robin Cooper is the inventor of the raspberry razor ('the razor that shaves off the tiny hairs from raspberries') and the colour greem. His first two books, *The Timewaster Letters* and *Return of the Timewaster Letters* were both huge bestsellers.

Robin Cooper might also be the pseudonym for Robert Popper. Robert is a writer and television producer, the co-creator and co-star of BBC2's award-winning comedy series *Look Around You* and producer of Channel 4's award-winning *Peep Show*.

www.robincooper.co.uk

4) Dropped hammer on ankle (my fault).
5) Trod in bucket of water (Tony's fault).
6) Sprained it whilst asleep (nightmare about the Olympics).

After waiting five hours in Accident and Emergency, during which time I saw a man in a neck brace trying to bite a nurse, we returned home. Rita is on crutches again.

Poor Rita. Still, managed to get through the day without having our 'discussion' . . .

Sunday January 2nd

Got up super early today, and after a breakfast of cereal, eggs, some more cereal and some more eggs, I wrote out my New Year's resolutions. It's a day late, but hopefully it shouldn't matter as I don't think I've changed that much in the past 24 hours!

Robin Cooper's (Official) 10 New Year's resolutions:

1. Start writing a diary (can tick that one off now!).
2. Stop writing so many letters.
3. Become a world-renowned (or at least locally-renowned) inventor.
4. Learn to whistle.
5. Tidy up shed.
6. Cut down on toffees (the eating of).
7. Visit Mother more.
8. Get Tony to stop using my shed as a drinking den (NB: URGENT).
9. Rectify employment situation.
10. Sort out Rita's wretched ankle problem FOR ONCE AND FOR ALL!

After my resolvements, I helped Rita wash, which was a bit of an ordeal (crutches slipping in shower), then did crossword. Have no idea what 'Greek hat face' is, but it seemed to fit (5, 3, 4).

4

Saturday January 1st

Rita fell down the stairs at twenty-two minutes past midnight on New Year's Day.

I had hoped for a better start to my diary – perhaps a poem glorifying the act of diarying, or a quote from a famous diarist, such as Shakespeare ('Wroteth another play today . . .'), but writing a diary is all about recording what actually happens. And sadly at 12:22, what actually happened was Rita falling down the stairs.

I was in the loft at the time, putting the finishing touches to my anti-bird device. Recently we've been having a lot of problems with pigeons and nesting birds (sparrows, pea-havens etc.) who've been making their home amongst the rafters.

My 'Bird Beddie' is designed to lure the winged beasts into a sort of holding pen. It's basically a mini tent made from an old dressing gown, a few bits of clothing and some cricket stumps. Once inside, the bird triggers a tape recorder, which plays a cassette of my friend, Tony Sutton, whistling some lullabies. The theory is that the bird, subdued by the gentle melodies, falls into a deep sleep, and all I have to do is simply remove it and release it into the wild.

That's the theory at least. In practice, the tent had collapsed and a rather chubby wood-pigeon was using a pair of my underpants as its nest.

When I heard the crash from below, I hurried downstairs to find Rita lying on her back, clutching her ankle.

'You'd better get the car,' she said. 'I've done it again.'

Rita and her ankle have never got on. Last year we made a succession of ankle-related visits to the hospital:

1) Fell down stairs (× 2).
2) Foot caught in seatbelt when getting out of car. Fell out of car.
3) Foot caught in seatbelt when getting into car. Fell into car, then out of car.

3

January

SPHERE

First published in Great Britain in 2007 by Sphere

Copyright © Robert Popper, 2007

Design of all letters, and features on pp. 71, 103, 107, 168, 243, 259
and 317 © Victorian Speedboat, 2007

The moral right of the author has been asserted.

A CIP catalogue record for this book
is available from the British Library.

ISBN 978-1-84744-042-6

Typeset in Melior by M Rules
Printed and bound in Great Britain by
Clays Ltd, St Ives

Sphere
An imprint of
Little, Brown Book Group
Brettenham House
Lancaster Place
London WC2E 7EN

A Member of the Hachette Livre Group of Companies

www.littlebrown.co.uk

The Timewaster Diaries

A Year in the Life of

ROBIN COOPER

sphere

In the afternoon Tony popped round – without Susan as usual – to wish us a happy New Year. He brought flowers for Rita (which looked suspiciously like the ones from Mr Alfonso's window box next door) and a can of ale for me. Since I do not drink ale (a fact Tony is only too well aware), he said, 'Oh I never knew that, Robin. Sorry about that, mate,' then finished it in one gulp.

The cheek!

Still haven't heard from Michael. It's been nearly a month now. Was feeling a little melancholy so went into his bedroom and sat down. Rita knocked on the door and joined me. I could see that she was also feeling sad so I put my arm around her, and together we remained there for about half an hour, looking out into our son's room.

It's funny – I'd never realized just how many photographs Michael has of his best friend Simon. I can't imagine myself having a framed photograph of Tony right by my bed, but I guess that's the younger generation for you!

In the evening I popped into the loft to check on the 'Bird Beddie' situation. Wood-pigeon was now using my dressing gown as a blanket, and lying underneath it as if he was actually in bed! Tried to retrieve it but received a nasty nip. If my invention is to take off – and I'm SURE it will – I will have to make a few refinements.

Monday January 3rd – Bank Holiday

Wrote a joke today. Was particularly pleased with it because it's a topical joke (apparently they're the hardest to write because of their topical nature):

> I say I say I say, do you know why they call it a 'bank holiday'?
> – Yes, because the banks are on holiday.
> I say I say I say, but do you know why the banks are on holiday?

– Yes, because the bank workers need a rest.
I say I say I say, but do you know why the bank workers
need a rest?
– No, I don't.
I say I say I say, because this joke has worn them out!

Read it out to Rita, who seemed to laugh (she insisted on putting her glasses on first so she could 'listen better'), but I'm not sure she got it, as she never really 'gets' jokes. When I asked her why she was laughing, she replied in the usual way, 'Because it's a joke'.

Afterwards I called Tony and treated him to a live performance. When I finished there was silence, and then Tony said, 'Could you repeat the joke please, Robin?'
    I retold the joke.
    'Once more.'
    This I did.
    After my third performance there was a very long pause indeed. I waited nervously. Suddenly Tony exploded in fits of laughter.

'That is the funniest joke I've ever heard in my life!' he said, coughing and spluttering into the phone. 'Tell me it again!'

Am going to send it into the local paper. They're running a joke competition at the moment ('Local Follies'), and this week's prize is a mini snooker table (plus ten cartons of washing powder). If Tony's reaction is anything to go by, I shall be mini snookering in no time at all.

I wish myself luck!

Tuesday January 4th

I am writing this tucked up in bed, while Rita is hobbling around the kitchen, putting the dishes away (and making a right old racket, I should add!), but I just wanted to let you know,

Dear Diary, how much I've been enjoying writing 'pon thy hallowed pages.

I have never written a diary before. I've written IN diaries before (i.e. Wed 9:30 dentist; Tues 4:30 plumber; Monday 2:00 Mr Camber re pigeon infestation etc.) but never written A diary, i.e. recorded my dos and don'ts in a daily fashion.

So, Dear Diary, let's drink to our glorious partnership. A partnership that will last a thousand years!

Hoorah!

Thursday January 6th

'Robin, what are you going to do about a job?'

Our 'discussion' has begun . . .

Rita finally confronted me about my 'misdemeanour' at the end of last year, and now there's a terrible atmosphere in the house.

I told her I regretted losing my job, but that working in the customer complaints department for a company that manufactured magnets was never going to propel the Coopers into the 'super league'. This only seemed to make things worse, though, as Rita replied, 'Thanks to your letters, we're now in the bottom division.'

She's right, I suppose. If I hadn't written all of those letters on company time or, more specifically, got caught writing all those letters on company time, then I'd be on the bus to and from work right now. Instead I find myself neither on the bus nor in work.

I tried to explain – as I have done so many times – that each letter was a potential goldmine, and that if just one of my ideas had been taken up – just ONE – we would both be living like Sir and Siress Richard Branson.

Such is the penalty one must pay as an inventor.

'Well you better hurry up and invent £500,' said Rita. 'You owe them that for the stamps.' And with that, she stormed (well, limped) out of the room.

Friday January 7th

Felt positively negative about everything today. I've really let myself down. Worse still, I've let Rita down. In fact, I'd even go so far as to say I've besmirched the Cooper name itself. I have become a besmircher, and no one likes a besmircher . . .

I have promised Rita that I will redeem myself and find a new job. I told her that I knew it was going to be hard, as I'm not as young as I used to be (although younger than I will be!) but that everything was going to be fine, as I still had a lot to offer – even at 52½.

With that in mind, I went into the shed and wrote out the following list:

What I (Robin Cooper) have to offer (at age 52½):

1) Myself (that goes without saying!).
2) I am punctual.
3) I am polite (I will always open a door for a lady, and close it for a gentleman).
4) Am very good with numbers (i.e. pi, which is roughly 3.2).
5a) I have experience working with others.
5b) BUT can also work on my own (i.e. in shed).
6) Can operate calculator and telephone (and both at same time).

After a while I grew a little tired, and so lay down on the floor with my head propped up against a soft bag of manure. Unfortunately I must have dozed off, because when Rita found me it was already 7pm. I'd been asleep for 6 hours! She was not happy, and wouldn't even let me have third helpings of potatoes at dinner.

Saturday January 8th

Wood-pigeon in loft still using dressing gown as bed. Could have sworn I heard it snoring today. Still has a nasty temper – and bite! Have named my winged nemesis 'Smithy', after the cartoon character 'Smithy Woodpecker'.

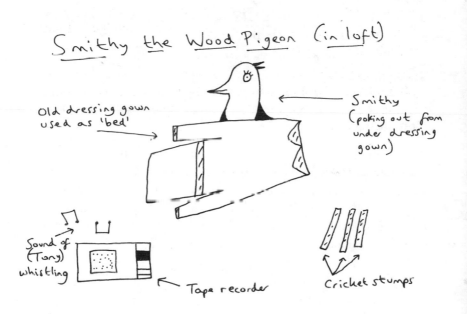

Smithy the Wood Pigeon (in loft)

Old dressing gown used as 'bed'

Smithy (poking out from under dressing gown)

Sound of (Tony) whistling

Tape recorder

Cricket stumps

Sunday January 9th

Oh hark! Hoorah! Michael finally phoned today.

Michael's now in Sydney (in Australia) and working part-time for a big company. Since it's a law firm, however, he said he couldn't give us his office number yet 'for legal reasons' and that his Australian mobile phone didn't connect to British ones 'because of the distance', but he was well, his friend Simon was well, and he was having a terrific year.

I can't tell you, Dear Diary, just how happy I was to hear my dear son's voice (well, I can tell you because I'm supposed to tell you everything – that's the nature of this human-diary relationship!). Anyway, I was beaming, and so was Rita – despite her hobble-ments.

In the evening, Rita's sister Linda popped round, and I opened a bottle of 'fizzy' (i.e. wine with fizzy bubbles in it) and we all toasted Michael's good health. Linda – who had earlier consulted an astrological book free with a lady's magazine – said that she was sure this was going to be a terrific year for the Coopers.

And why not . . .?!

Monday January 10th

Rita was back at work today, but as her ankle is still rather del-icate (she can't even wear a sock), I gave her a lift in. As usual Rita accused me of going too slowly ('you're not a driving instructor any more' etc.), and this soon escalated into an even bigger argument about my work situation, i.e. my non-work sit-uation. Oh alas . . .

After lunch (butter sandwiches – my favourite!) I put on my jacket, wrapped my scarf around me, and with a pocketful of trusty toffees, walked round to the job centre. Nay, it was time to officially seek gainful employment.

When I arrived, I stood outside, took a deep breath, waited a moment, took another deep breath, waited another moment, had a toffee, then entered.

I haven't been into a job centre for over 20 years,* but apart from a few more computers, it was pretty much the same: i.e. lots of men coughing. Took a couple of pamphlets, had a bit of a cough, came home and sat in the shed.

Bed at 11:11 (i.e. all the '11's!).

(Hello Dear Diary, this is my first footnote. Hoorah!) When I last visited a job centre, I was a printer's assistant, or, rather, former printer's assistant, who had fallen on hard times as a result of an 'incident'. The incident being somebody (well, me) accidentally leaving a tap running in the printworks overnight, causing all the machines to be destroyed, and a river of blue ink to flow into the carpet showroom next door, ruining the carpets – and my plans of becoming a printer.

Tuesday January 11th

Went to Mother's this evening. Brought her some grapes (seedless), and her beloved Reader's Digest magazine (also seedless!). This month's issue had an article all about 'ghost barges'. Apparently sightings are quite common, although I've certainly never seen one.

'Your hair looks . . . nice,' said Rita, as soon as we walked in – more out of shock than politeness, I think.

Mother's hair was completely blonde.

'Thank you dear,' said Mother, 'Mr Lawrence has given me a more natural look this week.'

Rita and I exchanged glances.

As ever, Mother's television set was on at full blast in the living room. In fact, it was so loud, that it caused her collection of mini glass bells (86), and mini china bells (64), to tinkle all around the room. What a tinkling!

Today she was watching a programme all about DIY. 'Robin, dear,' she said, 'doesn't that handsome man with the hammer remind you of your father?'

I think Mother's eyesight must be going the same way as her hearing: I don't remember Father being Chinese!

Wednesday January 12th

Have just realized that there's no such thing as 'Smithy' Woodpecker. It's 'Woodsy' Woodpecker. Silly me! I suppose 'Woodsy' is a more appropriate name for a wood-pigeon, but I'm sort of used to the name Smithy now – so Smithy it is.

Have to admit, I've also grown rather fond of the bird, so I've decided to let him carry on snoozing (and snoring) in peace. Haven't dared tell Rita what's going on, though. She's never really liked birds (since she was attacked by that jay), and I'm sure she'd insist I had it removed, or worse – de-beaked.

Thursday January 12th

Alas, I won't be playing mini snooker . . .

My joke didn't win the 'Local Follies' competition.

I was so disappointed, that I couldn't eat a thing for breakfast (although in the end I did manage to get down a couple of boiled eggs, a few pieces of toast and some cereal).

As an unbiased onlooker, I can safely say that my joke was far superior to that of the victor's. It was sharper, wittier and – most importantly – topical (which is the hardest type of joke to write, apparently). Here – and it pains me to write this – is the winning joke (by a 'Miss Lisa Bradley'):

> *What time is it when an elephant steps on your car?*
> *– Time to buy a new car!*

Now what's so funny about that, Miss Bradley?!

I am going to send a letter to the judges. I shall get to the bottom of this.

Friday January 14th

Tony popped round during his lunch break today, and when I told him the bad news about my joke, he reacted very strongly, shouting that it was all 'a rotten fix'. He even called the judges 'a bunch of crooked bast**ds!' and threw his can of Pennyfeather's ale against the wall. He was very upset. I think he was really looking forward to playing mini snooker with me.

Later, when Tony had calmed down (another can of Pennyfeather's), I mentioned that I was writing a diary.

'Can I read it?' he said
  'No, of course not,' I replied, 'it's private'.
  'Oh. Is it a sexy diary?' he asked.
  'Certainly not,' I said.
  'Why don't you put some sexy bits in it?'
  'Why would I want to do that?' I asked.
  'So that I can read it!' he replied, laughing so hard, that he actually swallowed his cigarette and burnt his throat.

Robin Cooper
Brondesbury Villas
London

Judges of the 'Local Follies' (Joke) Competition
The Brent Herald Local Newspaper
Victory House
2-9 Lyndhurst Road
London NW4

15th January

Dear Judges,

What is going on (with the situation I am about to describe below)?

Last week I formally and officially entered my joke into your 'Local Follies' joke competition, fully expecting to win (it was very good), and yet it was not deemed fit for victory.

How on earth a riddle about a clumsy elephant could beat one (mine) about a national and ROYALLY APPOINTED British holiday is a mystery to me.

I beg you to reconsider.

Best wishes,

Robin Cooper

Robin Cooper

P.S. I do not mind if you've already given away the ten packets of washing powder, but I was hoping for the mini snooker table. My friend, Tony Sutton, and I had planned a (mini) mini snooker tournament and were looking forward to some local press coverage. Come on – just think of the sales…!

Sunday January 16th

Phoned Tony to read him my (excellent) letter but had to speak to him via Susan because of his burnt throat. Could tell that they'd had another row by the way she kept calling him 'pig'.

Such is love . . .

Monday January 17th

Started using a new toothpaste today, called 'Mentathon 3000'. It's particularly minty. In fact, no sooner had my toothbrush entered my mouth, than I was overcome with a feeling of sheer invincibility. Such is the power of mint!

This sheer-invincibility feeling lasted until precisely 11:22am, when I telephoned my employer (or rather, ex-employer) Mr Fenton, of Fenton's Magnetic Supplies, to ask when I could come in and collect all my letters. Unfortunately, his answer was, 'I don't think we're quite ready for you yet.'

When I asked him how many letters there were exactly, he replied, 'Two thousand and thirty six bl**dy letters!' then hung up.

Strange. I could have sworn there were more.

Wednesday January 19th

Hoorah! I have an official meeting at the job centre on Thursday January 27th at 10:30 with a 'Mrs Paluine (must be a typing error) Palmer'. I wish myself luck!

After breakfast, I went to make some copies of my CV in Mr Singh's shop. Mr Singh has recently purchased a photocopying machine, which he claimed was 'the future of newsagency', as well as a laminating device ('Lamination is also part of the future, Robin').

One hour and five minutes later, I was walking out with 50

glorious copies of my curriculum vitatis, each one encased in bright green plastic sheeting. They look fantastic, and I'm sure everyone will want to meet me now. I know I would!

Sadly, Rita wasn't so keen. She said they looked 'more like menus', and that if I had any spare ones she could use them as 'place mats'.

The cheek!

Thursday January 20th

Was severely excited to receive my first letter of the year from my Swiss German penfriend, Gunter Schwartz, today. What exciting times!

I have been corresponding with Gunter for nearly 40 years now, and I can safely say that his English gets worse and worse with each letter . . .

Landsberger Strasse 60
CH-8006
Zürich
SWITZERLAND

Thursday the January [13]st

My dear friendly Robin,

New year welcomings to you!

I do hope the festivity's have not left you bereft of feeling. For me, I am one
in which I am not only to have been being but we do hope so.

Robin, I am sory to tell you again about the terrible situation with the house
handles. It is so bad that I have since atempted a repprimand but to no
effects. You would not believe it but I tell them otherwise.

What are we to be doing Robin? The house handles cannot be lifted or
even pulled along. When my father is trying to bind them with kindlung, this
caused so much slipage that it is making him a pain of the face.

How is Rita's ankle bonies? Did they decide what is best to her? Or did
they say otherwise? Please let me in the no. I am awaiting with impatience.

Zürich is full up with the snow. Hurry up sun and make water fast, I tell
them!

Hoidi is also sending her regardments.

Your ever friendly,

Gunter Schwartz

Gunter Schwartz

The 'house handles' saga has been going on for months now. Every letter seems to have some mysterious reference to 'house handles', but we have absolutely no idea what 'house handles' are. Unfortunately it's too late to ask now.

Instead, Rita and I wrote out the following list on the easy-wipe message board on the fridge.

'House Handles' (might be):

1) A type of door handle (but much heavier).
2) Straps of some sort (i.e. for a large bag or briefcase, although in his previous letter Gunter mentioned that house handles cannot be put on the shoulder – so probably unlikely).
3) Banisters (that keep snapping?).
4) An anvil (but I don't recall Gunter ever showing any interest in metalwork/blacksmithery, or anvils).
5) Something that is only ever used by Swiss Germans and no one else in the world.

We think it's probably number 5.

Friday January 21st

Bought a pair of binoculars in the charity shop today (£2.90). Saw a squirrel in close-up (such tiny hands), a mysterious turquoise button on the lawn, and right into Mr Alfonso's bedroom next door. After a while Mr Alfonso banged on his window, so I immediately switched focus to the button again.

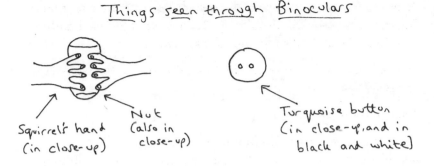

Things seen through Binoculars

Squirrel's hand (in close-up)

Nut (also in close-up)

Turquoise button (in close-up, and in black and white)

Sat in shed and scoured paper for jobs. No opportunities for budding inventors, but I did find the following:

1) Clerk in insurance office.
2) Clerk in other insurance office.
3) Product manager for 'International Perfume Company' (bit of a long-shot but might keep Rita happy due to potential free sprays/scented snaps etc,).
4) 'Self-Starting Above-the-line Resolutions Officer' in 'Exciting Forward-Thinking Company' (Not quite sure what this meant, but I'm certainly a self-starter and definitely an exciting forward thinker).

Wrote off to all the above, and enclosed a copy of my shiny new CV. Then cleaned my teeth again for ten minty minutes and popped out to the post box.

Stopped to have a look at the jobs advertised in Mr Singh's shop window. Was amazed at just what people advertise these days. Amongst the 'electricians, Spanish language teachers and gardeners' was an advert for '40 prams for hire' and another from an 'Italian lady (36-28-32)' offering 'professional bubble bath', whatever that means.

Five minutes later (and £2.25 poorer) I too had joined their hallowed ranks and become an official advertiser.

WANT TO DRIVE (A CAR)?

DO YOU???

WELL NOW YOU CAN, FOR I AM

ROBIN COOPER,

PROFESSIONAL (EX) DRIVING INSTRUCTOR

'Don't hesitate: learn to drive before it's too late!'

CALL NOW!!!

I wish myself luck!

Saturday January 22nd

A big day today: Rita finally came off crutches (or 'ankle sticks' as Tony calls them), and walked up and down the stairs with only the slightest of twinges. To celebrate, I bought her a box of chocolates (I ate the toffee ones) and then Linda came round to take her out to town for the day.

With the house to myself, I had a few licks of Mentathon 3000 (it really is the mintiest substance ever!), then popped into the loft to retrieve my tape machine. Was as quiet as possible as didn't want to disturb Smithy, who was lying in his 'bed' as usual, but appeared to have company (lady wood-pigeon).

When Rita returned home, I told her that I thought her hair looked nice, just in case she'd had it done (she hadn't but it always works), and made her a cup of tea. Think Rita is feeling a bit more perky, now that she's more mobile ankle-wise, and seems happy that I'm showing more of a positive attitude re job.

However, if she thinks I've given up the idea of becoming a world-famous/locally-famous inventor, she's got another thing coming! (I didn't tell her this though.)

Anyway, as a treat, I ordered us a takeaway for dinner, and together we did the bumper weekend crossword, followed by the Sudoku number puzzle. What a perfect evening: letters and numbers – and Robin and Rita – in perfect harmony!

Sunday January 23rd

A funny thing happened when I phoned Mother today. As usual she had her television set blaring in the background, so it was quite hard to hear what she was saying, but I could have sworn I heard her say something about 'meeting a new man'. When I mentioned this to Rita later on, she became very excited and made me call her again to see if it was really true.

'Meeting a new man?' Mother replied. 'No, I said I was eating some lamb.'

What a family!

Monday January 24th

How dare they?!

How DARE they . . .?!

(P.T.O. to witness an act of sheer and utter insolence . . .)

Brent Herald

2-9 Lyndhurst Road, London NW4

13th **January**

From: **Local Follies Department, The Brent Herald.**

To: **Robin Cooper**
Brondesbury Villas, London

Dear Mr Cooper,

I say I say I say,
Thank you for your letter,
I say I say I say,
I hope you're feeling better.

I say I say I say,
Sorry you didn't win.
I say I say I say,
But your joke went in the bin!

Yours sincerely,

Ted G Fetfus

Tuesday January 25th

Opened the shed door this morning to find Tony sprawled across the floor, clutching a can of Pennyfeather's ale, and sporting three nasty bumps on his head. When I asked him what had happened, he replied, 'Shoe, ash tray, clock.'

This could only mean one thing . . .

Susan.

Tony and Susan have been married now for 16 years, but I don't think they've been truly happy for about 5844 days.* To be fair, Tony probably isn't the easiest person to live with, although it must be hard being married to a woman who never goes out, and only ever wears pink.

I made Tony a cup of tea and a cup of coffee (his patented 'hangover cure'), brought him some toast (he got butter all over his moustache as usual) and lent him one of my shirts (which I'm sure I will never see again). Then, as it was late, I gave him a lift into work. We didn't say much on the way, although Tony did mention that he thought I was a 'very slow driver'.

The cheek!

*That's 16 years in total – including leap years – minus the wedding day (which Tony was too drunk to remember).

Wednesday January 26th

Didn't hear a word out of Tony all day, and no sign of him in the shed, so presume all is rosy in the Sutton household – unless he's been sleeping in his car again.

Saw a sad sight this afternoon. There was a lady tramp (trampette?) sprawled right across the bench on the high street. She must have been in her 60s and was ever so grubby, poor wretch. I took pity on her and gave her 50p and, when I looked at her closely, I noticed she had the kindest eyes I think I'd ever seen in my life so I gave her another 50p. She thanked me, and then took a big bite out of an onion.

By the way, no one at the local paper goes by the name of 'Ted G. Fetfus', and nobody has ever heard of him. I was incensed! That (mini) snooker table should have been mine!

I shall get to the bottom of this.

Thursday January 27th

I think I must have been very anxious about my big day with Mrs 'Paluine' Palmer at the job centre, as I had a terrible and terrifying dream last night . . .

My dream:

It was a boiling hot afternoon, and I was outside in the garden watering it. Suddenly a giant turquoise button (like the one I saw the other day through my binoculars but much bigger) appeared in the sky and started 'zapping' everything and everyone with a powerful turquoise-coloured ray. Whatever it zapped, disappeared: my shed, the apple tree (we don't have an apple tree) and the wheelbarrow (we do have a wheelbarrow). Next, the button moved over to Rita, who was lying asleep in our bed, which was also in the garden (we have certainly never put our bed out in the garden). I tried to cry out to her, but alas – no sound would come out of my mouth. It was too late. In an instant Rita was zapped, and she vanished into thin air. I tried to run but was rooted to the spot. I could feel the shadow of the enormous button covering my face, and then, just as the inevitable turquoise ray began to strike my chest, I woke up.

Stranger still was that when I went out into the garden (this is now no longer the dream but in my actual real life) I couldn't find the turquoise button anywhere. Definitely not the best way to start my big day.

Arrived twenty minutes early for my appointment, so stood outside and took a few minty licks of Mentathon 3000.

When I went into the job centre, the first thing I noticed about Mrs Palmer was her name badge: it actually said Mrs 'Paluine' Palmer. However, when I pointed out the mistake she replied, 'I know, there should be a double n.'

Fancy that!

Mrs 'Paluinne' Palmer asked me a bit about myself and my past history, and I told her everything I could. She sat there sipping her coffee throughout, but I was momentarily distracted when I noticed her using my laminated CV as a place mat.

Anyway, I think I may have gone into a bit too much detail, because when I told her about the inventing, my 'misdemeanour' with the letters, and my use of company stamps, envelopes and photocopier, she instructed me to 'wait here a minute while I consult a colleague.'

After much pointing and whispering, she came back, sat down again, then looked at me and said, 'Mr Cooper – have you considered early retirement?'

Oh alas . . .

Friday January 28th

I don't know what they put in that toothpaste, but as soon as I'd brushed my teeth this morning (and had a little nibble from the end of the tube), I shoved on my slippers and rushed out to the shed.

I have a new idea. A fantastic idea! It's a sure-fire billy-boy HIT! Be off with you 'early retirement'!

But before I got started – and like all good inventors – I made a quick inventory of everything inside my shed:

Shed Inventory (No. 19) as at 7:45am, Friday January 28th by Robin Cooper

9 × spades (various sizes)
Rake
Trowel
Towel
Broken deckchair
Atlas
1 × Pickwinkle (think it's called a pickwinkle, as it does look like a pickwinkle)
3 × bags manure (1 particularly soft bag)
(Anti) slug pellets
Table tennis table
Seeds
30 × empty cans of 'Pennyfeather's ale' (NB: Speak to Tony)
1 × toilet seat
Bleach (× 12 bottles)
Typewriter
Handkerchiefs
Pulley system
Packet of Biscuits
2 × bags of pegs
2 × marbles
Toolbox containing tools (NB: contents require separate list)
Vice
150 × nails
143 × screws
55 × pencils
Bandages/ankle couplings
3 × Plaster casts of Rita's leg (one signed by former hostage Brian Keenan, who we met two years ago outside a bank in Harrow)
Box of chalk

I couldn't finish off the list, as I was too excited to get stuck into my new idea.

So here it is. (I've written out the information as it would appear in professional print . . .)

New Idea by Robin Cooper:

Make way for the world's first combination between a crossword and a sudoku number puzzle, for 'Cooper's Crossoku' is truly a REVOLUTION in word and number gaming.

The Rules:

The player is faced with a crossword-like grid and a set of clues (as seen below):

COOPER'S CROSSOKU (NO. 1)

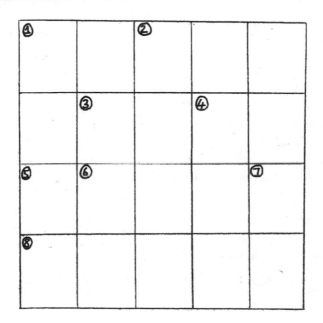

ACROSS

1) Unluckiness is contained within this four-legged monochromed mammal (2 words)
2) What is an 'a'? (3 words)
3) Famous novelist sadly deceased (4 words)
5) What did the man say who fell down the well? (5 words)
8) Lady yearned for exotic travel (5 words)

DOWN

1) Unwashed limb (2 words)
4) Male fruit-lover (3 words)
5) Unambitious life-form (2 words)
6) En France (transl.) (2 words)
7 What happened to the man in 5 across (2 words)

How to Play:

As you can see above, the clue for '1 Across' is 'Unluckiness is contained within this four-legged monochromed mammal', followed by '(2 words)'. The player must first think of this 2 worded answer (which is 'black cat'). The player or players (Cooper's Crossoku can be enjoyed by all the family) then count(s) up how many letters there are in this two worded answer, i.e. 5 (for 'black') and 3 (for 'cat'). He/she/they then physically write(s) down these numbers in the corresponding boxes of the crossoku grid, and then move(s) on to the next clue. The winner is when you finish it all. It's that simple.

Happy crossokuing!

SOLUTION

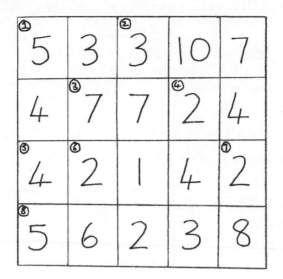

ACROSS
1) 5,3 (Black cat)
2) 3,10,7 (The indefinite article)
3) 7,7,2,4 (Charles Dickens is dead)
5) 4,2,1,4,2 (Help me O' help me)
8) 5,6,2,3,8 (Lynne wanted to see Pyramids)

DOWN
1) 5,4 (Dirty hand)
4) 2,4,6 (He eats apples)
5) 4,5 (Lazy squid)
6) 2,6 (In France)
7) 2,6 (An accident)

I doubt I'll even need to look for a job again. It's clear I'm set to become a millionaire!

Saturday January 29th

Tony couldn't understand my crossoku idea at all.

'It's a crossword but without words, and instead you use numbers made up from the words you get from the other words, but never use these words in answer form, only the numbers?'

'Yes.'

'But why?'

It pains me to say it, but sometimes it can be hard dealing with my intellectual inferior.

Sunday January 30th

Rita didn't understand my Cooper's Crossoku either.

'It's very complicated, Robin,' she said. 'Why are you using numbers instead of words?'

'Because that's the point.'

'I hope you're not going to be spending all your time trying to get this silly thing off the ground,' she said.

I replied, 'Yes', which I thought rather clever as it could be read both ways (i.e. 'Yes I will' or 'Yes I won't').

'Do you mean yes you will or yes you won't, Robin?' came her response.

I said nothing, but I think my silence spoke volumes.

Monday January 31st

After a vigorous bout of toothbrushing this morning, I went to check on my driving lessons advert in Mr Singh's window, as no one's replied so far.

Must admit, it did look a little drab compared to some of the others. I think the secret lies in using a coloured highlighter pen, because the 'Italian bubble-bath lady' had written the words 'All services offered' in bright orange, and there seemed to be quite a few men taking down her details.

Also realized why I've had no replies: I'd forgotten to include my telephone number!

February

Tuesday February 1st

Have written a poem about February, as it seems to be such an over-looked month . . .

'Ode to the Glorious Month of February' by Robin Cooper

February is the shortest month,
The shortest measured in days,
'Tis shorter than the month of March,
April, June and May(s).

Shorter still than August,
And July – oh months of sun,
And December with its winter coat,
Of snow and icy fun.

But what of old November,
January, September too?
Why these months are both longer,
Than February – yes 'tis true!

That only leaves October,
The tenth month of the lot,
But when compared to our friend, Feb,
Is it shorter?
No, it's not!

So let's put our hands together and pray . . .

The toast is . . .

FEBRUARY!!!

When I read it to Rita (after she had put on her glasses to 'listen better') she said it was 'Quite well written'. Tony wasn't too keen, however, and told me – in a rather aggressive tone – 'I've never liked poems, Robin. You know that.' (I didn't).

I do hope February will be a good month.

Wednesday February 2nd

And it is! (A good month).

Why?

Well, for two glorious Februarian reasons:

1) The organization advertising the position of 'Above-the-line Resolutions Officer' wrote back, requesting a meeting on February 22nd. I'm intrigued to find out what the job is.

2) Had my first reply to my advert. A rather softly spoken lady named Miss Marsh called to say that she wanted driving lessons. A date has been set: next Wednesday 9th February at 3:00pm (well I can hardly teach her at 3:00AM!!!!!).

Hoorah to one and all!

HOORAH!

Thursday February 3rd

Feel rather guilty. I have told a lie.

Rita asked me what I've been doing in the loft recently (real answer: bird observance), and I told her (unreal answer) that I've been giving the beams a 'rubdown' with sandpaper. When she asked me if this was 'really necessary', I said that smoother beams will help 'improve air-flow', and thus 'reduce heating costs'.

It's a terrible thing to say, Dear Diary, but were it not for her complete incomprehension of physics, her terrible fear of heights, and her irksome ankle, Rita would be up that ladder before you could say 'Please don't go up there!' and Smithy the woodpigeon would, alas, be homeless.

Friday February 4th

Posted my Cooper's Crossoku idea off to all the major newspapers (but NOT to the Brent Herald – they're in my bad books

34

at the moment). I wonder if a bidding war will ensue, with each publication fighting over the global, international, worldwide rights to my Cooper's Crossoku? I do hope so, and I wish myself luck!

Saw the trampette on the bench again. She was swigging from a bottle of 'Extra Discount Cider'. Think she must have remembered me, because when I walked by, she flashed me a huge mustard-coloured smile (she'd been eating mustard), so I gave her 50p, bringing my total trampal donation, thus far, up to £1.50.

Rita had invited Linda and Ian around for dinner, so in the afternoon I helped with the necessary preparements.

How I helped:

1) Bought some lovely halibut (I just love halibut!).
2) Peeled 16 potatoes.
3) Separated three yolks from three whites from three eggs.
4) Cleaned mirror in hall.
5) Emptied bins.

How I didn't help:

1) Broke vase.

After the above two words had occurred, Rita told me to 'leave her alone', so I went up to the loft to sand down the beams (i.e. check on Smithy). When I got there, I was amazed to find him actually out of his 'bed', but even more amazed to see him strutting about in my old pyjama top, his beak peaking out from one of the sleeves. Isn't nature wonderful!

Our evening with the in-laws was pretty uneventful. Linda talked about star signs as usual (in particular, something called 'the Capricorn effect') and Ian showed us the scar on his bottom again.

Rita and I must have seen that bottom about a dozen times by now.

Saturday February 5th

Mother popped round for tea this afternoon. She'd had her hair done again. This time it was practically pink (she described it as 'grapefruit'). I really wish Mother would stop going to see that Mr Lawrence: the man is 82, can hardly hold a pair of scissors, and has only one working eye. Mother always says that Mr Lawrence is a 'real gentleman', and has never tried to 'take advantage'.

Anyway, Rita made a lovely chocolate cake (I had three pieces, plus another secret piece in the kitchen), then Mother made us watch television for precisely 155 minutes.

What we watched:

1) Local news: story about a (local) woman who collects plastic bags (she had over 500, including 22 Harrods bags).
2) The final ten minutes of a drama about an extremely religious doctor. (I didn't know what was going on!).
3) The middle ten minutes of a documentary about Picasso. (Mother said the pictures 'frightened her', so we switched over to a programme about rocks.)
4) Programme about rocks (see above).
5) Adverts.
6) Two episodes of a DIY programme (the one with the Chinese man in it). Did learn how to un-block a loo, though.
7) Nature documentary about dogs. (Do dogs qualify as 'nature'?)
8) More adverts.
9) Local news again: same story about woman with bags.

I tell you, Dear Diary, if I have no luck as an inventor, I could always try my hand as a 'de-inventor' . . .

. . . I'd 'de-invent' the television!!!

Sunday February 6th

Nothing of any worth to report today. Found a marble in the shed.

Monday February 7th

As above (except the marble bit). Linda phoned to apologize for Ian's bottom.

Tuesday February 8th

Managed to get through to the editor of the Brent Herald (Mr Gary H. Meadows) this morning.

Mr Meadows told me that he'd launched an 'investigation' into the 'Fetfus affair', but had so far come up with no answers so I suggested he provided an official apology 'in the form of a mini snooker table'. Mr Meadows said he couldn't do that as it would mean 'physically going round to the winner's house and removing it from the bedroom of a 9-year-old girl'. The case continues.

Went for a walk with Rita in the evening. Her ankle is definitely improving (she's now in socks) and she managed to circumnavigate the entire block without tripping over. As a reward I made her a little 'modal' fashioned from tin foil, a safety pin and a match. Rita liked it so much, she pinned it to her nightie at bedtime, and even gave it a little kiss just before she went to sleep.

Such is love . . .

Wednesday February 9th – My driving lessons commence

Gave my first driving lesson to my new student, Miss Marsh, today. Must admit, I was a tad nervous, as I haven't driver-instructed for quite a few years. That said, I was certainly not as nervous as Miss Marsh: I had to ring her doorbell five times before she eventually peered out through her letterbox!

Most of the hour was spent coaxing Miss Marsh (small, be-cardiganed, about 50) out of her house and towards the car. When she finally made it to the vehicle (I used toffees as 'bait'), she insisted on sitting in the back seat, with me talking to her through the window from outside the car.

Since Miss Marsh wouldn't allow me to actually turn the key in the ignition, I spent the remaining minutes showing her diagrams of road signs from the Highway Code booklet. I doubt any of this went in, though, as she had her eyes closed the whole time. I've never met anyone so terrified of driving!

When the 'lesson' was over, Miss Marsh paid, told me she was 'really looking forward to next Wednesday', then scurried back into her abode.

I wonder if she'll progress to the front seat next week . . .?

Thursday February 10th

Rejection letters from the Times and the Telegraph re my Cooper's Crossoku puzzle.

The man from the Times opted for the word 'confusing', whilst the man from the Telegraph wrote 'very confusing'. I can only assume that the man from the Telegraph is slightly less intelligent than the man from the Times.

Tony popped round during his lunch break today. He told me there was a part-time position going at his work, but I didn't really like the sound of it (canning factory/conveyor belt/mashed potato/peas).

I told Tony not to tell Rita, which he promised, as she's been tearing out all sorts of job adverts from the newspaper recently (including one for a cleaner in a psychiatric prison), and thrusting them under my nose.

When Tony left, I telephoned my former boss, Mr Fenton, to find out when I could come and collect all of my letters, but his secretary said that he was 'still not ready to see me'. When I put the phone down, I really didn't know what to do with myself, so went up to the loft to see Smithy.

After such an eventful morning, it was rather comforting to find my beaked companion back in his 'bed', and for almost half an hour, and in complete silence (save a few 'coos'), Smithy and I observed each other across the rafters. I kept wondering what was going on inside his head (probably bed and worms), and no doubt he was thinking the same about me (mashed potato and peas).

It truly is amazing the bond that exists between man and bird.

Friday February 11th

Susan told Rita that Tony told me about the part-time potato and pea position, and that I told Tony that 'I would never work with potatoes and peas.' To make matters worse, Tony is taking Susan away for a romantic weekend.

Thanks a lot Anthony Lewis Sutton!

Rita was not in a very good mood after that. In an effort to cheer her up, I made her some soup (onion) which worked, surprisingly.

Hoorah for soup!

Saturday February 12th

Decided it was 'Be Nice to Rita Day', so took her out shopping and treated her to the following:

1) New blouse (with glittery tennis racquet insignia – Rita loves tennis!).
2) CD of 'Rod Stewart's Greatest Hits' (excluding 'I am Sailing', strangely enough).
3) Sequined gloves ('for the theatre' – which we never go to).
4) Coffee and a bun.

When we got back, I made Rita a Valentine's Day card in the shed (not sure it's one of my best efforts) then lay down on floor for a bit (comfy manure bag as pillow). Woke up an hour later with a beetle on my nose, then spotted another mound of empty ale cans stashed behind the table tennis table. I simply MUST have words with Tony.

Went to the cinema in the evening to see a film called 'Juliet's Progress'. Apparently Linda had recommended it to Rita, saying it was 'life-affirming'. Unfortunately the film – about a woman living with her manic-depressive stepfather in a bungalow – was more 'sleep-affirming', as we were both out cold within 20 minutes.

We haven't done that since our a-courting days!

Monday February 14th – Lord Valentine's Day

Gave Rita my homemade Valentine's card this morning.

I had intended to draw a picture of Rita drinking a glass of wine against a backdrop of love-hearts, but somewhere along the way, Rita morphed into a rabbit, and the glass of wine a chocolate egg.

When she opened it she said, 'It's very nice but it's more like a card you get for Easter really.'
    Rita did have a point.
    'Is it because of the rabbit?' I asked.
    'Partly,' she said, 'but also the chocolate egg.'
    I had to think about this.
    'Well, you've always loved rabbits, you love chocolate and you love eggs, so in a sense it's all about love.'
    'Yes, but what's the rabbit meant to be drinking out of the chocolate egg?'
    This question really took me by surprise.
    'Chocolate juice . . .?'

On reflection, I don't think my Valentine's card was particularly well thought out. Rita's card (a rose on a velvet cushion) was less imaginative than mine, but probably more in line with the actual event it was supposed to be celebrating (i.e. not Easter).

In the evening we went out for a special Valentine's dinner to our favourite restaurant in the entire (known) world, Signor Pantini's.

Happy Valentine's
Day (and Night!)
Rita . . .

Valentine's
Bunny

(Drinkable)
Chocolate
Egg

I had a cheese and tomato pizza (shaped like a heart), and Rita had a piece of lamb (also shaped like a heart). During the meal, Mr Pantini sung us some romantic Italian songs. He really does have a wonderful voice (although it is rather high for a man).

Rather annoyingly the couple on the next table – who must have been in their late 70s – insisted on kissing passionately throughout their meal. It was most off-putting, as I just could not stop thinking about Mother.

Tuesday February 15th

Icy cold today. Wore two pairs of socks.

Michael rang early this morning to wish his mother a belated happy Valentine's Day (such a thoughtful boy). All is well in Sydney, and last night he went out to a lovely French restaurant with his friend, Simon. Such is youth . . .

Tony joined me for lunch and we sat in the shed eating our butter sandwiches. Was going to have words with him re the canning factory/conveyor belt/potato/pea fiasco, plus the empty-ale-cans-behind-the-table-tennis-table saga, but stopped when I noticed a new bump just above his right eye. I don't think his romantic weekend with Susan went too well.

'I wish I hadn't bought her those high heels,' he said darkly, rubbing his forehead.

Wednesday February 16th

Driving lesson no. 2 with Miss Marsh.

Upon arrival I rang her bell several times but received no reply, so knocked on her neighbour's door to investigate. Unfortunately her neighbour didn't seem to understand much English, because when I asked if he knew where Miss Marsh was, he took me into his house and led me to his electric meter. To avoid embarrassment, I pretended to make a few readings, then left.

I returned to find Miss Marsh sitting in my car.

She was in the front seat.

Progress!

Admittedly it was the passenger seat, she did keep her eyes completely shut, and I was not allowed to make the car physically move – but still, I call that progress!

Some facts about Miss Marsh:

1) She has her hair in a 'limp' style (i.e. it's all limp, and sort of 'limps about' on her head).
2) She says she's 40 but I think she's 50.
3) She always seems to have a runny nose.
4) She wears a lot of green.
5) She smells a bit like rum 'n' raisin ice cream (my favourite!).

Later, I had a strange haircut, which seemed to make my hair longer, then came home and popped up see Smithy. However, as soon as I entered the loft, he flew off through a little hole in the roof. Perhaps my new hairstyle frightened him.

Returned to loft several times but Smithy didn't come back all day. I do hope he's OK.

Thursday February 17th

Crossoku rejection letters from the Daily Express and the Daily Independent.

The woman from the Daily Express seemed to agree with the man from the Times ('confusing'), whilst the man from the Daily Independent went one further ('baffling'). Never mind – still have the Guardian and the Daily Mail left. I wish myself luck!

Still no sign of Smithy. I've been worried sick. It's bitterly cold outside, and he left without his pyjamas. I'm sure wood-pigeon feathers are no protection against frostbite.

Friday February 18th

A howling, icy wind all day. Started the day in two pairs of socks. Ended the day in three.

Smithy still missing. Scoured the local area with binoculars, concentrating on rooftop aerials (good perching opportunities) and telegraph lines (ditto). Nay, 'twas a fruitless search.

Interesting telephone conversation with Mother this afternoon.

'I have a guest over,' she said. 'Mrs Clarke is here.'
    Mother has never liked Mrs Clarke.
    'How is she?' I asked.
    'The usual,' she replied. 'Horrible.'

Saturday February 19th

A very traumatic day.

Rita had gone out with Linda, and I was treating myself to a little lie-down in the shed. But just as I was nodding off, I heard the most dreadful shrieking noise coming from the garden. I looked out the window, and to my horrorment, saw Mr Alfonso's cat, Monty, grappling violently with Smithy.

Smithy was giving as good as he could get (clawing at whiskers, pecking at cat's pink nose etc.) but he was no match for the powerful Monty, who was pinning the poor bird down with his diabolical talons.

Quick as a flash, I rushed outside, grabbed the wretched feline by the scruff of his tail, and shook Smithy free. Monty raced off, miaowing. Smithy lay there limp and lifeless, his plumage in tatters.

I bent down, put my ear close to his beak and listened. No breathing. I rested my head gently on his little chest and waited for a heart beat. Nothing. I then went to check his pulse, but gave up when I couldn't find what constituted a wrist.

Smithy . . .

. . . was dead.

Why, oh why, oh why, oh why?????!!!!!!!

Stricken with grief, I carried my birdal friend back into the house, and walked solemnly up to the loft. There, I placed his body gently on top of his pyjamas, and with my eyes welling up, recanted the following (improvised) prayer.

Prayer for the Departed Soul of Smithy Cooper Esq.

O' bird of beauty,
Bird of mine,
I wish thee well,
For all of time.

The second verse didn't scan quite so well (due to emotions).

With thy wings so gilded,
That would make any heart milded (i.e. melted),
Your beak so sturdy,
That would make any man unworthy
Thank you Smithy,
For not being in any way pithy,
Rather for being such a fabulous bird,
That which I have ever heard (of).

And let us all say, amen.

Amen.

And so, as a mark of respect, I sat with Smithy for a few minutes, then made a slow, dignified descent of the ladder, each metal rung a veritable nail in my heart.

Oh Smithy (R.I.P.) . . .

Sunday February 20th

Felt completely shaken up this morning. In fact I was so upset, I couldn't even bring myself to go into the loft to retrieve the body (for burial/hygiene purposes).

Spent most of the day alone in shed. I really haven't felt this sad since our hamster, Hambles, got squashed. It's strange just how empty everything seems without Smithy. I suppose with Michael being away, Smithy had become almost a surrogate son to me.

Rita and I went to Linda and Ian's for dinner tonight, but I wasn't in the mood at all (told Rita I was depressed about the economy). According to Linda, Orion was 'in the ascendancy', thus my job interview on Tuesday will 'all go to plan'. According to Ian, however, it was necessary to show us his bottom again.

Somehow it just didn't feel right to be looking at another man's buttocks, whilst deep in mourning.

Monday February 21st – Smithy's 'funeral'

As soon as Rita left for work, I got dressed in my darkest clothes (black trousers, navy jacket, dark white shirt) and made my way up to the loft. It was time to give Smithy the simple yet dignified burial that he deserved (I'd set aside a little plot in the back garden, just behind the stinging nettles).

When I cast my eyes on Smithy's stiff little body, I'm not ashamed to say, Dear Diary, that a tear came to my eye – and another tear came to my other eye. But then, just as I went over to pick him up, I heard the following sound . . .

'Cough!'

I stood back.

The sound came again.

'Cough! Cough! Cough!'

It was Smithy – he was coughing himself back to life! It was a miracle! A veritable miracle! A miraculus veritabulatum!

After several more coughs/coughettes, Smithy wobbled to his feet, blinked a few times, looked me straight in the eye, and then let out an immense ball of spittle.

Hallelulah!

Smithy was back!

Felt ecstatically happy, and immediately helped myself to three bowls of rum 'n' raisin ice cream – never mind the expense!

Tuesday February 22nd – I am officially interviewed!

A very big day – my interview with the extremely vague company, whose full name is 'General Incorporated Business Solutions.' Wore my smart shoes (the ones with the pleats) and smart trousers (pleatless), and Rita gave me four kisses (a 'squaresworth') for luck!

At the offices I was met by a rather stocky 'army major' type, who introduced himself only as 'Henderson', and then shown a short introductory video all about the company.

The film featured a cartoon man with a moustache, explaining the benefits of something called 'Secondary Rhombic Thinking', and a business phenomenon known as 'Income Capacity Break-through' (or 'ICB'). I tried to take it all in but it was most complicated.

At the end of the film, Henderson handed me a form and asked me to fill it in. It was an 'aptitude test'.

The questions were baffling: 'Have you ever played tennis pro-fessionally?', 'Do you wear a watch . . .?' I tried my hardest to give the type of answer they might be looking for, but it was impossible to work out what that might be. One part of the test required me to draw a tortoise, for which coloured pencils were supplied. Henderson sat slurping his tea throughout, and I noticed he was using my laminated CV as a place mat.

After I'd finished, Henderson took my paper and asked me to wait for 15 minutes. Then a different man called 'Morris' (first name? Last name?) came into the room, and with a completely blank face said, 'Congratulations, you've got through to the next stage. We will be contacting you with the details.'

When I left, I realized I had forgotten to ask one very important question: 'What is the job?'

Wednesday February 23rd

Smithy making slow recovery since cat attack. Still wobbly on feet – and warbly in squawk. This morning he was shivering a lot, but when I tried to take his temperature, the thermometer kept slipping out of his beak. Estimated his temperature at 'room, plus or minus 9 degrees', but now can't really remember how I got to this figure, or what it actually means.

Anyway, will have to keep a close (and secret) eye on the patient.

47

Driving lesson no. 3: Miss Marsh finally sat in the driver's seat today, before quickly switching back to the passenger seat.

Noticed Miss Marsh's nose was particularly runny this afternoon. It even dripped on to the upholstery. She told me her condition was 'hereditary', and that her family had always been 'very susceptible to draughts'. Anyway, she's costing me a small fortune in tissues. I may even have to consider charging her extra.

It also appears that Miss Marsh's neighbour is still under the illusion that I'm an electrician because, just as I was leaving, he rushed out of his front door and beckoned me inside. Since he couldn't understand anything I said, I soon found myself fitting a new fuse to his table lamp.

Naturally I wouldn't accept payment, but to appear professional I took out a scrap of paper from my pocket, and asked him to sign it.

As Father used to say: 'If a job's worth doing, and no one else looks like they're going to do it for you, then you'll probably have to do it yourself in the end.'

Thursday February 24th

Have spent much of this week trying to work out exactly what I did to get through to the next stage of the interview. Was it my multi-purpose CV/place mat? My tortoise? The way I asked for the toilet at the end?

Tony is convinced I'm going to become a spy.

'I promise I won't tell anybody,' he said, swigging from his fifth can of Pennyfeather's, 'just as long as you get me some of those special gadgets they use.'

Did infuriatingly difficult crossword in the evening (why are horizontals always more difficult than verticals?), while Rita chatted to Fat Carol on the telephone.

As ever, Fat Carol had been having complications with her latest diet ('The Super Helio-Fix System'), and had apparently gained eleven pounds in three weeks 'just from eating cabbage and watercress'.

Rita and I are seeing Fat Carol on Sunday. Cabbage and watercress are most definitely off the menu!

Friday February 25th

The thaw has finally arrived, and I made a triumphant return to just one pair of socks.

Smithy doing well since his resurrection, although still a little dazed. Nursed him for about an hour (feather brushing/soothing words) then fed him some warm milky porridge, which he seemed to like, although he did leave the lumps.

Have told Rita that I am now varnishing the beams in the loft, in

order to help seal in any 'air lossage'. Have even taken to carrying a tub of varnish whenever I go up there – just in case she
checks. I do feel awfully guilty (but I still do it!).

Another rejection: the Guardian described my Crossoku puzzle
as 'cofnusing'. At first when I read their letter I was utterly
'cofnused' – that's until I realized I was meant to be 'confused'!
Fingers crossed for the Daily Mail . . .

Phone call in the afternoon from 'Henderson' of General
Incorporated Business Solutions. My second interview is next
week.

I wish myself luck!

Saturday February 26th

Another letter from Gunter. The mysterious 'house handles' saga
continues . . .

Landsberger Strasse 60
CH-8006
Zürich
SWITZERLAND

Sunday the February 20st

My dear friendly Robin,

I do hopes that all has been going. Here it has been generaly in motion, but then again we would not no otherwise!

Thank you for your letter which I have been reading on the countless occasions. I was very sad of you to learn of your job leaving you in the old year. Life can bring us many shocken, my dear Robin, each of which no one can posibly no where to turn. Do you go left or do you go right? No one nos otherwise.

Ear operation with leading Swiss surgeon.

I think I am telling you in my last communication about the house handles. What are we to be doing dear Robin? They are moving around so fast and are now no longer visible to us. We have been searching high and under but nothing is to be found. Now I am fearful of the electrik because of schnittung. I wish to myself that we had never been having the house handles, but Heidi thinks otherwise.

Heidi is also sending her regardments – and to Rita's ankle bonies.

Your ever friendly,

Gunter Schwartz

Gunter Schwartz

Oh dear. Even more confusing than ever. Rita and I have had to amend our list of 'house handles' possibilities on the easy-wipe message board in the kitchen.

'House Handles' might (also) be:

1) A suitcase on wheels. (Although in his last letter Gunter said that it couldn't be pulled along, so not sure.)
2) An electric circuit breaker of some kind. (Don't really know what an 'electric circuit breaker' is, so strictly speaking it shouldn't be on the list.)
3) Hot atoms???
4) Something else that is only ever used by Swiss Germans and no one else in the world.

We think it's probably number 4.

Sunday February 27th

There was panic in the Cooper household today . . .

With all the excitement of the past few days, Rita and I had completely forgotten that Fat Carol was coming over for lunch.

Fat Carol has been painting pictures of historical figures – as cats – for years. Unfortunately, Fat Carol gives Rita a new painting every time she visits. Even more unfortunately, Rita pretends she likes them. Further unfortunately, Fat Carol insists on helping to put up each new painting whenever she's round.

Fortunately, Fat Carol doesn't know that as soon as she leaves, we take her paintings down.

Fortunately still, I keep a detailed record of exactly where every cat painting hangs (there are 9 of them – Nelson, Churchill, Florence Nightingale, Napoleon, Beethoven, Harold Wilson, Charles de Gaulle, Frank Sinatra and someone called 'Princess Fifi de Mer'), so that prior to Fat Carol's arrival, I am able to re-hang them in exactly the right place.

'Nelson'
(as a cat)
by
Fat Carol
(But redrawn
by
Robin
Cooper)

Unfortunately, I'd lost the piece of paper. It was 12:35, and Fat Carol was arriving at 1.

Before you could say 'cats', I was up in the loft, gathering up all of the paintings. With hammer in hand, and Rita acting as director (of hammer action), I bashed in the last one ('Harold Wilson cat drinking milk from saucer outside No. 10') just as our guest was puffing her way up the drive.

As soon as she walked in, Fat Carol said, 'I've got a little surprise for you, Rita.'

We are now the proud owners of Mary Shelley, the author of Frankenstein, as a long-haired Persian!

Monday February 28th

My dream of becoming a Crossoku millionaire is finally over.

Letter from the Daily Mail: 'Your puzzle was, frankly, nonsense.'

Oh alas . . .

Talking of (not) becoming a millionaire, Rita has been growing increasingly concerned about our financial affairs. She's even started buying margarine instead of butter – and I absolutely hate margarine!

On top of that, her wretched ankle has been playing up again, which has only made her more irritable. The whole week she's been kicking me in her sleep, claiming it's due to a mixture of 'ankle twinges and worry'.

I now have a bruise on my shin in the shape of France.

March

Tuesday March 1st

Popped round to Mother's today. She needed a new plug for her kettle. Was surprised to see her as a brunette. That Mr Lawrence has a lot to answer for.

As usual her television set was blaring. This time it was a quiz show.

'This is my favourite programme,' said Mother. 'That man just won a car, a dishwasher and some linen.'

A rather elderly man – wearing the name badge 'Norman' – was standing on a set made to resemble a tropical island (sand, palm trees, plastic gulls). Next to him, a brand-new dishwasher was being emptied by a glamorous lady, while an even more glamorous lady was folding up some linen and putting it on top of the dishwasher. Norman was holding an inflatable porpoise (although it may have been a baby dolphin), which he waved into the camera.

My mother pointed at the television
   'I'm on it next week,' she said.
   'Really Mother?' I asked.
   'Yes, I got a letter from the programme.'

To my amazement she produced a letter – addressed to her – on official BBC headed paper. I copied it out . . .

Dear Mrs Cooper,

We are delighted to confirm your appearance on our programme, 'Linegan's Luck', on Friday March 11th. The show will record at 5pm but we will need you to be at the studio from 1pm so that we can go through the procedure with you.

We have organized a car to collect you from your home at 12pm, as well as a car to take you back home after the recording. Lunch and refreshments will be served throughout the day.

We do hope you have a fantastic time on the programme and we would like to wish you all of Linegan's luck. Who knows, you may be driving away in our top prize – a brand-new car!

Kind regards,

Emma Attwood

Assistant Producer, Linegan's Luck

'How did this happen?' I asked.

   'I phoned the number and got through to the man,' she said. 'Do you think I should wear a hat?'

I can see my mother with some new linen. I can even see her with a dishwasher. But in a brand-new motor car? At 76 . . .?!

Wednesday March 2nd

Was visited again by the giant turquoise button last night. Button zapped shed, Mother, car and the BBC. Am rather concerned that this is going to become a recurring nightmare. It's all rather ominous . . .

Driving lesson no. 4. Am pleased to say that we are continuing with our progress. We haven't driven anywhere as yet, or even turned the car on, but Miss Marsh seems to know her Highway Code pretty well by now. Her strongest subject is probably 'stopping distances'. As a joke I told her that it was time she learnt her 'starting distances', but she just looked back at me, blinking.

Just as I was leaving, I saw her electrically challenged neighbour again. He held his table lamp up to the window, flicked it on and off a few times, and gave me a thumbs up.

A happy customer!

Thursday March 3rd

Rita got stuck in the bathroom this morning. When I let her out, she said that she'd been banging on the door for twenty minutes. I must have slept through it all!

From what I remember, I was in the middle of a smashing dream, in which Smithy and I were flying high above the Pyramids (in Egypt). I even had my own set of wings – and there wasn't a turquoise button in sight!

Anyway, must remember to fix bathroom door.

Friday March 4th – I am officially interviewed again!

My second interview with General Incorporated Business Solutions (or 'MI5' as Tony calls them).

Once again I was met by the mysterious Henderson, who was now sporting a small (and equally mysterious) moustache. He led me into a large meeting room where there were three other applicants, Paul Ball, Mike Peters and Mike Peters. That's not a spelling mistake – there were actually two men with the same name. Fancy that!

Fortunately they were quite different in appearance: Mike Peters was short and stumpy (a bit like a squashed cake), whereas Mike Peters was tall and thin (a wafer?).

It's funny, as I have never met another Robin Cooper in my life, although I was once introduced to a 'Robert Carter', which I thought was pretty close.

Anyway, Henderson informed us that we were all going to be 'battling it out' for the one job that was available. I was terribly nervous, but didn't dare think about putting a toffee in my mouth. (Well, I did think about it, but I didn't do it!)

Next, we were each given a hand-held keyboard device and asked to tap out the answers to a series of quick-fire maths problems. All our responses were being recorded by a bulky-looking machine in the corner of the room, which made a noise a bit like a bus. Henderson told us it was called a 'Mathemindulator' and that it had cost the company nearly £20,000. Paul Ball gasped.

The problems were pretty tough, but I've always been good with numbers. For example I can do my 14 times table quicker than my 10s – which does come in handy at times – and I can divide most things neatly into thirds.

Afterwards, we were split into pairs, consisting of two people per pair. The pairs were:

1) Team A: Robin Cooper (myself) and Paul Ball.
2) Team B: Mike Peters and Mike Peters.

Paul Ball was a particularly nervous chap, and I noticed he kept swallowing the whole time, which only made me want to swallow too. I also noticed that he was missing a thumb.

'How did you do that?' I asked.
    'A man bit it off by mistake,' he replied, before swallowing.

The task: each team was given a box containing three household objects. Whenever Henderson clapped his hands, we had to take out one of them and try to 'sell' it to him, as if we were professional salesmen.

Team A (us) went first:

Henderson handclap number 1:
Small length of hosepipe: I said that it could be used to water small flowers, such as dandelions. Henderson replied, 'A dandelion is not a flower. It's a weed.' I quickly re-named the item a 'weed-waterer'. I think Henderson was impressed, as I saw him make a 'ticking' motion with his pen.

Henderson handclap number 2:
A lady's shoe: Paul Ball said it was a very special piece of footwear, 'once worn by Cinderella'. Henderson barked,

'Nonsense. Cinderella is completely made up!' Paul Ball swallowed. I swallowed too, then told him that it was the 'perfect gift for any one-legged businesswoman on the go'. Another tick!

Henderson handclap number 3:

A stone: by this point Paul Ball was swallowing so much that I had decided it was all down to me. However I was so stuck (how do you sell a stone?) that I resorted to a joke: 'You can exchange this stone,' I said, 'for £14' (i.e. '£' as in pounds, but also 'lb' as in pounds (lbs)). Henderson thought about this for a moment, then chuckled. Our third tick!

Overall, I think we performed better than the Mike Peters' duo: halfway through their presentation they had quite a bad argument, which resulted in a broken eggcup.

At the end of the session, Henderson stood up and said, 'Thank you, gentlemen. You will be hearing from us soon.'

I wish myself luck!

Saturday March 5th

Haven't stopped eating toffees all day. Am a nervous wreck! I can't stop thinking about the interview. Did I do well? Or did I do unwell? Rita soon grew tired of me and my toffeeness, and gave me a number of menial tasks to carry out, in order to take my mind off things:

Rita's Menial tasks:

1) Find a place for all the elastic bands in the house. I found 96 and put them in an envelope marked '95 elastic bands'. (I then put an elastic band around the envelope.)
2) Clean out kitchen dustbin with detergent. (A horrid task as there was a rotten peach at the bottom of the bin that resembled a fluffy, decaying egg.)
3) Wipe greasy fingerprints from all light switches. (Actually quite a pleasant thing to do.)

4) Tidy up shed. (I told her I will do this 'in my own time'.)
5) Fix bathroom door. (Forgot).

Must admit I felt a lot better after that. No more toffees went into my mouth all day – and only three went in at night.

Sunday March 6th – National Mother's Day

Michael rang this morning to wish Rita a happy Mother's Day (such a devoted lad). All seemed to be going well out in Sydney, and Michael ensured us that he was fine for money, even though he was still having to share a room with his friend, Simon.

For lunch, Rita and I took Mother – who's a 'natural' blonde again by the way – to a rather fancy restaurant in London.

Unfortunately, I think it was a bit too fancy for her . . .

'Haven't you got proper tea here?' Mother said to the waiter.
   'I'm sorry, madam,' he replied, 'that is proper tea. It's Earl Grey.'
   'No, proper tea,' she said. 'You know – PG Tips?'

We shan't be going there again.

P.S. – Smithy looking much healthier today (slightly rosy cheeks) and also eating much better (6 beetles, 1 ant).

Monday March 7th

Mother has been driving me absolutely mad about her 'Linegan's Luck' quiz show programme. She's been calling me every day at exactly 12:44pm to remind me to watch. I still can't believe she's going to be on national (British) television. They're filming in four days' time!

Anyway, I finally sat down and watched an entire episode today: Three contestants move around a snakes and ladders-style board on the throw of a die but, as the show has a nautical feel, eels are used instead of snakes, and rope ladders instead of normal ladders. Linegan is the quizmaster – a jolly pirate character with a stuffed parrot, called 'Master Beaky', on his shoulder.

Depending on which square they land on, the contestants answer questions on a variety of subjects. Today it was 'Rivers', 'Cooking for Pleasure', 'The Home', and the 'Linegan's Mystery' category. If they land on a 'Walk the Plank' square they miss a turn, if they land on a 'Pieces of Eight' square they get 8 points, and if they land on a 'Barrel of Rum' square, they win a prize (but never rum, strangely).

All in all a very hectic and noisy programme, culminating in a 'Mrs Margaret Hepworth', 43, from Ipswich, winning a motorbike.

A car is one thing – but my mother on a Triumph 600 is quite another!

Tuesday March 8th

I've been looking back through the pages of my hallowed diary, and have just realized that I never got round to finishing my shed inventory.

So here it is . . .

Shed Inventory (No. 19 contd.) as at 11:30am, Tuesday March 8th by Robin Cooper

> 4 × cardboard boxes
> Packet of mints
> Lawnmower no. 1 (broken)
> Lawnmower no. 2 (half-broken)
> Lawnmower no. 3 (quarter-broken)
> 6 × Packets of seeds
> Spare table tennis net
> Brent Herald from 8th August 1993. Headline: 'Local Man
>   Falls Down Well'
> Box of pins

Spare hammer head (not the shark, but from a hammer!)
Book on knots
'Practise' rope (with knots in it)
3 × marbles (they get everywhere!)
Map of Bournemouth
Additional 11 empty cans of Pennyfeather's ale (NB: Speak
  to Tony)
6 × Hoover bags (3 empty, 3 full)
Plastic pot
Can of motor oil
Pruning glove (i.e. 1 glove)
Feisil Powder (have no idea what it's for. It just says 'Feisil
  Powder')
2 × pin cushions
(Home-made) Ceremonial bugle
Badge featuring the words 'I love wild flowers' (found it on
  a coach journey)
Packet of iron filings
Butter dish

Unfortunately, I didn't have time to finish off the list, due to bag
of manure (i.e. being too comfy) (i.e. I fell asleep).

Wednesday March 9th

Driving lesson no. 5.

The march (or should that be 'marsh', as in 'Miss Marsh'!) of
progress continues. At last, the car has been switched on! Yes,
I was finally allowed to turn the key in the ignition, although
again, no physical movement of the vehicle was permitted.

I have tried to ask Miss Marsh what it is that terrifies her so
much about driving, but all she ever says is 'the driving'.

We still have a lot to do.

Thursday March 10th

After lunching on margarine sandwiches (it's just not the same any more), and checking on Smithy (99% recovery – one feather still bent), I telephoned Fenton's Magnetic Supplies again. I really felt it was time I collected my letters, as there had to be at least a dozen terrific, world-shattering, money-making ideas amongst them.

To my surprise, Mr Fenton himself took the call:
'We found some more of your letters last week,' he said. 'They were in the boiler room.'
'Oh dear,' I said.
'Yes. Oh dear,' he replied.

There was quite a long pause. I tried to think of what to say.

'So how many is that then?' I asked.
'Three thousand and eleven bl**dy letters.'
Down went the phone.
Luckily they didn't look behind the fire hose!

Friday March 11th – Mother is a (veritable) TV star!

With such an exciting day ahead of me, I have decided to write directly into my diary, and record events as and when they happen. I suppose you could call it 'live diarying'!

6:15am It is now. I am writing this, having awoken. The bit I wrote before (i.e. above) was 'then' (i.e. about 6:13). Think I'll go back to sleep now as am feeling a little confused.
7:32 Just got out of bed. Am going to take shower and then get dressed.
8:25 Eat breakfast (2 eggs, cereal, 4 pieces toast, crumpet, 2 cups of tea).
9:15 Go to shed. Have little lie down.
10:15 Drive to Mother's. Writing this bit at the traffic lights (is that illegal?).

10:37 Arrive at Mother's. Mother's hair is orange. She insists it is 'red'.

11:20 Still feeling hungry, so eat bun with jam. Mother eats nothing, as is 'too nervous'.

11:40 Have spent twenty minutes trying to dissuade Mother from wearing a hat. 'When have you ever seen a quiz show contestant wearing a hat?' I ask. 'Mr Perry Constance from Lincoln wore one in series 3,' she replies.

12:02 Fancy car with tinted windows collects us. Driver is wearing a hat. So is Mother.

13:05 Arrive at Teddington Studios and met by a 'production runner' called Lucy. Lucy receives shouted instructions via a man via a walkie-talkie. There seems to be some problem with the sinks in the 'green room'. What is a 'green room'? We follow Lucy to room marked 'green room' and wait in corridor while Lucy checks sinks. Have quick peek inside. Room is not green. Lots of bowls of crisps are laid out. 'Perhaps they are filming a crisp commercial in there,' says Mother.

13:10 Another girl on a walkie-talkie meets us in corridor and takes us to canteen for lunch. Mother eats soup. I eat soup. Then I eat chicken with potatoes and peas. Then fruit crumble with custard. Then another crumble (with cream).

14:03 Mother is shown to her dressing room, which has lots of bright bulbs around the mirror, fresh towels and a big bowl of fruit.

14:10 I am taken into 'make-up'. Foundation is applied. I do not know why this is happening.

14:15 Make-up woman tells me there has been a mistake. Foundation is removed.

14:25 Back to Mother's dressing room. I eat pear from big bowl of fruit. Wardrobe assistant enters with rail of clothes to suggest some 'alternative outfits'. None of these include a hat. Mother refuses. Wardrobe assistant leaves.

14:35 Wardrobe Supervisor enters. Discussion revolves around hat. Mother will not budge. Wardrobe Supervisor leaves. I eat another pear.

14:40 Producer enters. Producer discusses 'hat' issue. Mother mentions Perry Constance. Producer informs Mother that Mr Constance was 'mentally unstable'.

14:55 Hat comes off in return for Marks and Spencer vouchers (£10).

15:00 Knock at the door. It's 'Linegan' himself (Clive Henley), who looks very different without his pirate wig. Also notice he doesn't seem to pronounce the letter 'g' at the end of words (i.e. 'I am really lookin' forward to an excitin' show tonight . . . Once the show gets goin' we'll all be havin' a lot of fun' etc.).

15:15 Mother introduced to other contestants: Nick, a welder from Coventry; Lisa, a housewife from Dorset; and Gerald, a retired explorer from Bath (I've never seen an explorer in real life before). Gerald comments on my mother's hair ('wonderful colour'). Mother blushes.

15:20 Taken to studio floor. So many lights! There were lights on the ceiling, lights on the walls, lights on the floor. There were even lights on the lights!

15:25 Mother and contestants do a 'practice run'. A different man plays the part of Linegan (in my opinion he was better, actually). Mother keeps looking into the cameras. I notice Gerald keeps looking at Mother. Director comes into the studio. Mother told not to look into cameras. Gerald told not to look at Mother. Gerald blushes.

15:50 Rehearsal ends. Mother is hungry.

15:55 Fetch crumble from canteen and take to Mother's dressing room. Pass a woman in a nurse's outfit. I ask who she is. Am told she is a nurse. I don't know why I asked. Mother leaves crumble due to 'nerves'. I finish crumble.

16:00 Mother into make-up. Mother asks lady if she remembers Perry Constance. Make-up lady replies, 'We don't like to talk about that man, after what he did.'

16:40 Mother fully dressed (minus hat!). Last-minute 'swotting up' on facts from Reader's Digest magazines.

16:50 Am shown to my seat in the studio by Lucy the production runner via blocked sinks (now unblocked). The audience seem very excited. Eat a toffee.

16:55 A 'warm-up' man named Frank Parr makes some jokes to 'warm us up' (although it's already pretty warm in the studio!). His funniest joke was: 'Did you hear what happened to the man who invented Polos?' (We all replied 'No?!') 'He made a mint!'

17:05 The music starts and the show begins. I am so excited! Linegan, now in full pirate costume, with Master Beaky the parrot on shoulder, enters and introduces all the contestants. Mother is introduced last, 'From London, Mrs Hilary Cooper!' Mother walks on to the set. Audience clap politely. I make a loud 'whooping' noise. I can't believe it – my mother is actually on a television show! Make whooping noise again.

17:10 The game begins. Mother is first to play. She throws a 3 and moves along 3 places. 'Your specialist subject?' 'Mountains,' she replies. Since when has my mother known anything about mountains?

Linegan: 'Mrs Cooper. What is the highest mountain in the Western hemisphere?'

Mother: 'The highest mountain in the where?'

Linegan: 'In the Western Hemisphere?'

Mother looks confused. Oh dear . . .

Mother: 'I know it . . . I know it . . .'

Come on Mother. Think!

Mother: 'Is it . . . the acon-gaja?' (I think that's what she said).

Linegan: 'Correct!'

I am stunned! How did she know that?! Mother moves up board again, lands on 'Barrel of Rum' square and wins food hamper. (I do hope there are toffees in there!) I applaud loudly. Master Beaky squawks. Suddenly remember giving Mother a special issue of the Reader's Digest all about mountain ranges. Good old Reader's Digest! Eat another toffee.

17:20 It is impossible to note all this down. Everything is happening so fast. Game is just too exciting. So many lights! Mother doing very well indeed and keeps climbing board. Just answered 3 questions correctly on 'Reptilian Life' ('The gecko', 'Locusts', 'Poisonous glands'). I never realized just how much she knew about everything. When did she get so clever? I must start reading those Reader's Digests myself. Mother wins a set of 24 'Linegan's Luck' pens (they look very nice) and a dishwasher. I think Gerald is still looking at her.

17:25 Welder has descended three eels and walked the plank twice. He is knocked off the show. Is he crying? Gerald is definitely looking at my mother. Director comes into the studio and has words with him again.

17:30 Mother lands on 'Barrel of Rum' square. Wins weekend to Paris and another food hamper. (More toffees!) This is incredible!

17:35 Lisa is asked to name three British Weathermen. She answers: 'Roger the Rabbit'. Stunned silence in studio. Lisa is eliminated.

17:38 Now only Gerald and Mother remain. The studio lights are dimmed. Dramatic music plays. There is a 'hush' in the audience. Chew toffee very quietly. Have never felt so nervous in all my life. Gerald gives Mother a kiss. Director talks to Gerald again.

17:45 After a short round on 'General Knowledge', Gerald and Mother are on equal points.

'We are now enterin' the final round. Our contestants are now goin' head-to-head,' proclaims Linegan. 'One question. One answer. And at the end – one winner.' Feel sick with nerves. Gerald and Mother are led to a barnacle-encrusted podium and made to face each other. The lights dim even more. My heart is pounding. I am physically sweating. Mother looks worried. 'May I have a glass of water please?' she asks. It is quickly brought to her. I can see her hands shaking. She can hardly hold the glass. Oh dear . . .

The game continues . . .

Gerald throws a six and gets to choose the final subject. He chooses 'The History of Ferrari'. My heart stops pounding and sinks into my stomach. I take out my toffee and put it into a paper hankie. 'The History of Ferrari'? Mother is surely doomed.

17:47 Linegan: 'Now take your time. If you get this right, you will be winnin' "Linegan's Luck".'

Gerald: 'OK.'

Linegan: 'Mr Gerald Hale, what was the first production Ferrari to feature a mid-engine V8 layout? Was it the Ferrari Testarossa, the Ferrari Spider, or the Ferrari 308 GT4?'

Gerald: 'Was it . . . the Ferrari Spider . . .?'

Linegan: 'Is that definitely your answer?'

Gerald: 'Yes.'

There is a long pause. Please put us out of our misery . . .

Linegan: 'Incorrect!'

Gasps from the audience. I shout out, 'Come on, Mother!' (I can't help myself!)

Mother replies, 'That's my son!'

There is a ripple of laughter.

Linegan turns to Mother. Mother takes a deep breath.

Linegan: 'Mrs Cooper. If you answer this correctly, you're goin' to be walkin' away the winner.'

Mother: 'Thank you, Mr Linegan.'

Linegan: 'Mrs Hilary Cooper. What was the first production Ferrari to feature a mid-engine V8? Was it the Ferrari Testarossa, the Ferrari Spider, or the Ferrari 308 GT4?'

Mother: 'Oh, I did read something about cars last week. Was it . . . the Ferrari 308 GT4?'

Another long pause. Even longer than before . . .

Linegan: 'Mrs Cooper . . .?'

Mother: 'Yes?'

Linegan:' Is that definitely your final answer?'

Mother: 'Yes . . .'

An even longer pause, eclipsing the previous one by at least a factor of two . . .

Linegan: 'You have just won yourself a car!'

The lights go up! The music strikes up! I stand up! The audience stands up! I cannot believe it! I literally cannot believe it! My mother has won! She has won a car (Nissan)! She's the official winner! Linegan kisses Mother. Mother kisses Master Beaky. Gerald kisses Mother. Mother kisses Gerald. She's won! Hoorah! Hoorah! Pop two toffees into my mouth!

I am now back at home, and it is way past midnight. Tonight has been one of the most exciting nights of my life. I simply cannot sleep! Am writing this in the kitchen eating a margarine sandwich which, for the first time, tastes even better than butter!

When I told Rita, she almost fell down the stairs again! The phone hasn't stopped ringing either: Linda said she knew that Mother would win 'because Virgos are born lucky', and Tony asked if he could have one of the food hampers ('She won't need two of them', he said).

The whole day has been like one long dream. I still can't believe it. My mother – a quiz show champ!

DAY PASS

PASS NO: 01463

NAME: Robin Cooper (Mr.)

DATE: 11th of March (Friday)

STUDIO: 6

PRODUCTION: Linegan's Luck (mother is on it)

Property of Teddington Studios.
Please return to Security Desk if found.

Saturday March 12th

Mother invited us over for a celebratory lunch today. She greeted us with a glass of champagne ('from the hamper') in one hand, and a dried apricot ('from the other hamper') in the other. I noticed she was still wearing her 'Linegan's Luck' name badge.

Inside the living room was her friend-she-doesn't-like, Mrs Clarke, and, to my surprise, a tall, distinguished-looking, grey-haired gentleman, who was sitting in the armchair, and eating from a packet of exotic crisps.

It was the retired explorer and 'Linegan's Luck' quiz show rival, Gerald Hale. What on earth was he doing there?!

Mother seemed very excited to introduce us . . .

'Gerald's been to the Sahara!' she announced.
  'Oh, that was a long time ago, Hilary,' he replied. (He called her 'Hilary'!)
  'Gerald's eaten dog!' said Mother, impressed.

Mother had clearly taken a shine to this Gerald chap. Not only was her television switched off the whole afternoon, but she appeared to have adopted a new and more 'refined' laugh (old laugh 'ha, ha, ha!'. New laugh 'nyah, nyah, nyah!').

What's more, when she caught Mrs Clarke chatting to Gerald later on, she leaned over and said, 'I think it's best if you leave now, Mrs Clarke. The family are here.'

Spent the rest of the time eating luxury toffees (I ate 11, but pretended it was 9), watching Mother get increasingly giggly on 'pop', and listening to Gerald's exploratory exploits (nest of scorpions, frost-bitten chin). We left when Mother started to dance the foxtrot.

Not a lot was said on the journey home, although Rita did say that she thought Gerald was 'charming'.

I wonder how long all this will last . . . ?

P.S. – Mother gave me the set of Linegan's Luck pens (the logo sparkles in the light), and Rita a jar of 'luxury apricot mustard' (with real apricot chunks). I think Rita was a little disappointed, as I'm pretty sure she had her eye on the pens.

Sunday March 13th

I must remember to fix the bathroom door! Rita keeps getting trapped inside!

Last night Rita wrote me a reminder note on brightly coloured paper, and stuck it above my side of the bed. It kept falling off on to my face in the middle of the night, and scaring the life out of me, but I daren't throw it away.

Mother was in a particularly merry mood on the telephone tonight, and kept referring to me as her 'little Robin'. I asked her if she was drinking champagne, as I could distinctly hear bubbles fizzing in the background, but she flatly (excuse the pun!) denied it. No mention of Gerald, though.

Didn't fix the door today (forgot) but will definitely fix it tomorrow (unless I forget).

Monday March 14th

Still no news from General Incorporated Business Solutions re job. Still no progress re fixing the bathroom door.

Tuesday March 15th

It's snowing in March! There was snow everywhere this morning. There must have been at least 4 inches on the ground. Poor worms.

Rita hates the snow – for obvious ankly reasons – but I love it. Today I wore my wellies (I love wearing my wellies) as well as two scarves (I also love wearing two scarves!). Mr Alfonso from next door is clearly a fan of snow too, as he spent hours making a snowman in his drive. He told me that he'd even taken the day off work, especially. I suppose when you're a headmaster you can do that sort of thing.

Mr Alfonso's snowman was a real work of art: not only was it life-size (if snowmen existed) but extremely lifelike. It was sporting a pair of sunglasses and a clump of, what looked like, real hair for its beard. It was only then that I noticed Mr Alfonso was completely beardless!

With the temperature falling rapidly tonight, I popped into the loft to check on Smithy. Was relieved to find him back in his pyjamas.

Such a sensible bird.

Wednesday March 16th

What a terrible, awful, horrendous, bad, dreadful, awful, appalling, poor, horrific, awful day . . .

I got stuck in the bathroom.

For ten hours!

I had just taken my morning bath, but, when I went to open the door, the wretched handle came off in my hand. Rita had just left for work and there was no one to help me. Oh, if only I had trained Smithy to pick locks with his beak . . .

As if this wasn't bad enough, I'd left my towel and all of my clothes in the bedroom and so was completely in the nuddy. To keep warm I took dips in the bath (until the hot water ran out) and then wrapped the tiny yellow bath rug around my waist to preserve body heat. What a sorry state I was in.

Soon I was really shivering, but I remembered a programme I'd once seen about a man who had swum in a lake somewhere (Norway? Northampton?), so I took the jar of petroleum jelly from the bathroom cabinet and rubbed it all over myself (not the jar of course, but the contents). This had the positive effect of raising my temperature by a couple of degrees, but the negative effect (since I had foolishly smeared it all over the soles of my feet) of me slipping all over the floor.

With absolutely no way of telling the time, I was clueless as to how long it would be before Rita would be returning home, by which time I could have:

a) Frozen to death
b) Starved to death (there was only a bar of lemon soap to eat)
c) Drowned to death (in cold bath)
d) Slipped to death

Was this the end? Was this how I was to go? Smothered from head to foot in thick grease, wearing nothing but a thin strip of yellow polyester . . .?

With no time to lose, I emptied out a bottle of bubble bath, then snipped off the end of the bottle with Rita's nail clippers (and while I was at it, trimmed my toenails) so that it formed a tube. Swaddling my feet in tissue paper to avoid slippage, I mounted the sink, stuck the end of the bottle through the tiny window above the mirror and bellowed through the device.

My improvised megaphone was a success. No sooner had my bellowing begun than a large, scruffy lady, pushing a supermarket trolley along the pavement, turned round. I recognized her at once. It was the grubby trampette from the bench. She was my only hope.

'I need you to telephone my wife at work,' I said. 'Her name is Rita Cooper. She will come and rescue me.'

'But I don't have a telephone,' the trampette replied.

'You will have to use a telephone box.'

'But I don't have any money.'

'You will have to reverse the charges.'

'How do I do that?' she asked.

Oh dear! I explained the concept of reversing the charges (actually quite a complicated concept to explain), then threw her a stick of lipstick, which she used to write down Rita's number on her hand.

Whilst she was away, I kept my spirits up by nibbling at a tube of Mentathon 3000, but its sheer mintiness only made me chillier. Finally – and to my great relief – the trampette returned.

I asked her what Rita said, and she pulled up one of her grubby sleeves and read from her arm.

'I'm very busy. I'll be home when I'm finished. You'll just have to wait.'

Oh dear.

She then pulled up her other sleeve.

'Perhaps now you'll remember to fix the bl**dy door!'

I thanked the trampette for her efforts and told her she could keep the lipstick. For good measure I also threw her a tin of talcum powder and a half-used tube of calamine lotion. Finally, I asked her what her name was.

'They call me Old Milly,' she replied. And with that, she was off.

Several hours later, Rita arrived home with Tony, who forced the door open with his foot.

'Nice skirt,' He said, pointing to the bath rug around my waist, then left.

I am not talking to Rita, and she is not talking to me.

Thursday March 17th

Bathroom door fixed.

Did not utter a single word to Rita all day. She will simply have to learn the hard way.

Friday March 18th

Mr Alfonso spent at least half an hour fussing over his snowman this morning. He used a toothbrush to comb its beard, and a can of Mr Sheen spray to polish its sunglasses. What a perfectionist! (But then again, headmasters are always perfectionists.)

Still not speaking to Rita, and silence reigns in the Cooper household. In fact, it was so quiet today, you could hear a pin drop. I know, because I tried. You could even hear a needle drop. I know, because I tried that too.

Tony popped round in the evening, but I strictly forbad him from conversing with Rita, and led him straight through to the shed. Unfortunately Tony wasn't in a particularly chatty mood (argument with Susan re lawnmower, i.e. Tony's refusal to use it), and he left shortly afterwards.

Sat in shed alone, shivering with cold and disappointment then went back into house for more quietude, which was soon broken by a knock at the front door. It was Mr Alfonso.

'I just wanted to let you know that there's a thief in the neighbourhood,' he said, pointing towards his snowman. The sunglasses were gone.

'Oh dear,' I said, 'who would do a such a thing?'

I shall be having serious words with a certain Mr T. Sutton . . .

Saturday March 19th

Crack open the trumpets . . .

Da-da-da-da-da-da-daaaaaaaa . . .!

**General Incorporated
Business Solutions**

Unit 80
Victory Business Park
Barn Way
London NW2

17th March

Robin Cooper
Brondesbury Villas
London

Dear Mr Cooper,

We are pleased to inform you that you have successfully completed the second part of our interview process. We would therefore like to offer you the position of ABOVE-THE-LINE RESOLUTIONS OFFICER.

Your starting date is Monday April 4th. Your daily hours shall be from 9:30am – 5·30pm.

Your salary shall be £XX,XXX.XX per annum.*

We look forward to welcoming you as part of our exciting, forward-thinking organization.

Yours sincerely,

Henderson (Mr)
Chief Directional Above-the-Line Manager

At last, the waiting's over! I have a job! I am officially to be in full employment, and we shall make a triumphant return to butter! Well done Robin Cooper! You have done it! Well done I!

Since I'm not talking to Rita (and she not to me), I said nothing to her about my good news, although I'm sure she could tell something was up: I spent most of the day strutting around the house, humming the tune to 'Congratulations'!

Did find it extremely difficult not to tell anyone (I mentioned it in passing to Smithy, but he merely pecked at his pyjama buttons), so I invited Tony round, and informed him in the shed. Tony congratulated me, and swore that he would not breathe a soul to anyone – not even to Susan.

'What's the job then?' he asked.

I quickly thrust a can of Pennyfeather's into his hand, and instantly Tony's mind wandered.

I suppose it would be nice to know what General Incorporated Business Solutions actually do, and what 'Above-the-line Resolutions Officer' really means, but I'm sure I'll find out when I start.

I have covered up my salary with Xs just in case somebody secretly reads my diary, and finds out how much I am physically (and fiscally) worth.

Sunday March 20th – the official 1st day of spring

Rita can be such a stubborn woman! We are STILL not talking. We're now communicating via a series of notes, nods and knocks (one for 'yes', two for 'no', three for 'maybe' and four for 'knock again please'). It is most tiresome.

Called Mother at around 11:30 this morning, and a man answered the telephone. It was Gerald Hale: 'I'm afraid Hilary is just getting dressed at the moment,' he said. 'Can you call back later, please?'

I was shocked, but tried to comfort myself that this was just a 'phase' Mother was going through (rather like the time she started wearing gloves indoors). I didn't call back.

Later, saw Old Milly on her bench.

'I didn't recognize you with your clothes on!' she said loudly, causing a father and his daughter to look round.

I thanked Old Milly once again for her help, and presented her with three shiny, new 50p coins, bringing my total trampal donation up to £3.

By the way, Rita's lipstick appears to have been put to good use: Old Milly was wearing it on her lips – and all round her eyes.

Monday March 21st

'Have you seen my lipstick anywhere?' Rita wrote this morning.

I shrugged, then knocked twice at the table.

After a desperately quiet evening at home, I resolved to do something – anything – to get me through this awful period of solitude.

And thus was born . . .

The 'Conversation Spindle' (see over).

Robin Cooper's Conversation Spindle:

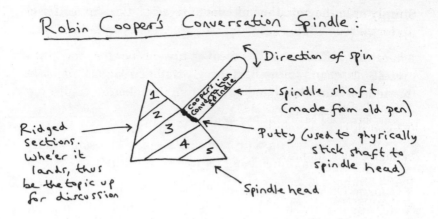

Direction of spin

Spindle shaft (made from old pen)

Putty (used to physically stick shaft to spindle head)

Ridged sections. Whe'er it lands, thus be the topic up for discussion

Spindle head

NB: You will note that only 5 topics are shown here. That is because the other 5 (i.e. 6-10) are on the other side of the spindle!

Fashioned from pieces of cardboard, an old pen and some putty, the Conversation Spindle (1 to infinity players) is an ideal way to start a conversation. As can be seen: written along the base of the spindle is a series of numbers, each one corresponding to a different topic of conversation. Thusly:

1. Life
2. Holidays abroad
3. Food and drink
4. Space travel
5. Birds
6. Bridges
7. Badges
8. Spin Again
9. Lord Halifax
10. Driving

Simply spin the spindle and whe'er it lands, thus be the topic up for conversation. Happy spinning! (And happy spindling!)

After throwing a 4, I had a rather interesting conversation (with myself) about the future of Space Travel. One part of me said that man would be walking on Mars within a decade, whilst the other part disagreed. We also discussed Mars, the chocolate bar (I liked it, but I also didn't).

What a clever man I am!

P.S. – Mother's 'Linegan's Luck' prize car finally arrived today, and apparently it came all wrapped up in a huge red ribbon and bow. Mother was thrilled. She LOVES ribbons and bows!

Tuesday March 22nd

Was (silently) excited to receive another letter from Gunter today . . .

Landsberger Strasse 60
CH-8006
Zürich
SWITZERLAND

Wednesday the March [16]st

My dear friendly Robin,

Thank you for your letter. I am wishing you good lucks with your jobs meeting.

I am thinking it has been such a long time my dear Robin that we have been writing to each selves but now we can talk in the face to face. Yes – it is the good news! I am saying this because Heidi and myself will be visiting in your beatiful land. We come on the Friday June 10 for four days. Is this acceptible or do you no otherwise?

We have no good news on the other hands regarding the house handles. What are we to do? Hans and Lotte Schwimberg were so shocken that they were in their auto before they had completed their eating!

The house handles is also causing the bad air and is dirty everwhere. Now Heidi is walking around the house with a stoffen in orders to keep it clean.

Please do let me no if our visit pleases you or otherwise.

Your ever friendly,

Gunter Schwartz

Günter Schwartz

Rita checked the wall calendar in the kitchen, then gave a little nod. And so it's official . . .

After 206 letters, 12 postcards and 3 packages (two of them containing bratwurst, the other a poster entitled 'Zurich by Night'), I am finally going to meet my Swiss German penfriend of 39 years, Herr Gunter (don't know his middle name) Schwartz.

I've only ever spoken to Gunter twice on the telephone (Gunter's spoken English is worse than his written English), and seen just one photo of him (from 1982) so I have no idea what he's really, actually like. As for Heidi, I can only guess.

But what's more exciting: perhaps now we will get to find out what the mysterious 'house handles' are!

And so, Rita and I quietly wrote out a new list on the easy-wipe message board:

'House Handles' might (actually) be:

1) A toaster that constantly burns the toast. ('Bad air and is dirty everywhere'   ?)
2) A mal-functioning portable toilet. (Surely it can't be that!)
3) Something that is only ever used by Swiss Germans and no one else in the world.

We think it's probably number 3, but all will become clear in exactly 80 days' time.

Hoorah!

Wednesday March 23rd

Began the day with a spin on my Conversation Spindle. Unfortunately I threw another 4, so had to discuss Space Travel (with myself) again. Will man ever walk on Venus? The answer: yes, and also no.

As last week's driving lesson was cancelled (due to unforeseen 'bathroom problems'), I'd arranged a double lesson for today.

However, after spending a week at home with a silent wife, the prospect of spending two more hours in a stationary vehicle with an (almost) equally silent non-wife quite literally filled me with dread.

It was time to take drastic action.

After lulling Miss Marsh into a false sense of security (toffees, tissues and questions on road hump signage), I did something to her that I have never done before . . .

I turned the key in the ignition, put my foot on the acceleration pedal and began to drive.

At first Miss Marsh looked at me without saying a word.

And then the screaming started.

I managed to make it as far as the mini roundabout before Miss Marsh yanked on the handbrake and we skidded to a halt, narrowly missing what looked like a very pregnant dog.* In an instant, Miss Marsh flung open the door and ran down the road at full speed. I tried to catch up with her, but she was:

a) Too fast.
b) Wearing more suitable footwear for running (i.e. 'sporty' shoes) than me (brogues).

Within seconds she had scurried back into her home, and bolted the door shut. I was left physically panting in the driveway.

Oh alas . . .

*On closer inspection, it turned out to be two dogs just lying on top of each other.

Thursday March 24th

Went to see Mother's prize car today. It still had its red ribbon tied around it!

I asked Mother if I could take her for a little drive, but she declined, saying, 'I don't want to break the bow.' Then offered to give her some driving lessons, and she replied, 'Thank you, Robin, but Gerald has already said he will teach me.'

The cheek!

In-laws came over for an exceptionally awkward dinner tonight. With Rita and I still on un-speaking terms, the ladies (i.e. Linda and Rita) ate in the living room, while the men (i.e. Ian and I) sat in the kitchen.

Since Ian has never been one for 'chit-chat', I fetched my Conversation Spindle from the shed. Unfortunately Ian threw a 4, three times in a row (this HAS to be a design fault), so I found myself having a further three conversations about wretched Space Travel.

Ian's and I's (3) Space Travel Discussions:

1) 'What is space dust?' Basically dust that's in space. (Very short conversation.)
2) 'Is there life on the moon?' Ian thought there might be rudimentary life forms living underneath the moon's crust, which he called 'lunar crabs'.
3) 'Flying to the sun.' We both agreed that such a trip would be foolhardy.

On balance, however, I do think my Conversation Spindle was a success: for the first time in months, Ian didn't show me his bottom!

Friday March 25th – Good Friday

Life in the Cooper abode has become pretty unbearable, but if Rita thinks she can win this 'silenting contest', she is very much misguided. After Mother and Father's terrible argument during the 1966 World Cup Final, I lived in a household in which neither parent uttered a single word to each other for nearly 13 years (although Father would occasionally read the paper out loud in a heavy German accent just to annoy Mother).

Didn't really do much today. Visited Smithy (i.e. 'varnished beams' – eh, Dear Diary!), and ate a macaroon in the shed.

Later, when I saw Mr Alfonso sweeping up the remains of his snowman (or rather, 'slushman'), I hurried outside for a chat. At last someone to talk to! Was dismayed to find he'd caught bronchitis and had completely lost his voice.

Oh the irony . . .

Sunday March 27th – Easter Sunday

Clocks went forward last night, but I'd accidentally put all the clocks back an hour. Spent the day in a state of temporal confusement. I didn't know if I was coming or going! Other than that, came up with a new and revolutionary way of eating grapes.

The Robin Cooper Grape-Eating Method:

1) Bite into a grape (as normal).
2) BUT don't spit out the pips.
3) Using your tongue, push the pips under your upper lip.
4) Repeat the process, storing all pips under your lip as you go.
5) When you have finished eating your bunch/bowl of grapes, simply spit out all the (stored) pips in one go, thus saving yourself time and – no doubt – money.
6) This doesn't work for seedless grapes.

NB – call Patent Office.

Monday March 28th – Easter Monday

After 232 hours of uninterrupted unutterization, Rita was the first to snap.

'Quick!' she shouted. 'Get the car – I've done it again!'

Method: slippery grape pips on kitchen floor.

Result: re-sprained ankle.

Conclusion: frantic drive to Accident and Emergency.

I can't say I'm happy about what happened (although I did win the silenting contest) but I do think we were both relieved to be on speaking terms again. After ten days of enforced nothingness there was just so much to talk about, and we chatted away like two teenagers (in their early fifties).

I began, of course, by telling Rita my fantastic employment news. She was completely overjoyed, and kissed me thrice. Only later did she inform me that she already knew.

Thanks again Anthony Lewis Sutton!

We left with Rita back on crutches, but I'd wager there wasn't a happier couple in the hospital – or indeed the entire health authority region – than Robin and Rita Cooper.

Tuesday March 29th

Spent all morning looking after Rita (soup and Easter egg) and generally helping with her hobblements.

Then, at 12:45, I received the phone call.

'You can come in between 2:15 and 2:30 today.'

Yes! After three months of waiting, Mr Fenton, and Fenton's Magnetic Supplies Ltd, were finally 'ready' for me.

Despite the whole letters 'misdemeanour' and subsequent 'please will you leave the building' scenario, I was actually rather excited about seeing my former colleagues again, and wondered what they'd all say when I told them about my new job (providing it wasn't, 'What is it?').

Oddly enough, I was also looking forward to see Mr Fenton again, even though the last time I saw him he threw an electro-magnetic stapling device at my head.

And so, at 2:14 this afternoon, I pulled into the car park, put a toffee in my mouth, walked calmly up to the front of the building and pressed the buzzer. To my total dismay, I was told – via the external intercom – that I was 'not to enter the premises'.

Instead I was made to wait outside, while Mr Fenton's secretary fetched my (12) boxes of letters.

Thus, with the rain beating down 'pon my heavy brow, I carried each of the boxes back to my car, threw one last look at my old place of work and then, with a solitary 'toot' of my horn, drove off.

I am not too proud to admit that I did shed a little tear on the way home.

Oh alas . . .

Wednesday March 30th

Haven't heard a thing from Miss Marsh since our 'incident' last week, so was unsure as to what to expect when I turned up at her house today.

Miss Marsh greeted me very formally at the front door.

'Mr Cooper,' she said, 'I just want to let you know that during the past week I have had a lot of time to really think things over.'

Oh dear, I thought.

'And I feel that, because of everything that's happened between us, perhaps we should . . .'

She paused. I decided to put myself out of the misery.
   'Call it a day?' I said.
   '. . . take things a little slower,' she replied.

I didn't expect that!

And so Miss Marsh sat in the back seat with her eyes closed while I read from the trusty Highway Code booklet, making sure the vehicle remained fully – and completely – stationary.

It's safe to say that we've now gone right back to square one, but to be honest, Dear Diary, I was happy to be there.

Hoorah!

April

But it didn't stop there. Mr Fenton started driving me home at the end of each working day. He'd even insist that I lay down in the back of the car. 'Use the travel blanket, Robin,' he would say. 'You must be very tired'. Mr Fenton was ever so insistent.

I, of course, being unaware of Tony's letter, suspected nothing (and hence, did use the travel blanket).

It was only when Rita and I returned from a full expenses-paid weekend to Mr and Mrs Fenton's holiday villa in Majorca that Tony finally admitted to me what he had done.

Mr Fenton was not happy (and gave Tony a very 'thick lip').

Thus, when I woke up this morning, ten familiar words filled my head:

1)What 2) has 3) Tony 4) got 5) in 6) plan 7) for 8) me 9) this 10) year?

No sooner had I got out of bed than there was a knock at the door. I opened it. It was a policeman.
    'Good morning, sir,' he said.
    'Morning,' I replied.
    'Did you know there's a gorilla on your roof?'

I stepped outside. A ladder was propped up by the side of the house and sitting rather forlornly on the roof was a gorilla, or rather a man dressed as a gorilla. He was swigging from a can of ale.

'Morning Tony!' I said.
    'April Fool's!' came the rather weak reply.
    'I think you'd better come down now,' called the policeman. Tony received a caution ('I'm not going to talk to you sir, unless you remove that gorilla mask') and had his can of Pennyfeather's confiscated.

'What were you doing up there?' I asked.
    'I told you,' said Tony. 'April Fool's – I was going to throw bananas at you from the roof.'

'But where are your bananas?'

'I forgot to bring them. I don't think I'd thought it through properly.'

Tony looked confused.

'How's Susan?' I asked.

There was a long pause, then Tony said, 'Robin, can I sleep in your shed tonight?' Oh sooth . . .

Saturday April 2nd

Started looking through some of my precious letters this morning but when Rita found out what I was doing, she yelled at me, 'Leave them alone – they're nothing but trouble!' before threatening to 'hide them away'.

'Well then, hide them away,' I replied, 'I'm bound to find them!'*

Rita took pity on Tony and let him sleep in Michael's room last night. When I brought him his trademark cup of tea and cup of coffee 'hangover cure' this morning, I noticed that he'd moved all of Michael's framed photos from the bedside table.

'Sorry, Robin,' he said, 'I just couldn't sleep with all those pictures of your son's friend in his swimming trunks next to me.' Tony was in a terrible state. He refused a shower ('I had a wash yesterday') then drank his boiling hot drinks down in two gulps (i.e. one gulp per cup).

Later, Tony tried phoning Susan but she kept hanging up on him, so Rita said that he could stay 'as long as he liked'. In fact, Rita fussed over him all day. She even combed his hair!

I know Tony is having a hard time at the moment, but I'm about to start a very important new job on Monday as an Above-the-line Resolutions Officer and no one seems to be making a fuss of me.

*I've always been good at finding things: I once found a missing set of house keys in the microwave, a mislaid cufflink in the fridge, and Rita's lost purse in an optician's dustbin (and it wasn't even her optician!).

Sunday April 3rd

Dreadful night's sleep. Had another one of my turquoise button dreams again. It was a different setting this time (I was on the moon) but with the same, terrible consequences (button zapped me, spaceship, Conversation Spindle, offices of General Incorporated Business Solutions – which were on the moon – then the moon itself). I do wish all this turquoise zapping would stop.

Woke up extremely agitated and found it quite hard to believe that in just 24 hours, I'd be entering a new and exciting chapter of my life.

With that in mind, I decided to take stock of how things had been going – on a personal level – for me, personally. So, after a light breakfast (3 eggs, 2 bowls of cereal, one apple, one pear, 4 biscuits), I went down to the shed, and looked back at my list of New Year's Resolutions . . .

How Well Have I Fared? (Re: Robin Cooper's (Official) 10 New Year's Resolutions)

1. **Start writing a diary.**
   Well, I've done that, and look – I'm still doing it!
2. **Stop writing so many letters.**
   I've also done that. (NB – Remember to go through boxes of letters for good ideas/inventions – whether Rita likes it or not!)
3. **Become a world-renowned (or at least locally-renowned) inventor**.
   Haven't quite achieved this yet. Need a brand-new FANTASTIC idea v soon. (See point 2.)
4. **Learn to whistle**.
   I doubt an Above-the-line Resolutions Officer will ever be called upon to utilize this skill, so I can safely disregard this point.
5. **Tidy up shed**.
   NB: Speak to Tony re empty ale can detritus.

6. **Cut down on toffees (the eating of)**.

   I am only eating approx. 3 toffees a day and approx. 3 at night. This is a marked improvement. I award myself a toffee!

7. **Visit Mother more**.

   I suppose I could try harder (by visiting more) but it is a bit difficult at the moment, vis-à-vis her and Gerald Hale.

8. **Get Tony to stop using my shed as a drinking den (NB: URGENT)**.

   See point 5.

9. **Rectify employment situation**.

   I have done so. That is the reason for me looking back at this list in a reflective manner!

10. **Sort out Rita's wretched ankle problem FOR ONCE AND FOR ALL!**

    This, unfortunately, has not yet physically occurred.

Totting up the above, I award myself a score of 4 out of 10 (i.e. a point each for resolutions 1, 2, 7 and 9).

However, as resolution 4 (whistling) is now invalid, my new score now becomes 4 out of 9 – not bad going after only 3 months. What's more, if I continue at this rate, then by the end of the year I'll have a final score of 16 out of 9. Hoorah!

Tony is still with us, and Rita is still fussing over him. Despite her hobblements, she made a full Sunday lunch today including Yorkshire puddings (Tony ate two). She even made an apple crumble – something she hasn't done for ages – and Tony finished off all the custard!

In the evening I left Rita and Tony playing cards in the living room, saying I needed my 'beauty' sleep for my big day tomorrow. Tony replied that it was 'beastly' sleep, and Rita laughed as loud as a horse.

Saddened and somewhat dejected, I went up to the bedroom. On the bed was a note. It read: 'To my wonderful husband, good luck with your big day tomorrow. I am very proud of you. Your loving wife, Rita.'

Well, Dear Diary, I was ever so touched. It really made me think just how lucky I was to have tripped over Rita's ankle on the number 8 bus, some 25 years ago.

Oh thank you Rita, thank you ankle – but most of all, thank you London Transport Ltd.

Monday April 4th – I am an (official) employee!

My first day in my new job.

After eight solid hours above-the-line resolutioning for General Incorporated Business Solutions, I can safely say that I still have no idea what General Incorporated Business Solutions actually do.

The office is all 'open plan', with each of us working from, what Henderson called, 'workstations'. These are sort of private dens measuring roughly 8 feet by 8 feet, marked out by mini walls running at waist height.

In my den is a chair, a desk, a pen-holder (I'm using my 'Linegan's Luck' pens to convey professionalism), a modern computer (with instruction manual – phew!), a phone (with a sticker that says 'internal calls only'), a small radiator and, strangely, two waste-paper baskets. There is also a tea and coffee machine at the back of the office, but I was too nervous to use it due to an over-abundance of buttons (33).

My role – as it appeared to me – was to input data from photo-copied sheets of paper, known as 'Data Forms', into the computer and then to telephone a series of code numbers through to a department called 'Data Control'.

Finally, at the end of the day, a lady from 'Configuration' tele-phones me with another set of numbers, which I have to write down and then put in an envelope marked for the attention of 'N9 Portcastle'.

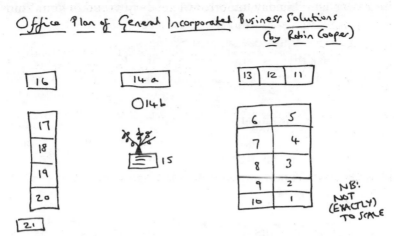

Office Plan of General Incorporated Business Solutions
(by Robin Cooper)

KEY (to the above – not a actual 'key' to open the (office) door!!!)

1) Workstation 1 – Empty (apart from large sheet of 'bubble wrap')
2) Workstation 2 – Delineation Department, manned by Watkins (Mr)
3) Workstation 3 – Accounts. Thin man with freckles
4) Workstation 4 – Empty. Currently housing broken facsimile machine and dirty cutlery tray
5) Workstation 5 – Business Indexing. Corville (Mr). I already don't like him
6) Workstation 6 – International Department. Patel (Mr). Quite quiet. Likes planes
7) Workstation 7 – Re-insurance Department. Wilson (Mr). Mid 10's. Sleeps a lot
8) Workstation 8 – Something called 'Staffordshire Holdings' or perhaps 'Hivings'. Not sure. Occupied by Morris (Mr), who wears a large watch
9) Workstation 9 – Resolutions Department. Me! i.e. Cooper (Mr), i.e. Robin Cooper (me)
10) Workstation 10 – Empty, apart from 24 pack of correction fluid
11) Toilet (out of order)
12) Toilet (unisex)
13) Tea & Coffee machine (very complicated)
14a) Henderson's office, with view of car park and skip
14b) Henderson's stool. Henderson likes to sit on it after lunch
15) Plant (possibly an 'Anglian Yucca')
16) Photocopying room, manned by Lewis (Mr), who must be at least 85
17) Configuration Department. Never see anyone in there, but they always answer their phone when you ring!
18) Meeting Room 1
19) Meeting Room 2
20) Huskings Department. No idea what this is. Run by a man called (confusingly) 'Hiskins'
21) Water fountain (broken)

What the data forms mean, what the code numbers refer to, and who or what 'N9 Portcastle' may be is a complete mystery. As all the staff (I counted 22) were working so diligently, I felt it unwise to ask them what we were actually doing. I did consider quizzing Henderson, but his moustache – which has grown enormously since I last saw him – frightened me.

Came home absolutely shattered (terrible bus journey – woman sick on stairs) and went straight to bed. In fact, I was so tired, I had nothing to eat all evening, although I did come downstairs later for a light snack (chicken legs, carrots, ice cream, cup of tea and some biscuits).

P.S. – Pleased to learn that Tony and Susan are, for the moment at least, reunited. Although not too pleased to find three empty cans of ale in Michael's sock drawer – and a gorilla suit under the bed.

Tuesday April 5th

Lots of data-inputting today. Completed 92 data forms in total. Can't quite tell if that's a good thing or a bad thing but I'm still in my job, so I must be doing something right – whatever that may be!

Rita keeps telling me not to worry about what the company does, and just to concentrate on 'not being sacked'. That's easy for her to say, but she's not the one who has to type in mysterious information relating to something/someone known as 'Dr Duck'.

Popped over to Mother's this evening. That Gerald Hale has clearly not bothered giving Mother a single driving lesson yet. In fact, I don't even think he's opened the car door, as the vehicle was still sitting in the driveway with its ribbon round it. Didn't say anything though (well, Rita wouldn't let me).

Anyway, when we walked in, Gerald was sitting in the living room armchair, dressed in a rather tight safari suit, and drinking a glass of champagne. He then got up, did a bit of a bow, and kissed Rita's hand. Rita physically blushed!

More explorer stories . . .

According to Gerald, he was the first man ever to take huskies to the Sahara. However, as the heat was too much for the dogs, he had to switch to camels, halfway. To be honest, I could have told him that myself!

Mother still hanging on to Gerald's every word. Rita still calling him 'charming'. I'm not convinced, though – I could have sworn I saw him wiping his hands on the tablecloth.

Wednesday April 6th

Finally plucked up the courage to use the complicated tea and coffee machine at work today. Couldn't find the 'tea' button, so made myself a cup of hot water with milk. To my surprise, it was actually rather nice (the equivalent in liquid form to a sandwich without the bread, I suppose), and I'm even drinking a cup right now as I write this, tucked up in my lovely warm bed!

Also realized something strange today: there are absolutely no women at work. It's all men. I wonder why . . .?

Thursday April 7th

Completed 108 data forms today. Not bad going, I thought, although all this resolution work is pretty exhausting. Also, I've been locked away in the shed most evenings, making Rita a very special surprise birthday present for Sunday.

Poor Rita. This will be her third birthday in a row that she'll be celebrating with ankle grumblings, so I really want to make it a day she never forgets.

P.S. – Having another cup of (non) tea!

Friday April 8th

The past week has been very exciting, as I appear to be making an impression at General Incorporated Business Solutions. Yesterday Henderson commented that I was 'shaping up into a very promising Resolutions Officer', so I gave myself an (imaginary) gold star!

Apart from Corville in 'Business Indexing' (horrid, shrill-voiced man), the office is still a very quiet place to work in. In fact, it's the sort of place where, if you sneeze (as I did the other day after eating a plum), no one says 'bless you' (no one did).

Luckily the Cooper household has become an all-round happier place since I started my new job. Rita's ankle is slowly improving (she's in socks again), Michael phoned twice in one week (Simon and he are now taking dancing lessons), but best of all – we're back to butter again.

Roll on the good times!

Saturday April 9th

Driving lessons have been moved to Saturday mornings. Miss Marsh is still in the back seat with her runny nose, her closed eyes and her limp hair. I think we've moved from square one to square zero.

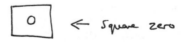

Told Miss Marsh that I thought she would definitely pass her test first time – if it was a test for passengers! Could have sworn I saw her laughing into her tissue.

Finally finished making Rita's surprise present this morning. It's a 'beauty set', consisting of a lipstick and a tub of talcum powder – both made by me. Have named the brand, 'Cooper's Mystique', which I think has a certain 'mystique' about it.

At the moment, however, the products aren't quite of 'marketable' quality, as the lipstick leaks a bit, and the talc is a tad lumpy.

As back-up, I've bought her a calligraphy set (Rita has always had very neat handwriting) but, just to make 100% certain, I popped into town after lunch to see if there was anything else I could find her.

Passed 'Peter's Pet Supplies' and thought about getting Rita a pet, as I'm sure she'd enjoy the company whenever I'm in the shed. Had a look around, but couldn't make up my mind, so wrote out the following list to help me:

PETER'S PET SUPPLIES

"...we're animal magic...!"

Pet for Rita?

ANIMAL	PROS	CONS
Dog	friendly	Might bite
Cat	Neat	Rita hates them
Mouse	Cheap	squeaks
Bird	Also cheap	Also squeaks
Goldfish	Even cheaper	Forgetful
Hamster	Used to have one ('Hambles')	Nibbled Rita
Rabbit	Hops 'daintily'	Carrots v. expensive
~~Snake~~	~~A 'talking point'~~	~~Poison~~
Tortoise	slow	Too slow
Horse	Loyal/will pull cart	Sneezes a lot

Decided against an animal, so went next door and bought myself a big bag of toffees instead.

Sunday April 10th – Rita's birthday

My Cooper's Mystique range wasn't a great success . . .

When Rita found out that the lipstick contained beetroot, and the talcum powder was basically just flour, my home-made beauty set went straight down the sink. Oh well!

Luckily, Rita liked her calligraphy set so much that all was soon forgiven. In fact, she even wrote me a thank you note in her fanciest handwriting. It said: 'My deare Robin, Thou artst the finest husbande a ladie could hope fore.'

Thank the Lord for pens!

Later, took Rita to Signor Pantini's for dinner and when we walked into the restaurant . . .

'Surprise!'

Waiting inside were Linda and Ian, Tony (minus Susan as usual), Mary Stafford (Rita's depressed/depressing friend from work), Fat Carol, Mother (brunette) and Gerald (tight safari suit and white scarf).

Rita was so touched that when Mr Pantini started singing (he really does have an incredibly high voice), she burst into tears. This soon set depressed/depressing Mary off and also, rather strangely, Ian.

But all in all, 'twas a wonderful evening . . .

Fat Carol presented Rita with a painting of President Nixon (as a bob-tailed lynx), Linda gave her a video entitled 'Aries and You' (we don't have a video recorder), Ian did a trick with his bottom, and we all toasted Rita with delicious fizzy wine.

Happy birthday my darling Rita!

P.S. Am a little bit tipsy.
P.P.S. Am very tipsy.
P.P.S. I don't feel well.

Monday April 11th

Had a bad head this morning. Had a bad head this afternoon. Had a bad head this evening. Oh Lord Bacchus, oh Duke and Duchess Drink . . .

Somehow managed to get through a day's resolutioning without incident, but I swear that I will never let a dram of alcohol pass my lips again. Not one dram. Not one dramette. Not even a dramini.

Tuesday April 12th

Have been trying my hardest to decipher the data forms at work. I just can't make heads or tails of them (think that's the right expression). Tony has been begging me all week to smuggle a data form out of the building so that he can take a look at it. He's still convinced that I'm a spy, and even called me 'James Bond' the other day.

So, at 5:30 today – and against my better nature – I secretly scrunched one of them up into a ball, popped it into my mouth and strolled towards the exit.

Just as I reached the door, Henderson tapped me on the shoulder. Oh dear . . .

'Good night, Cooper,' he said.

Quick as a flash, I pointed to my bloated cheek and mumbled 'dentist' as best I could.

'Too many toffees!' he remarked, before walking off.

Perhaps Tony is right. Perhaps I'd make a good 'double zero seven'.

Wednesday April 13th

'A-chooo!'
  'Bless you.'
  'Thank you.'

I think I've finally made a friend at work! (See above). His name is Wilson (I daren't ask his first name) and he works as a 'Re-insurance Officer' (I daren't ask what that is either).

Whilst of a polite disposition, Wilson isn't the sort of person I would normally choose as my friend (although I could say the same about a certain Mr T. Sutton!), as he does have a tendency towards gloominess, and seems to be permanently drowsy.

On Monday, Henderson caught Wilson napping at his desk, and gave him a very angry and very verbal warning, in which he threatened dismissal. So when I spotted Wilson re-napping just 15 minutes later, I quickly threw a box of staples at him, and woke him up just in time. Wilson was in a lot of pain (the box of staples hit him right in the teeth), but grateful nonetheless.

Since then, Wilson has lent me a couple of biros (in exchange for toffees) and we've really hit it off. Well, when I say 'hit it off', I mean we're still at the 'Please can I borrow a biro?' 'Certainly. If you give me a toffee' stage, but 'friends are friends' as the saying goes.

Conversation with Tony tonight. 'I've made a detailed analysis of that form you gave me,' He said
  'Oh yes,' I said, excited. 'What does it mean then?'
  'I'm not quite sure,' he replied, 'but I think they might be aliens.'

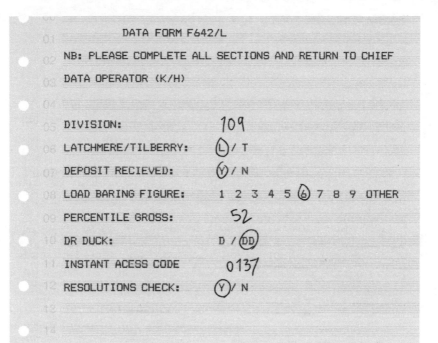

```
            DATA FORM F642/L

NB: PLEASE COMPLETE ALL SECTIONS AND RETURN TO CHIEF

DATA OPERATOR (K/H)


DIVISION:                 109

LATCHMERE/TILBERRY:      (L)/ T

DEPOSIT RECIEVED:        (Y)/ N

LOAD BARING FIGURE:      1  2  3  4  5 (6) 7  8  9  OTHER

PERCENTILE GROSS:         52

DR DUCK:                  D /(DD)

INSTANT ACESS CODE       0137

RESOLUTIONS CHECK:       (Y)/ N
```

Just WHAT does it all mean . . .?!

Thursday April 14th

Everyone seemed to be eating on the bus this morning. An old man was chomping on a hard-boiled egg, a young lady was biting an avocado as if it were an apple, and an extremely tubby man with 4 chins was scoffing a succession of Quality Street chocolates straight out of a plastic bag. I wonder what he'd done with the original box? (Perhaps he'd swallowed it!)

Not wanting to be left out, I popped a toffee in my mouth and took a refreshing lick of Mentathon 3000. That'll teach them!

Friday April 15th

Rita really seems to be enjoying the calligraphy set I bought her. When I returned from work today, she was in the living room teaching depressed/depressing Mary how to calligraphize.

I have always been fond of depressed/depressing Mary, but do feel rather sorry for her since she still lives with her parents, both of whom are in their late 90s. As a result, depressed/depressing Mary rarely gets to go out, and, whenever she does, she normally ends up quite emotional. Rita told me that she once tried to eat clay.

Hence, when I asked depressed/depressing Mary to show me what she'd been writing (it looked like the word 'chains' in tiny italic handwriting), she got extremely agitated and immediately tore up her work. I apologized, but Rita hobbled over to me and told me to 'leave the room at once!'.

I don't think I'll ever truly understand the female person.

Saturday April 16th

Pretty uneventful driving lesson this afternoon (explained emergency stops, changed bulb in neighbour's fridge), although Miss Marsh did say something rather interesting: 'Don't you think life would be so much better if mankind had never invented the wheel?'

Was relieved to come home to an empty house. With Rita out with Linda all day, now was my chance to look for all my boxes of letters.

I was shocked! I found them hidden behind the big cupboard in the loft!

How on earth did Rita get them up there?! Apart from her fear of heights, she can hardly walk at the moment, let alone negotiate a rickety aluminium ladder. Plus, each box must weigh at least two roast chickens.

And what if she had seen Smithy . . .?

This is all very worrying.

Anyway, I eventually settled down and had a good, long read, while Smithy merrily hopped about. I must say – and without blowing my own trumpet – there really were some super ideas for new products in there (including a blowless trumpet, funnily enough!).

Here are my favourites . . .

List of good inventions, by Robin Cooper:

1) Beef Scarecrows: Quite simple really – scarecrows made from beef. Both frightening (to crows) and environmentally friendly (to man). Unfortunately they were also edible to crows (and man) (i.e. Tony).

2) Robin Cooper's Revolutionary New Dart Board: I felt it was time to give the old-fashioned darts board a well overdue 'make-over'. My idea was for a new (non round) dartboard, with added triangular sections for triple score. Some dart players suggested it was a little 'complicated' however.

3) Parmaynu the Ping-Pong Bat. A delightful character with a friendly demeanour, Parmaynu was designed as the 'face of table tennis' and a figurehead for ping-pong players the world over (see below). Books, films and cereals were planned (but never physically realized).

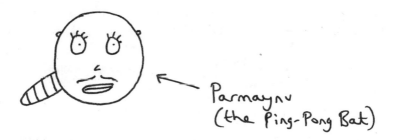

Parmaynu
(the Ping-Pong Bat)

4) Greem: An entirely new, never-seen-before colour (not

entirely unlike green), set to revolutionize the world of the visual arts and vision in general. Alas, it didn't.

5) Waspard – Whilst bees make honey, wasps can make (a form of) mustard, apparently. Wasp mustard, or 'Waspard', never really got off the ground due to the rather hazardous extraction process. Taste was also an issue.

6) The Boar'ngalow – A single-floored wooden dwelling, specially designed for domesticated boars to live in. Actual production prevented by issues pertaining to environmental health (specifically, boars escaping).

7) The Imsimil-berati-lahn. As its name suggests, a noise reduction device. When placed in the home or office, the Imsimil-berati-lahn reduces all sounds by a factor of 25. The prototype would have been a great success, had it not amplified sounds by a factor of 25.

8) Cleani-Vox (the 'Speaking Soap'). A bar of soap that physically tells you when your hands are clean. It measures the amount of dirt that is left on your hands, then plays a tape-recorded message (of Tony's voice) via the in-built mini speaker, letting you know when to stop washing. On hindsight, I suspect size may have been an obstacle.

9) The raspberry razor – Self-explanatory really. A razor used to shave off the tiny hairs from raspberries. Perfect for the particularly fussy cook and anyone allergic to fruit hair. Sadly, customers were hard to find.

10) The blowless trumpet (see above).

It's such a shame that the great British manufacturing community never quite took up any of these wonderful ideas. I'm certain that each one could still be of great benefit, not only to the British people, but also to mankind – and womankind – in general. All they need is a little 'fine tuning'.

Have resolved to step up my inventing projects. Verily will I show the world!

Sunday April 17th

Tea at Mother's.

Gerald was slouched in the armchair when we walked in. Once again he was in his tight safari suit, drinking champagne, and also once again he kissed Rita's hand.

I do wish he wouldn't do that.

Was going to say something to him about Mother's driving lessons (car still untouched in driveway in its ribbon and bow) but Rita threw me such a nasty look (sort of like a sneer but with an added dramatic twistage of her nose) that I decided to 'keep my tongue' (i.e. I didn't say anything – I think that's what the expression means).

Mother spent most of the afternoon rushing around Gerald as usual. She kept feeding him luxury truffles, and even fetched his slippers from the bedroom. What were his slippers doing in the bedroom? She's even started calling him 'Gerryboo'.

I must say, it really is strange to see Mother so happy with another man. I can't remember her being this happy when Father was alive (except perhaps for when he was in another room).

Later, I found out that it was Tony who carried my boxes of letters up to the loft, in exchange for the apple crumble we had two Sundays ago.

I called Tony and had angry words.

'You betrayed me for the price of a dessert,' I said.
'What could I do, Robin?' he said. 'You know I love crumble.'

He went on . . .
'By the way, did you know there's a bird in your loft?'
'Yes,' I replied. 'Why?'
'I'd be careful if I were you. The thing's got a nasty bite.'

Good old Smithy!

Monday April 18th

Had a chat with drowsy Wilson at the tea and coffee machine today (Henderson has ordered him to drink one cup of black coffee every hour, due to repeat slumbering offences). In an effort to squeeze some information out of him, I mentioned that I thought it was a bit odd that there were no women working with us, and Wilson replied, 'Well, what we do isn't really women's work, is it?'

'Isn't it?' I thought (but didn't dare say out loud).

I suppose I must be a spy then!

Tuesday April 19th

The extremely tubby man with the 4 chins was on the bus again this morning with his plastic bag full of chocolates. Today his total was a staggering 31 – and with no recourse to sips of water. Think he must be part camel!

Spoke to Michael in Sydney tonight. Unfortunately, he'd hurt his back practising his dancing at the weekend, so Simon had to give him a special massage. I do hope he's properly qualified.

Wednesday April 20th

My one and only work friend, Wilson, has been sacked.

Word has it that he was caught snoozing underneath Henderson's car. Quite what he was doing there in the first place, no one seems to know. What a shame. I shall have to find myself a new Wilson (i.e. friend).

After work, I went for a little walk with Rita along the high street. She's no longer crutch-dependent and is back to her normal legs again. Saw Old Milly out on her bench as usual. She was in a particularly sorry state, with strange blue markings all over her face. On closer inspection these turned out to be small

112

grids of 'noughts and crosses,' which she must have drawn all over herself in biro.

When we passed, she was adding a 'nought' in one of the boxes on her chin, using a cracked make-up mirror to guide her. I gave her my customary 50p (total trampal donation: £3.50) and explained to Rita that Old Milly was the lady who telephoned her while I was stuck in the bathroom. Rita said 'thank you', then Old Milly said:

'Did you know we've both got something in common?'

'Really?' asked Rita. 'What's that?'

'We've both seen your husband naked!'

I don't think Rita likes Old Milly very much.

Thursday April 21st

The entire office was on its best behaviour today. The Chairman, a small white-haired man named Mr Stevens, was paying us a visit.

Henderson, whose moustache looked neater than ever, accompanied Mr Stevens on his walkabout and, when they reached my workstation, Henderson actually introduced me as their 'star employee'.

Mr Stevens said, 'Yes, I've heard about you. They say you're doing a grand job.'

'Thank you, sir,' I replied. 'I try to do my best.' (What else could I say?)

'So what exactly do you do?' he asked.

Oh dear.

'I'm an Above-the-line Resolutions Officer,' I replied.

'I know that,' he said, 'but what does an Above-the-line Resolutions Officer do on a day-to-day basis?'

Oh dear, oh dear.

I looked at Henderson.

Henderson looked at me.

I looked at Mr Stevens.

Mr Stevens looked at Henderson.

Henderson looked at Mr Stevens, then Henderson looked at me.

This was it . . .

'Well, as an Above-the-line Resolutions Officer, I officiate all the various details pertaining to the business in as resolute manner as possible, paying particular attention to all those factors that physically fall on top of the actual line of business . . . that we are in.'

Mr Stevens looked at me.

I looked at Mr Stevens.

Mr Stevens looked at Henderson.

Henderson looked at Mr Stevens.

Mr Stevens looked back at me.

I looked back at Mr Stevens.

Mr Stevens looked at Henderson.

'My, he is good!' said Mr Stevens. 'What a clever chap!'

As soon as they left, I shoved three toffees into my mouth and guzzled half a tube of toothpaste.

Tube of Mentathon 3000 (toothpaste)   Three toffees (in their wrappers)

Friday April 22nd

That's it!

I have an idea! A new idea! A FABULOUS idea! It's a sure-fire, runaway, billy-boy HIT!!!!

And I owe it ALL to the 4-chinned, chocolate eating, non-drinking camel-man on the bus!

Why?

Well . . .

What if one were to combine the deliciousness of a chocolate bar with the thirst-quenchingness of a glass of water?

Thus was born . . .

'Aqua Choc'.

Aqua Choc is – quite simply – the first chocolate bar in the WORLD with a water centre.

The moment you bite into it, you instantly receive a mouthful of refreshing – and delicious – water. In fact, you could even say it's the most mouth-watering chocolate (soon to be) on the market!

I was hardly able to concentrate at work (due to the above) and as soon as I got home, I telephoned Tony. He agreed at once that it was a 'brilliant idea' and that we were sure to become – as he put it – 'the new Cadbury's brothers'.

Am keeping this quiet from Rita at the moment. She tripped over Mr Alfonso's cat, Monty, in the driveway yesterday, and has been rather irritable since. In fact, she kicked me so hard in bed last night, that I now have a bruise on my shin in the shape of Wales.

Anyway, Tony and I are to begin work on 'Project X' (our secret name for the Aqua Choc project) this Sunday.

(Aqua) Chocs Away!!!!!!!!!!!!

Saturday April 23rd

Miss Marsh couldn't stop smiling all through her lesson today. When I asked her what was the matter (Miss Marsh smiling is normally a worrying sign) she went bright red, and then told me that it was just because she was happy with her new hairstyle (I hadn't even noticed, but I pretended I had).

Instead of its usual 'limp' style, Miss Marsh's hair was sort of done up like a mound of 'buns', with clumps of hair modelled into sort of 'mini buns', which were in turn connected to slightly larger buns, all feeding into a central bun 'unit'. It was quite effective actually – if you're going for the bun 'effect', I suppose.

Miss Marsh was in such a good mood that she even sat in the driver's seat, held the steering wheel, and mimed driving for about ten minutes, while I handed her tissues.

We are suddenly making real progress.

Afterwards, spent over £20 on chocolate bars in Mr Singh's shop. Hid them behind table tennis table in shed. Tony and I will need them in the production of our prototype.

Life, Dear Diary, is ever so exciting at the moment!

Sunday April 24th

Project X (Secret name for Aqua Choc) day:

Tony had agreed to meet me in the shed at 9:30 sharp this morning. At 10:15, when he'd still not arrived, I gave him a call, but a very weary-sounding Susan answered, saying 'I don't know where he is, and I don't care where he is!' before hanging up.

I tried Tony's mobular telephone, but only got through to his voice-answering system. I didn't leave a message (I never know how to – is it before or after the 'beepage'?).

Not one to be deterred, I decided to press on alone, but after about twenty minutes I grew tired and so had a little lie-down on the floor. Unfortunately I fell fast asleep.

Several hours later, the shed door was burst open and I was rudely awoken. It was Tony. He was drunk. Very drunk.

'Sorry I'm late,' he said (Tony was 8 hours 10 minutes late to be precise), 'but I bumped into an old friend.'

In stumbled a large ginger-haired man with no front teeth.

'You remember Jimmy,' said Tony.

I had never met Jimmy in my entire life.

'Oh yes,' I replied, 'nice to see you again, Jimmy.'

'Have we met?' said Jimmy.

For the next thirty minutes Tony and Jimmy regaled me with 'blue' jokes (none of which I will print here, Dear Diary), whilst swigging can upon can of Pennyfeather's ale. To cap it all, they ate their way through at least £6 of chocolate.

I shall be charging Tony for misappropriation of stock. Technically, that's office theft.

Since there was no way of kicking them out, I left them in the shed, and went back into the house for dinner (soup, lamb, potatoes, carrots, peas, trifle and whipped cream, chocolate biscuits, an apple). I think I heard Tony stumble out at about 10pm. I presume Jimmy left with him.

I should never have gone into partnership with Tony. When will I EVER learn?

Monday April 25th

Rita woke me at 6 this morning, saying, 'Robin, there's a big, ginger-haired man relieving himself in the garden.'

It was Jimmy.

I waited calmly for Jimmy to finish his 'business', then not-so-calmly chased him down the drive with a mop. Rita called me her 'hero' and promptly awarded me a pentagon's worth of kisses (i.e. 5).

I do hope I never see Jimmy again (or rather, he never sees me again . . .).

Work was busy as usual. More forms. More resolutioning. It really is a wonderful business, and I'm sure General Incorporated Business Solutions are leaders in their field (whatever the field is).

Tidied up shed when I got home. It was an absolute pigsty. There were half-eaten chocolate bars and crushed ale cans everywhere. I even found one of Jimmy's socks in there.* I shall be having very serious words with Tony.

Forgot to say. Read the Sunday Times 'Rich List' supplement yesterday. Very depressing read. One man made £40 million just from chairs. Chairs!

*I know it's Jimmy's because Tony never wears socks – even in winter.

Tuesday April 26th

Went to Signor Pantini's for dinner with Mother and Gerald tonight. Picked them up on the way first, and noticed that the ribbon and bow are still tied around Mother's car. When WILL Gerald start giving her those famous driving lessons? Of course, Rita forbad me from saying anything. I hate being forbad!

Anyway, ended up having quite an annoying meal, as mother kept calling Gerald, 'Gerryboo' and Gerald kept calling Mother, 'Hilaryboo'.

Tried to listen to Mr Pantini singing (his voice was particularly high tonight) but Gerald insisted on telling us more of his 'adventure' stories:

1) Polar bear stampede in Arctic ('We fought them off hand to paw').
2) Escape from hungry cannibals ('They were very, very hungry').
3) Venomous moth in Tanzania ('One bite and you can't move your legs').

Am sure the last time I heard these, the polar bears were penguins, the cannibals were pygmies, and the moth was a mouse that nibbled a lot.

To make things worse, I had to pay for the entire meal since Gerald had accidentally 'mislaid' his wallet. I noticed he'd ordered the lobster and an £18 bottle of wine – plus the most expensive sorbet on the menu ('Milanese coconut de luxe').

Wednesday April 27th

Was woken very early this morning by an awful choking sound. Looked out of the window to see that wretched cat, Monty, skulking around Mr Alfonso's tulips, and coughing up enormous fur balls. One of them was the size of a profiterole!

Saw Tony tonight. He finally apologized for his behaviour on Sunday, but when I told him about Jimmy sleeping in the shed and then using our garden as his toilet, he looked at me blankly and, with all seriousness, said, 'Who's Jimmy?'

What do they put in that Pennyfeather's stuff?

Thursday April 28th

Another exciting letter from Gunter today . . .

Landsberger Strasse 60
CH-8006
Zürich
SWITZERLAND

Thursday the April ²¹th

My dear friendly Robin,

I am very deligted that you are finally in the working again. You explain your job but I think that I am not understanding of it. What are you doings there Robin?

Here in Zürich life is good. Heidi is passing her exam G.M.B. (I do not no the words in England) and she had big smiles all day. She is also wearing the ticket with proudness.

Small water damage in roof of auto.

I think I am mentioning the house handles in my letter of last. It is now being very bad because they are aktiv at night and it has been hard for us sleeping because of the sounds. Heidi has put stoffen in the ears but still she is hearing. The officer from Central Platz is giving us stickung boxes but we have had no result. Did you be doing this with your house handles Robin or did you do otherwise?

We are both very exciting to see you. We have making all the nessesary arrangings and will be arriving in your land on Friday June 10 at 10:15 in the morning at London Airways. Will you be so kind as to carry us, or will you do otherwise?

Looking forward with impatiance.

Your ever friendly

Gunter Schwartz

Gunter Schwartz

As soon as we were both back from work, Rita took out a piece of her 'calligrapher's parchment paper' and, with her special italics pen, wrote out a familiar list.

'House handles' might be:

1) Alarm clocks that keep going off at night(?).
2) A tinnitus-inducing device (whatever that may be).
3) Cuckoo clocks that make a lot of noise (it is Switzerland after all).
4) Something that is only ever used by Swiss Germans and no one else in the world.

We think it's probably number 4. Anyway, all will become clear in just 43 days.

Friday April 29th

Started talking to Patel today from the International Department (yes, they even do whatever it is they do in other countries!). We met at the tea and coffee machine. He helped me locate the 'tea' button.

Patel's a friendly sort of chap, but only seems to talk about aeroplanes. He's completely obsessed! He even wears a badge featuring a different plane every day (today it was a 747, yesterday it was a 737).

As a joke, I told him that I was 'very fond of aviation', as it was the 'only way to fly!' He laughed so much (well, it was a good joke) that Henderson came out of his office, and told us both to get back to our workstations!

This is all very exciting. Patel may well become my new Wilson . . .

P.S. – Washed Smithy's pyjamas tonight.

Saturday April 30th

Today's driving lesson was a veritable landmark in the Cooper-Marsh vehicular eruditional two-way relationship (or 'C-MVE2WR' in initials!).

Not only was the engine actually switched on, but Miss Marsh (whose hair was still in buns) even asked me to 'take the hand-brake off and make the car move' (her actual words).

Of course I was in the driving seat, and we only drove to the end of her driveway, but Miss Marsh managed to keep her eyes open the whole time (something that will certainly come in handy when she's behind the wheel), and afterwards she even asked me to reverse the car back up to her house.

Well done Miss Marsh. Well done I! And well done buns!

May

Sunday May 1st – 'May Day – May Day!' (To be read as if in an emergency!!)

Project X (Secret name for Aqua Choc) day 2:

Tony kept to his word, and arrived on time for our second meeting today. He was even wearing a suit. When I asked him why, he said, 'So as to appear professional.'

There wasn't much I could say to that!

Anyway, for the next five hours – and without a Pennyfeather's in sight – Tony and I worked solidly (and soberly) as a team. Our main aim was to figure out the best way to physically get water to go inside a chocolate bar and then to actually stay there (i.e. not leak everywhere).

Finally, we came up with our solution:

1) Slice open an ordinary household chocolate bar using razor blade.

2) Bevel out mini 'well' in chocolate using mini chisel.

3) Drip distilled water (from Tony's garage, which he has assured me is safe to drink) into mini well, using a pipette.

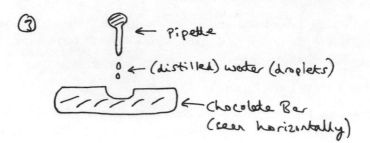

4) Re-seal chocolate bar, using melted chocolate as 'cement'.

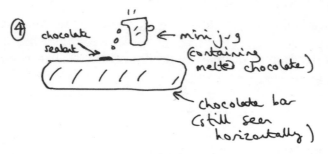

5) Smooth down cemented edges with plastic smoothing instrument (i.e. protractor).

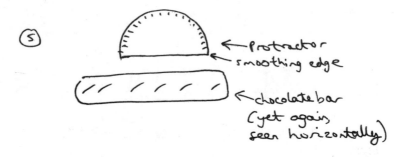

6) Hey presto! Aqua Choc is born!

Once we had completed our first prototype, Tony and I shook hands in an official manner (i.e. firmly), and then invited Rita into the shed to become the world's first official Aqua Choc taster.

The tasting didn't go quite to plan.

The water filling went down the wrong hole. Rita had a choking fit. Tony gave her a whack on the back. Rita slipped and lost her balance. Tony tried to catch her but failed. Rita fell out of the shed and resprained her ankle.

Oh alas . . .

Monday May 2nd – Bank Holiday

Tony came round early this morning to apologize to Rita. He gave her a big bunch of tulips, which looked like he'd picked them himself (from Mr Alfonso's garden), but Rita was touched and so asked him to stay for lunch. As usual, Tony obliged.

After yesterday's Aqua Choc debacle, I felt we could all do with a bit of cheering up. So, after lunch, I composed a new (and I think, very funny) Bank Holiday joke.

> *I say I say I say, what did the bank say to the building society?*
> *– I don't know, what did the bank say to the building society?*
> *I say I say I say, have a think, then.*

– I have thought long and hard but I just don't know.
I say I say I say, would you like me to tell you the answer?
– Yes, I would.
I say I say I say, what did the bank say to the building soci-
ety?
– I don't know.
I say I say I say – neither do I – because I've forgotten
now!!!!!!!!!

Understandably, Rita wasn't really in the mood (and also could-
n't find her glasses to 'listen' properly), but Tony loved it, and
said that it was 'even funnier' than my last one.

Have resolved to send it into the local paper again – despite what
happened last time. Hopefully it will win the competition (a set
of 'professional squash racquets' plus ten cartons of washing
powder) and they'll be no more of that 'Ted G. Fetfus' nonsense.

I wish myself luck!

Wednesday May 4th

New tea and coffee machine installed at work, which has even
more buttons (40) than the last one. Went to have a good look at
it, and noticed there was even an option for salt – dispensed in
cubes! Made myself a cup of tea (with one salt) but it wasn't
very nice (too salty) so promptly added one sugar, which more
or less cancelled it out.

Thursday May 5th

Smithy's lady friend is back.

Presumably he wooed her with his fresh, clean pyjamas (which
were a better fit, actually, as they'd shrunk slightly in the wash).

Watched the two 'love birds' (sorry, I couldn't resist!) quietly for
a bit (lots of neck rubbing and close-contact-cooing) then
politely made my exit.

All that wonderful cooing made me think of all the – no less – wonderful sounds in the world (there must be at least a million), and so here are my top 20 favourite sounds.

Robin Cooper's Top 20 Favourite Sounds (in the world):

1) 'Coooooo' (Smithy/wood-pigeons in general).
2) 'Kirl siiiiiii' (envelope being opened).
3) 'Scrahh scrahh' (pen 'pon paper).
4) 'Thrlirrr' (butter 'pon bread).
5) 'Robin' (hearing my name – but only if it's followed by good news!).
6) 'Bzzzzzzzz' (Bumble bee – but only if it's friendly!).
7) 'Kir-kirll, kirl-kirll' (toffee being unwrapped), 'Khr-rumph' (then chewed).
8) 'Nyeaaah' (My shed door opening) (NB: oil hinges).
9) 'Sfiiiiih' (Bus hydraulic system).
10) 'Sfih' (My head hitting my pillow at night).
11) 'Donnnnnng!' (Big Ben).
12) 'Dinnnnnng!' (Little Len).
13) 'Hello' (greeting).
14) 'Tseh' (the tearing of a tissue).
15) 'Fffut!' (Pickwinkle in use).
16) 'Slriii' (A lick of Mentathon 3000) (or any quality toothpaste).
17) I can't think of any more (that's not a sound, but an apology).
18) Oh – here's one: '   ' (the sound of silence!).
19) And another: '   ' (Inside a monastery!).
20) I almost forgot – 'Schmah!' (A kiss from Rita!).

Perhaps I could do a list for all the senses (tasting, seeing, hearing (see above), touching etc.). I could even publish them in a professionally published book. I could call it 'Robin Cooper's SENSE-IBLE lists!'

I'm sure it would become a bestsenser! (i.e. bestseller).

Friday May 6th

Had another cup of tea with salt today. I don't know why really. Perhaps I'm developing a bit of a 'salt tooth'. Anyway, managed to get most of it down. Patel (Harrier jet badge) took a sip and told me it tasted of 'runway grit'. We both laughed quite loudly, before Henderson tapped angrily on his window. Patel has definitely become my new Wilson. Hoorah!

After dinner, depressed/depressing Mary came over to see Rita, and the two of them sat calligraphizing in the living room. Depressed/depressing Mary now has a calligraphy set of her own, which looked even better than Rita's (it even had purple ink).

Soon afterwards Linda walked in, carrying a large plastic bag. 'Look what Ian bought me,' she said. Inside was an incredibly expensive-looking calligraphy set, surpassing anything that Rita or depressed/depressing Mary had. Their faces dropped.

'It's all gold ink,' said Linda. 'Real gold.'

I think I can see what's coming . . .

Saturday May 7th

Rita bought a new pen this morning. It cost £45. £45 for a pen!

I was not happy, but Rita assured me that it was 'very useful for the letter S', and 'very good value for money'. After lunch (and after calling Linda and depressed/depressing Mary to tell them all about it), Rita used the pen to copy out an old poem from a magazine, called 'Lady Grey and the Parlour Maid'.

When Rita was out of the room, I secretly counted up all the Ss. There were precisely 25 of them: 'was', 'enters', 'curtsies', 'cleans', 'suddenly', 'spots', 'mouse', 'cheese', 'mistress', 'shouts', 'hits', 'pleads', 'stop', 'ignores', 'banishes', 'street', 'streets', 'misery'.

25 Ss! That's £1.80 per 'S'! Hardly 'value for money', I thought.

By the way, there seemed to be more buns on Miss Marsh's head today. In fact, there was a whole new cluster right behind her left ear. Anyway, we (i.e. I) drove round the block twice, and Miss Marsh managed to keep her eyes open the whole time.

Think I can safely say that Miss Marsh's confidence is directly proportional to hair bunnage.

Sunday May 8th

With the sun out, and Rita back in socks (hoorah!), we went to Regent's Park, London NW1 (don't know rest of postcode but will endeavour to find out) for a picnic with Mother and Gerald.

The Cooper Picnic Menu:

French bread
(Non French) bread
Flask of tea
Flask of soup (flask broke in car, when we drove over new and
    never seen before road bump at end of street. I shall be writ-
    ing to council)
Assorted salad items
Bar of Aqua Choc (but no one would try it)
Cold roast potatoes (× 12)
Butter (hoorah!)
Hams (assortment of)
Ketchup
Cinnamon (I don't know why Rita brought that)
Turkey slices (× 20)
Plain yoghurt (× 1 for Rita)
Jam (flavour unknown, as label missing. Rita suspected it was
    blackcurrant. Gerald insisted it was banana)
Crisps (× 5 packets – one each – plus one spare for me)
Apples (1 × cox, 3 × pippins, 1 × toffee (apple))
Pears (2 × conference)
Lemonade
Toffees (author's own!)

Smashing grub (see above for details), although it would have been nicer if Gerald hadn't gone into quite so much detail about his international culinary exploits. Just as I was biting into my turkey sandwich, he launched into a rather graphic story about the time he was forced to eat his own sewage in Borneo.

By the way, Gerald offered to pay for half the food, but then discovered that he'd 'mislaid' his wallet again.

Monday May 9th

Turquoise button returned last night, but this time the dream ended quite differently . . .

It began as normal (i.e. with lots of zapping – Regent's Park, Gerald, turkey sandwiches, ketchup etc.), but then, just as I was about to become a 'zappee', Miss Marsh suddenly jumped in front of me (this is in my dream, and not in my bedroom!!!) and took the full force of the giant button's deadly beam. I never knew Miss Marsh was that brave!

But what happened next was even more amazing – her hair buns started to absorb all the rays, and throb bright turquoise. Then there was an enormous flash, and Miss Marsh was transformed into a sort of triangular shaped, hat-wearing 'being' (who was now male), called 'Cardinal Wig-Wam Tommy'. Cardinal Wig-Wam Tommy removed his hat, pointed it at the craft, and fired a huge missile right out of the end.

Bullseye!

It hit! The giant turquoise button exploded – and I was saved!

Hoorah for Miss Marsh! Hoorah for Cardinal Wig-Wam Tommy!

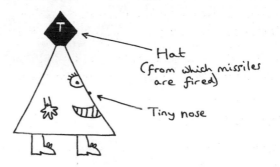

Cardinal Wig-Wam Tommy (Miss Marsh in 'dream form')

Hat
(from which missiles
are fired)

Tiny nose

Tuesday May 10th

Spoke to Michael in Sydney this morning. Unfortunately his back's still been playing up, so Simon's had to continue with his massages. Luckily he's not charged Michael a thing, but then I suppose that's what friends are for.

P.S. – sit's snow svery slate, sand sam swriting sthis ssecretly swith SRita's snew spen sthat's smeant sto sbe sgood sfor SSs. SActually sit sis! Slook: Ssssssssssssssssssss Sssssssssssssssssssssssssssssssssssssssssssssssssss S s s s s s s s s s s s s s s s s s s s s s s Ssssssssssssssssssssssssssssssssssssssssssssssssssssssssssssssss ssssssss

196 Ss. That's 23p an 's'. At last, we've got our money's worth!

Wednesday May 11th

A woman has started working at General Incorporated Business Solutions (which probably means that we're not spies after all). Have no idea what she does but she's in workstation 1, has red hair and seems to wear an awful lot of perfume. I'm sure she

133

uses it as air freshener as well, as I've smelt it a couple of times in the unisex toilet after she's left. Have heard she's a divorcee.

Speaking of women, I popped into the loft this evening and found Smithy still entertaining his lady friend. I didn't stay long. What's more, his pyjamas were off.

Such is love . . .

Thursday May 12th

Ever since our picnic last Sunday, I've been trying to find out the rest of the postcode for London's Regent's Park, but it turns out that there is no rest of the postcode. It's just 'NW1'. Fancy that! Well, at least I've put that mystery to bed, and can continue with my life.

New Data Form (R1045a) issued at work today. Even more baffling than the last ('Dr Duck' has been replaced with 'Dr Gull'). According to Henderson, the changeover was 'vital', so as to 'bring us in line with Europe and the rest of the world'.

Tony now suspects Mossad.

By the way, there was only one 'Linegan's Luck' pen in my penholder this morning. Am sure there were two when I left the office last night. Strange.

Friday May 13th (i.e. Friday the 13th, i.e. unlucky for some . . . see below)

Woke up with horrid mouth pain today (i.e. toothache) and then this arrived . . .

Brent Herald

2-9 Lyndhurst Road, London NW4

11ᵗʰ May

From: Local Follics Department, The Brent Herald.

To: Robin Cooper
Brondesbury Villas, London

Dear Mr Cooper,

I say I say I say,
Your second joke we got,
I say I say I say,
But win, it did not.

I say I say I say,
It really was quite bad,
I say I say I say,
We think you are quite mad!

Yours sincerely,

Ted G Fetfus

The Fetfus Affair has reared its ugly head yet again.

I was so incensed, so enraged, so utterly livid that Rita had to physically restrain me from calling the police ('999'). This is an outrage of the most outrageous kind. Those professional squash racquets had my name (metaphorically) written all over them.

I shall get to the bottom of this!

Saturday May 14th

Woke up in such a bad mood today that I had to cancel my driving lesson. Think Miss Marsh was secretly relieved, though, as she said 'Oh good' when I told her. (I didn't mention anything about the whole 'Cardinal Wig-Wam Tommy' business.)

Tony got very angry when I broke him the terrible news about the joke competition. He crushed his ale can with his bare hands, flung it across the shed (I'm getting quite used to this now), and swore violently (that too), using a combination of words beginning with 'b' and 's'. (I will NEVER get used to that.)

After Tony left, I seethed in shed for rest of the day, while Rita sat in the living room, copying out Queen Elizabeth I's signature from a book on Tudor women. Unfortunately I don't think she was concentrating hard enough (ice-skating on television at same time), as she added an extra 'I' on the end, and was therefore left with a piece of paper bearing the name of our present (and glorious) Queen. I didn't say anything, but I'm pretty sure that forging the signature of a living monarch ranks as treason.

Luckily there wasn't a policeman about. Rita could have been hanged.

Monday May 16th

Had a very angry conversation with the editor of the Brent Herald (Gary H. Meadows) at lunchtime today. Once again, he denied all knowledge of the letter, and of the culprit. I asked if they had any spare squash racquets in the office, but he merely smirked. I told him that I couldn't abide smirkers, to which he smirked again, and then hung up.

The absolute cheek!

And so, after much deliberation, the directors of Aqua Choc Inc. (i.e. Tony Sutton and I) have decided that the best ways to get our own back are the following (things):

1) Finish making our bars of delicious (but 'choke-free') Aqua Choc.
2) Sell them in professional confectionary shops up and down the land.
3) Then, when the Brent Herald comes a-knocking for free samples (for 'review' purposes), we jolly well tell them where to go!
4) Failing that, Tony will personally 'smash the editor's little teeth in'.
5) Hopefully we will only need to action points 1–3.

P.S. – Secretly tore up Rita's illicit forgery this evening, then burnt the shreds of paper in the back garden, and scattered the ashes down Mr Alfonso's drain. They can hang Mr Alfonso, but no one will hang my Rita!

Tuesday May 17th

Tooth still hurting. Think it's my left dorsal molar (or is that birds?)*. Have been brushing with/nibbling at Mentathon 3000, but it doesn't seem to help – although it still tastes nice! Have therefore booked the dreaded dentist for Saturday . . .

> Oh dentist be gentle,
> Dentist be kind,
> Do not cause affliction,
> Unto this man of mine (i.e. me).

*Actually, do birds have teeth?

Wednesday May 18th

Da-da-da-daaaaaaaa! Tony and I have made a breakthrough with Aqua Choc.

We've finally worked out a way to slow down the speed at which the water centre flows from the chocolate 'well' and into the customer's mouth – thus preventing possible asphyxiation (always bad for business).

The secret lies in the 'resealing' process: i.e. using a thicker chocolate sealant, which reduces surface area of roof of 'well', creating lower volume of water held and, in turn, gentler flow of liquid into customer's mouth, thereby ensuring smoother taste, and survival of customer.

Offered Rita a bite of our new, improved Aqua Choc but she simply refused. That woman can be SO stubborn sometimes.

Thursday May 19th

Ate a bar of Aqua Choc on the bus this morning. It was delicious (and refreshing). Shame the chocolate-eating man with the 4 chins wasn't around. I'm sure he'd have enjoyed it too.

Another pen missing from my pen-holder this morning. I was absolutely livid. I cannot bear people touching my things without my (verbal/written) permission. How dare they?! I feel defiled! Absolutely defiled!

It is clear there is an office thief about but, mark my words, Dear Diary, I shall catch them red-handed (or rather blue-handed, as they are blue pens) – at whatever cost.

Friday May 20th

Think Tony and I have our first customer . . .

As luck would have it, the man with the 4 chins sat next to me on the bus this morning, and we got chatting. His name is Philip

Teff, he's 43, and he works for a company in north London that promotes Norfolk.

I told him that I'd noticed he was a chocolate lover ('I have the odd one every now and then,' he replied) and offered him a bite of my Aqua Choc. Luckily he loved it (and wasn't asphyxiated). In fact, he said that it was 'like a snack and a drink all in one'* and instantly placed an order for five bars.

Roll on the good times!

*NB – this could make a good slogan.

Saturday May 21st

The dreaded dentist today.

I really don't know why I still go to Dr Davis. He's such an unpleasant man, and not a particularly good dentist either. Last time, he gave me a filling which fell out two days later when I got the hiccups. I may be no tooth expert, but I'm pretty sure that fillings should be 'hiccup-proof'.

I'd only been in the chair for a couple of minutes when I needed to answer the call of nature, so I asked Dr Davis – very politely – if I could use his toilet. He sighed loudly (into my mouth) and said, 'Well, don't be long.' Dr Davis's toilet is actually a bathroom. With a bath in it. I don't know why there's a bath in it. When would a dentist ever need to take a bath? Today, however, the bath was actually running.

When I got back in the chair I said, 'Do you know that your bath is running?' but Dr Davis sighed loudly into my mouth again and replied, 'Just keep still, Mr Cooper.'

Unfortunately I couldn't relax. I kept wondering what would happen if his bath overflowed. The bathroom was directly above the surgery, and so the whole tub could have come crashing down through the ceiling and flattened us both! I think Dr Davis

sensed my anxiety because, out of nowhere, he suddenly bellowed, 'Stop worrying about the bl**dy bath, and keep your
mouth open!'

Very painful filling. Simply MUST find a new dentist.

Quite difficult to teach Miss Marsh afterwards due to benumbed
mouth, but after psyching herself up (2 toffees, 6 tissues) Miss
Marsh actually took the wheel, released the handbrake, and let
the car move forward down her drive. Hoorah!

Next week, we're switching on the engine.

Sunday May 22nd

Spent most of the morning making up Philip Teff's Aqua Choc
order (Tony was supposed to assist, but naturally didn't turn
up). Must admit it was quite a fiddly procedure, as I kept getting
chocolate everywhere, and nearly lobbed off the top of my
thumb with the blasted razor blade.

After that, Rita and I went for a disappointing lunch at Linda
and Ian's. I must say, sometimes it really is hard to believe that
Linda is actually Rita's sister because she always serves such
meagre portions. On my plate were four roast potatoes (Rita
gives me between five and seven), 33 peas (I get 50 at home,
minimum), 1 piece of chicken (I'm used to three times this
amount) and only two scoops of ice cream (Rita always serves
four, plus I automatically get seconds).

I don't know how Ian puts up with it!

By the way, Linda is clearly bent on stirring things with Rita at
the moment. After lunch, she showed Rita her new calligraphy
pen, which was 'from Japan' and complete with a rotating, electronic nib.

Lunch at Linda's (seen from above)

Plate → ○ ○ 8 ← Roast potatoes (×4)

Pears (×33) →

chicken (1 piece)

Ice cream (2 scoops)

← Bowl

'It's perfect for Os and much better than your "s" pen!' she said, drawing Os all over her paper napkin (actually it was pretty good for Os). Rita sat there seething, but luckily we left before Ian got his bottom out.

I'm glad I'm not a sister.

Monday May 23rd

Gave Philip Teff his 5 bars of Aqua Choc this morning, in exchange for £2.50 plus a brochure all about Norfolk. He ate them all on the bus, and immediately placed an order for 10 more. Hoorah!

Mother (whose hair was 'natural' blonde again) popped round to see us this evening. When we asked where Gerald was she replied, 'He was meant to come with me, but at the last minute he took the car out for a spin instead.'

I couldn't believe it!

'Gerald's been driving your car?' I said.

'Yes, I put the insurance in his name. He thought it would be a good idea.'

'Has he given you any lessons yet?' I asked.

'No. Not yet. Gerryboo's been very busy recently'.

I gave Rita a look, but she didn't respond. Unfortunately I don't think we're on the same wavelength vis-à-vis Gerald Hale. Rita still thinks he's 'charming', and only the other day she described him as 'dashing'. I'm really not too sure about this Gerald Hale fellow . . .

Tuesday May 24th

Miss Marsh transformed herself into superhero, Cardinal Wig-Wam Tommy again last night.

She (well, he) saved me from an almost certain zapping, but sadly was too late to stop Ian from having his bottom obliterated.

I wonder if it's time for me to say something. Perhaps I should thank her . . .?

By the way, cleaned up the loft this evening (feathers, droppings, beetle casings etc.). Smithy used to be such a tidy bird, but lately he's really let himself go. Shame.

Wednesday May 25th

Secretly checked all workstations in the office today. No sign of any of my missing 'Linegan's Luck' pens, or devices used by petty thieves (torches, gloves, trapdoors etc.) to carry out writing-implement-related crimes. The case continues.

Linda finally apologized to Rita for her behaviour on Sunday. Apparently she'd been very 'emotional' of late. Tried to listen in on their telephone conversation (with a wine glass pressed up against the wall). Think I heard the word 'menopause' mentioned a couple of times.

P.S. – It is now five minutes past midnight, and I've just been woken by a loud knock at the door. It was Tony. He'd had another 'bust up' with Susan, and was in such a state

(Pennyfeather's) that he started to get undressed in the hallway! In the end I had to lead a completely naked man upstairs and guide him into Michael's bedroom. Thank the Lord Michael is away. Whatever would he think?

Thursday May 26th

Philip Teff likes Aqua Choc so much (he guzzled all 10 bars in just under 6 minutes today) that he's agreed to provide us with an official and hand-written affi-david (I never know how to spell that word) as to the quality of our product. Hoorah!

Smithy situation back to normal. It appears his lady friend has 'flown the coup' (as in 'coo'!), and Smithy's pyjamas – I'm pleased to say – are back on.

Tony staying another night, and Rita combed his hair again – with my comb!

Friday May 27th

Aqua Choc is ready to go . . .

Cooper & Sutton Chocolatiers
Brondesbury Villas
London

The Chairman/Chairwoman
Cadbury's (Delicious) Chocolates
Bournville Lane
Bournville
Birmingham
B30 2LU

27th May

Dear Sir/Madam,

Make way for a REVOLUTION in chocolate engineering…

Cooper & Sutton Chocolatiers proudly present the world's most refreshing chocolate bar that has ever and will ever exist(ed).

We're talkin' about AQUA CHOC!

Yes – AQUA CHOC!

AQUA CHOC is the only chocolate bar in the (known) universe featuring a delicious FRESH WATER FILLING.

It's like a snack and a drink all in one!

AQUA CHOC is perfect for:

- Thirsty chocolate eaters
- Busy mothers
- People 'on the go'
- Desert dwellers

That is why you CANNOT afford to miss out on the OPPORTUNITY of a LIFETIME.

So – book a meeting with Cooper & Sutton to sample AQUA CHOC live and we GUARANTEE you'll want to go into production (with AQUA CHOC) within minutes!

What are you waiting for?

Call NOW!

We look forward to hearing from you,

Robin Cooper   Tony Sutton

> I, Philip Howard Lee Teff, being of sound body
> and mind, do hereby testify that I have tasted
> Aqua Choc of my own free will, and that it was
> very, very nice.
> Signed:
>
> _[signature]_
>
> PHILIP H. L. TEFF

I wish myself (and Tony) luck!

Saturday May 28th

We have lift off!

Despite the fact that Miss Marsh's hair was bunless today (i.e. back to original 'limp' style), she turned the key in the ignition, put the car into first gear and physically moved the vehicle down her driveway, and onto the actual road.

We made it as far as the little roundabout at the end of the street before Miss Marsh became 'nauseous', and her nose started running rather heavily. I mopped her face with tissues, popped a toffee into her mouth, then drove her back home, before fixing her neighbour's toaster (he paid me in toast).

Well, I think that merits a semi hoorah . . .

Hoo!

Popped into Mother's on the way back. Car in driveway looking a little shabby (general bird messings, plus the words 'clean me' written in dust by unknown hand). Was surprised to find Mother and Gerald still in their dressing gowns – at 4:30 in the afternoon. Noticed Gerald has particularly small feet for a man.

Also noticed that Gerald still hasn't paid me for the picnic (or the restaurant).

Sunday May 29th

Susan finally allowed Tony back home this morning. Don't think he was too pleased. Needless to say he didn't bother tidying up Michael's room before he left. I found 9 empty cans of Pennyfeather's in the sock drawer, and a rather unsavoury magazine (and I can tell you – Dear Diary – that it was certainly NOT the Reader's Digest) under the bed.

I shall HAVE to have words.

P.S. – Just saw a family of earwigs scurrying around the bathroom. I assume they're a family as there were two large ones and two little ones, and they did all seem to stick together.

Tuesday May 31st

Bitterly excited to receive this latest missive (letter) from Gunter today . . .

Landsberger Strasse 60
CH-8006
Zürich
SWITZERLAND

Wednesday the May [25]st

My dear friendly Robin,

I do trust that you are well and of good spirit.

As you no, we will be arriving in your land in so little time, that I think we are to be no less possible than that which it is! And what better way than to ask one-selves that question than to do it for ones-selfs! Better that than looking around for nothings. Or do you no otherwise?

Packing, puckung and bringing the accompinaments with is so important, I think, for Heidi, that she must always be with the containers and so many clothings. But then again the women may not no otherwise. I think Rita may be the similar too?

Implant in foot of tree.

I believe that I am telling you about the house handles. Again this is something that we are living through in the mornings and the nights. Now the schriekung is magnified many times because of the heatness. Hans and Lotte Schwimberg suffered a great shocken when they were sleeping in the house and Doktor Ehlers attended rapidly.

I think you can see that we will be needing the holidays!

I will be reaching you by telephoning before we take to the skys. We are all in excitement.

Your ever friendly,

Gunter Schwartz

Günter Schwartz

SP – We are wishing you a joyous birthday for the week in actual.

New £52 pen (complete with built-in digital stopwatch) in hand, Rita wrote out a now very familiar list on the easy-wipe message board . . .

'House Handles' might (well) be:

1) A substance that expands with the heat, causing a nasty noise ('loud rubber'?)
2) A ghost. I don't really believe in them, but I do know two people who claim to have seen them:
   i) Mother swears she once saw the ghost of Sir Winston Churchill in her bedroom (just as she was getting undressed).
   ii) Adrian Chalk – the skinniest boy in my school – who swore he saw his OWN spirit, walking three steps in front of him – at ALL times. (He left after two terms.)
3) Something that Hans and Lotte Schwimberg (whoever they may be) are both allergic to. What that is, we don't know (pollen machines??)
4) Something that is only ever used by Swiss Germans and no one else in the world.

We think it's probably number 4, although Tony – who popped in tonight for a bun – added his own number 5:

5) Handles for the house.

Ten days to go . . .

June

Thursday June 2nd – My birthday! (see below!)

Happy birthday to me,
Happy birthday to me,
Happy birthday dear Robin,
Happy birthday to me.

For I'm a jolly good fellow,
For I'm a jolly good fellow,
For I'm a jolly good fe-e-llooooooow,
And sewsayor (I've never understood that word) of
us.

And sewsayor of us,
And sewsayor of us,
For I'm a jolly good fellow,
For I'm a jolly good fellow,
For I'm a jolly good fe-e-llooooooow,
Which (or is it 'that'?) nobody can deny!

Happy Birthday Robin! Happy Birthday I!!!!

53 today! Hooroh!!!!!!!!!!!!

Yes, as can be seen from above, it's my official 53rd birthday today – and what a birthday it was! It began with Rita making me breakfast in bed . . .

My (birthday) breakfast:

1) 3 × boiled eggs
2) Soldiers (not real soldiers but bread ones!)
3) 2 × cups of tea
4) 1 × tomato (mainly for garnish, but I did eat it)
5) 1 × bowl of cereal
6) 2 × bananas
7) 3 × pieces of toast
8) 1 × yoghurt (Rita ate this)

Then there was the best bit: the physical giving of presents . . .

My presents:

1)   1 × shirt (replacement for the one I 'lent' Tony months ago)
2)   2 × socks (i.e. 1 × pair)
3)   Bumper book of crosswords (hoorah!)
4)   New stripey tie for work ('flattering' vertical stripes)
5)   Radio for the shed (to physically listen to)
6)   An orange (Rita always gives me an orange on my birthday. I think it began as a private joke about 15 years ago, but neither of can remember what the joke was, or what the orange signifies)
7)   A hexagonal's worth of kisses (i.e. 6!)

Additional presents/cards:

1)   Card from mother containing £10 (the same amount since 1984, before which it was normally a cheque for £8)
2)   A video entitled 'Gemini and You' from Linda and Ian (we don't have a video recorder)
3)   Card from Miss Marsh (don't think Rita was too happy about the three Xs she'd put at the bottom)
4)   A very stylish birthday card from Michael in Sydney, featuring the face of Liza Minelli.

Next, there was work . . .

Everyone sung 'happy birthday' (see above for words) and I even got a kiss from the perfume-wearing, red-haired woman in workstation 1 (which meant that for the rest of the day, my face reeked of her face).

At lunch, my loyal friend Patel presented me with an oversized birthday card (featuring an image of a smiling Concorde) signed by my colleagues. I was deeply touched (and later, took it to the toilet and checked all the signatures to see if anyone had been using my pens).

After work – and after I had thoroughly scrubbed at my face with a pumice stone – Rita and I went to Signor Pantini's for a slap-up meal. Sadly, Mr Pantini was unwell, so we had to make do with a tape recording of him singing in his distinctive falsetto. But, still – what a voice!

Thus, in a nutshell, there endeth another glorious birthday (and birthnight) in the life of Mr Robin Cooper. A year older I may be – but a year older I am! Hoorah!

P.S. – I notice Tony didn't send a card.

Saturday June 4th

Car physically moving again. Miss Marsh at the wheel. Ran over a banana in the road, and Miss Marsh made me get out of the car and clean the tyre, just in case the vehicle 'overturned'. After that, she said that it was still 'too dangerous to drive', and so walked back home. Lesson only lasted 8 minutes!

Later, a most unusual thing happened. I was crosswording with Rita in the living room, when I suddenly heard the front door being opened. I leapt to my feet, and ran to the hallway.

Tony was letting himself into our house – with a set of our keys!

Before I could say anything, he slammed the door behind him (think he was a bit worse for wear, ale-wise) and, without even acknowledging me, marched right up the stairs, and straight into Michael's bedroom.

'Who gave Tony keys?' I asked Rita.

'Oh, I did,' she replied. 'It's much less fuss for everybody now'.

I really can't decide if this is a bad thing, or a very bad thing.

Sunday June 5th

Tony arose at about 1pm today. He looked even more of a shambles than usual (and that's a lot of shambles) and when I brought him his trademark cup of tea and cup of coffee, I noticed a fresh Susan-inflicted bump on his forehead.

'Clock?' I asked.

'Clog,' he replied.

Am sure Tony's forgotten about my birthday, but thought it best not to say anything. Besides, his birthday presents (when he remembers) usually leave something to be desired. Last year he gave me a cardigan – my OWN cardigan – one that I'd lent him three years earlier!

Monday June 6th

Pens still being swiped from my desk. Apart from Henderson's office (which has a large 'out of bounds' sign in the window), I've checked all the nooks and all the crannies, but still the thief remains at large. Think I shall have to lay low for a while. Hopefully the villain will reveal himself/herself via some logistical error. Apparently that was how they caught Crippen.

Fat Carol came over this evening, but luckily I found my secret piece of paper listing all the locations of her historic cat paintings. Got Tony to help hang them up (but didn't let him do the hammering-in bit due to Pennyfeather's imbibation), and Fat Carol didn't even suspect a thing.

Phew!

We are now the proud owners of Henry VIII – as a long-haired ginger tabby – and his six Tudor kitten wives!

King Henry VIII and Co! (or rather, 'and Cats'!!!)
by Fat Carol
(But redrawn by Robin Cooper)

key:
① King Henry VIII
② Catherine of Aragon
③ Anne Boleyn
④ Jane Seymour
⑤ Anne of Cleves
⑥ Kathryn Howard
⑦ Katherine Parr

Tuesday June 7th

Gunter telephoned today to discuss travel details for his trip to London. Was really shocked at just how bad his spoken English was. He'd even forgotten the word for 'hello' (which is 'hello').

Spent most of the time trying to work out exactly which airport Gunter and Heidi were meant to be arriving at, since Gunter couldn't remember if it was 'Heathwick' or 'Gatrow' (it was actually Stansted).

Just before he hang up, Gunter announced, 'This will be being the most important journey I ever have to be undertaken. It will be the greatest times of my lifes.'

I don't know why, but I'm beginning to feel a little bit nervous about Friday.

Wednesday June 8th

The Coopers are in full spring-cleaning mode for our Swiss German visitors.

Our Preparements:

1) Crumbs wiped from behind/beneath/beyond toaster (there must have been at least 90).
2) Fresh J-cloths in kitchen.
3) Un-fresh J-cloths in bin.
4) New soap (mandarin) in bathroom.
5) Curtains dusted (I can't see the point of doing this: the dust goes everywhere, and then just ends back on the curtains).
6) White loo paper replaced with lavender loo paper (didn't enjoy doing this, as loo-roll socket kept springing back and knocking my wrist out of joint).
7) Greasy fingerprints wiped from light sockets (I actually quite enjoy doing this).

By the way, Tony is still with us, but I think he's been using my razor, as it's completely clogged up with hair. The strange thing is, Tony still has his moustache, and his face is all as stubbly as usual, so I really don't know which part of his body he's been shaving.

Don't think I'll ask either.

Thursday June 9th

Rita and I have been thinking about our big day tomorrow, and wondering exactly what Gunter looks like.

From the one photo we have of him (Gunter on a horse, in a hat, eating an ice cream, Vienna, 1982) it's almost impossible to tell, as most of his features are obscured by his hat, his ice cream, and a donkey, which was standing in the way.

For some reason I've always pictured Gunter as being medium-sized, with very straight hair, and possibly a middle parting.

Rita, on the other hand, sees him as tall, slender and blond. (I hope he's not too tall, too slender and too blond!)

Anyway, to prevent any arrival-based confusion at the airport, I fashioned a banner out of cardboard, saying: 'THE ENTIRE GLORIOUS NATION OF GREAT BRITAIN WELCOMES GUNTER AND HEIDI SCHWARTZ – WELCOME O' GUESTS!'

Was quite pleased with it, although Rita said that it was 'unnecessarily large', and Tony pointed out that 'Britain' was actually spelt 'Brittin'.

Talking of Tony, he finally went back home tonight. Had to clear up his room as usual, and this time I found 12 'empties' in Michael's sock drawer, plus two pieces of buttered toast in the bed. Something simply MUST be done!

Friday June 10th – Gunter's official arrival in Great Britain

Gunter's plane was delayed, so had to wait for three hours in arrivals. Felt a little self-conscious walking around with my banner. Rita was right. It really was far too large (at least 10 times larger than anyone else's sign) – why is she always right?!

Anyway, our predictions of Gunter's appearance couldn't have been more wrong . . .

Gunter is actually no more than about 5 feet 2 in height, chubbular in shape, and has the curliest hair I have ever seen on a man. I suppose, if I had to compare him to anything, I'd say he looked a bit like a seal with a perm.

Gunter greeted me warmly (but didn't even mention my massive banner), kissed me twice on both cheeks, and presented me with a gift of an oversized Emmenthal.

At last, after 39 years of regular correspondencing, I was finally face to face (and cheek to cheek) with my dear Swiss German penfriend. Hoorah!

I then realized that Heidi wasn't around, but, when I asked Gunter where she was, he simply replied, 'She will follow.'

We waited for a couple of minutes – pretty much in silence – before Gunter turned to me, nodded towards the exit sign, and said, 'Shall we . . .?'. I enquired once more about Heidi, but he just said the same thing, 'She will follow.'

And so we left – without her!

For someone who could barely string a sentence together in English, Gunter talked incessantly during our drive home. His main topics seemed to be 'sanding harbours', 'battery doctors', and something called 'schwein matrons'. I calculated that I understood about 30% of what he said, and he 15% of what I said. Thus a total two-way comprehension value of 45% was established. This didn't bode well for the weekend.

Got home, and as soon as we walked in, Rita said, 'Where's Heidi?'
    'She will follow,' I replied (what else could I say?).
    'Ja, she will follow,' chimed Gunter.

After Gunter had unpacked, taken his shower, and carefully blow-dried his hair (he brought two hairdryers with him – one of them for 'the urgent matters'), we all sat down to lunch. During soup (onion), Rita looked at me and gave me a little pre-arranged nod. It was time . . .

I turned to our guest and, as innocently as possible, said, 'How are the house handles, Gunter?'

At once Gunter started gasping: 'Schrecklich! Schrecklich! I cannot talk about the house handles. Not now! I am coming to get away from it!'

Oh dear. I suppose we will just have to try another approach tomorrow.

When we finished, I offered to show Gunter all the letters he'd sent me over the years, as I thought it would be a good way of really getting to know one another. Gunter seemed excited at first and replied, 'That is wunderbar, Robin! Really wunderbar! But now I sleep.'

And with that, he got up from the table, walked out of the room, and went straight up to bed!

Gunter didn't emerge until about 7, when he came back into the living room, and sat straight down at the dining table again. Rita asked if he was all right, and if he wanted to watch a bit of television or go for a walk, but Gunter replied, 'Thank you, but now I eat.'

The cheek!

After our (enforced) meal, I offered to take Gunter out for the evening, but he said he was 'feeling in the fantastic' and seemed quite content on sitting in our armchair, flicking through the TV channels, playing with his feet, and eating the cheese he had brought for us.

He really isn't quite what we expected.

Saturday June 11th

What a day . . .

Rita and I had planned to take Gunter (and Heidi – who has still not 'followed' by the way) out to see the sights of London. I'd even prepared a special map of our route, which I'd annotated in five different colours (red, green, light blue, dark blue, and just blue).

Over breakfast, I showed Gunter the map, and his eyes lit up: 'That is truly wunderbar Robin!' he said, 'But London, I have already seen.'

Rita and I were stunned. We'd always been led to believe that this was Gunter's first trip to Great Britain.

'When have you seen London?' said Rita.

'Oh, we have it in Switzerland, in the television. The Buckingham, the Westminster, the Oxford. It is very nice. But I have seen it now.'

'I see,' I said, somewhat deflated. 'So where would you like to go instead?'

'To Critter Land,' said Gunter.

'Critter Land?' said Rita.

'Critter Land,' said Gunter, handing us a slim colour brochure, featuring a man wearing a giant ant's head on the front.

And so, at 10.15 this morning, we set off down the M25 to Critter Land, ('the UK's most exciting insect-themed adventure park'). Gunter could hardly contain his excitement, and even broke into a yodel.

In all my life I have never been to such a horrendous place! I got completely soaked on the 'Larvae Lake Plunge', was almost sick during the 'Giant Mosquito Net Chucker', and practically decapitated on the 'Mandibles of Death' ride. I am never going to Critter Land again.

We'd only been back at home for a few minutes, when suddenly there was an awful commotion from Gunter's bedroom. Rita and I rushed upstairs (well, Rita hobbled upstairs) to find Gunter deep in shock. There was a naked man asleep in his bed! (No points for guessing who it was . . .)

I know I should have been angrier with Tony, but after everything Gunter had put me through that day, I was secretly rather pleased.

Tony eventually got dressed and left the house – but not before finishing off his can of Pennyfeather's, and calling me a 'bl**dy Judas'.

Good old Tony!

Sunday June 12th

This morning I was woken at 7:30 by a knock at the front door. I opened it to find a tall, thin lady in her late 40s, with a soft hat pulled over her hair, a small case in one hand, and a fixed grin on her face.

'Hello?' I said. 'Can I help you?'

'Robin?' came the reply.

'Yes,' I answered.

'Ich bin Heidi,' she said.

Hoorah! Heidi DID follow!

I led Heidi into the living room, and rushed upstairs to wake Gunter, but he didn't seem that bothered at all. In fact, he rolled over and went straight back to sleep!

After eventually getting up, showering and blow-drying his hair with both hair dryers (leaving me to make small talk for forty minutes with Heidi, who spoke no English), Gunter came downstairs, and greeted his wife as if her sudden arrival was the most natural thing in the world.

'I tell you she will follow!' he said.

These Swiss Germans are peculiar.

Rita and I asked Gunter if there was anything special that Heidi might like to do for the day, and our guests discussed the matter in German for quite some time. Then Heidi opened up her handbag, and handed us a familiar-looking brochure.

'Critter Land'.

Half an hour later, Rita, I, Gunter, Heidi, and a worse-for-wear Tony (who had camped out in the shed all night) were travelling back down the M25, while our Swiss German guests treated us to 20 minutes of (semi) close-harmony yodelling.

Gunter bought a hat with tentacles, Rita won a wormery, Tony fell in the Larvae Lake, I coughed up a beetle grub, and Heidi just sat on a bench all day and watched.

161

Came back. Dried off (Gunter used both his hairdryers again), then took Gunter and Heidi out to Signor Pantini's for dinner. Mr Pantini sung some wonderful (high pitched) love songs, and Gunter and Heidi even joined in a bit, but had to stop when customers complained about the 'clash of styles'. Then tried to make conversation with Heidi, who merely smiled and nodded at everything we said.

When Rita mentioned 'house handles', however, Heidi let out a loud shriek.

'We don't want to be thinking of that now!' exclaimed Gunter. 'House handles nicht!' replied Heidi.

The mystery of the millennium continues.

Monday June 13th – Gunter and Heidi's official departure from Great Britain

Alas, we never did get to find out what 'house handles' are, but . . .

Gunter tried a piece of my Aqua Choc this morning, and (despite a minor choking) said that he thought it was 'absolute wunderbar!' Not only that, but apparently he knows a very important man, called Herr Buller, who is the director of a leading and PROFESSIONAL, chocolate-making company in Zurich!

Gunter promised me that he'd speak to Herr Buller as soon as he got home, and that he'd even try to set up an OFFICIAL meeting between me (Cooper) and he (Buller) in Zurich. Gunter also assured me that Herr Buller eats chocolate, and also drinks water.

Bingo! I've (potentially) hit the big time!

Rita and I promised to visit in November, and I tell you, Dear Diary – I already can't wait! Hopefully we'll be travelling there not only for pleasure – but for business too!

A tearful goodbye at the airport (well, Gunter was in tears, Heidi was still smiling), plus lots of emotional cheek-kissing. Finally, as Gunter disappeared into passport control, he called out to me 'You have been the greatest friend since man!'

Auf wiedersehen, Gunter.

Auf wiedersehen, my friend.

Tuesday June 14th

Rejection letter from Cadbury's re Aqua Choc. Alas, Tony and I will not be the next Cadbury's Brothers. Will have to write to Mars, and perhaps we will become the next 'Mars Brothers'. (Chocolate) fingers crossed . . .

The Cooper household feels an emptier place altogether without our Swiss German friends. I keep expecting to come downstairs to find Gunter sitting in the armchair, eating cheese and picking his feet.

Oh happy times!

Wednesday June 15th

4-chinned Philip Teff placed an order for another 10 Aqua Chocs on the bus this morning. This is a very good sign indeed (despite the fact that I now have to physically make the blasted things again). He also gave me another interesting brochure all about Norfolk: apparently, King Canute once had a holiday home there.

Gunter phoned tonight to thank us for our hospitality (or 'hospitalizing' as he put it). It was smashing to hear his voice again, even though he still couldn't remember the word for 'hello' (which is still 'hello').

P.S. – Another one of my pens was swiped from my pen-holder today. This is an UTTER outrage!

Thursday June 16th

Mother called from an airport this evening. I asked her what she was doing there.

'Remember the programme I was on?' she replied

'Yes, of course,' I said.

'Remember I won a trip to Paris?'

'Yes.'

'Well, I'm going off today, and I'm treating Gerryboo.'

'Bonjour Robin!' said Gerald in the background.

Oh dear.

Mother then rattled off a list of televisual programmes she wanted recording (including one about the casino industry for Gerald). I tried to tell her that we don't have a video recorder but she'd hung up by then. Her last words were 'Gerryboo, dear, if you really like that video camera, then let me buy it for you.'

This is all getting very worrying.

Friday June 17th

A most unbelievable event has occurred. Was fetching the earwig repellent down from the loft (Rita finally spotted the earwig family in the bathroom), when I noticed Smithy behaving rather oddly.

He was sitting bolt upright (Smithy usually slouches), with his face scrunched up (do birds have 'faces' or is there another term for a 'bird face'?) and generally looked very odd indeed. I went to see what was the matter, when suddenly Smithy arched his body back, fluttered his wings, and then let out the most enormous burp I have heard (from a bird).

I gazed on in amazement . . .

Smithy laid an egg. A real egg.

Smithy was a mother!

I cannot tell you, Dear Diary, how completely overjoyed I was. In fact I CAN tell you – and I just did! In fact I was so utterly thrilled that I even danced a little jig all round the loft (until I banged my head quite hard on one of the low-lying beams) in sheer celebration.

Since this clearly meant that Smithy was actually a girl bird, I decided – after a bit of dizzy deliberation – to rename him (i.e. her) 'Smithie'.

Hoorah for Smithie! Hoorah for her!

Saturday June 18th

After our recent banana escapade, Miss Marsh made a full inspection of my car tyres for any 'errant fruit skins'. Luckily my vehicle passed the test!

Got up to third gear today (top speed: 14 mph) before Miss Marsh said she was feeling 'dizzy' and her nose started to drip all over the upholstery again. Apparently she was suffering from a 'spring cold'.

Came back, wiped seats, then went up to loft.

Smithie had laid another egg! (I wondered what that loud burping sound was this morning).

I'm in a real pickle: should I tell Rita or should I not tell Rita? If I tell her that I've been secretly keeping a bird (and now potential future birds) in the loft all this time, she'll absolutely kill me, and if I don't tell her, but she finds out somehow (i.e. she suddenly becomes psychic/Tony gives the game away/ankle heals and she walks up ladder) then I'm dead too.

I'm in a non-win-non-win situation. I really don't know what to do.

Sunday June 19th – National Father's Day

Rita made me a couple of boiled eggs for breakfast this morning, but I couldn't eat them. Somehow it just didn't feel right. Told her I had a bit of a 'funny tummy'.

After breakfast, Michael called from Sydney to wish me a happy Father's Day. Hoorah! He even said I was the 'best dad in the world'. He was right – I am! (With the exception of His Royal Highness the Duke of Edinburgh of course.)

Only chatted for about a minute before Rita took the phone. Think Michael was upset about something, as Rita moved into the living room and shut the door. Tried listening (with wine glass pressed up to the wall) but couldn't make out exactly what was the matter. Think it had something to do with a pair of shorts Michael had lent Simon, though.

Monday June 20th – The first day of Wibbledon! (we always call it that in this house!)

Mother phoned from Paris this evening. She said that she'd decided to extend the holiday for a few more days as a 'special treat' for Gerald. I told her I was pleased (although I wasn't really), and when I put the phone down, Rita told me to stop being a 'Mr Misery Guts' (I hate it when she calls me that).

Popped up to loft before bedtime for last minute 'varnishing'. Smithie sitting quite proudly on her two eggs. I wonder if she'll have twins?

Tuesday June 21st

Didn't eat my boiled eggs again this morning. I just couldn't do it. Said I had another tummy ache. Unfortunately Rita made me take some medicine, which tasted so horrible I ended up having a real tummy ache, then having to take some more just to get rid of it!

By the way, Rita, Linda and depressed/depressing Mary have formally agreed an amnesty on excessively expensive pen-purchasing. This is all well and good, but I wish they'd done this last week: it might have saved me the £59.99 I forked out on an 'Ignatium scroll pen', whatever that may be. As part of their 'peace treaty', the ladies are also forming a 'local calligraphy group', open to themselves, as well as to members of the local community. Rita seemed very excited.

I think it's a terrific idea, and hopefully it will take Rita's mind off her ankle twinges. Last night Rita kicked me so hard in bed that I'm walking around with a bruise on my shin in the shape of former West Germany.

Wednesday June 22nd

It pains me to say this, but my good friend Patel has become Suspect Number One in the ongoing case of 'Cooper v the Office Pen Swiper'.

I had just returned from the unisex toilet (red-haired lady in workstation 1 has changed to an even more potent perfume, which smells strongly of tomato), when I found Patel crawling under my desk on his hands and knees. I asked him what he was doing, and he said that he was 'looking for his badge' (Boeing 757), which he claimed had 'fallen off' his shirt.

'How very convenient,' I thought (but of course did not say this out loud). Will have to keep my eye on Patel and his pen-related shen-e-annigans (never know how to spell that word).

P.S. – Rejection from Mars re Aqua Choc. Alas, Tony and I will never become the next Mars Brothers. However, we may still become the next 'British Chocolate Conglomerates Brothers' – (chocolate) fingers crossed . . .

Thursday June 23rd

Am very annoyed with Rita. I strictly forbad her from having anything to do with that 'rag', the Brent Herald. And what did she do. . .?

How could she lend her support (and my pennies) to those filthy pamphleteers? How could she betray me so? My very own wife!

Friday June 24th

Mother and Gerald got back from France, and came over for dinner this evening. When Gerald walked in, he was wearing his tight safari suit – but this time with a beret on his head! He also called Rita 'madam mwazelle' (but in French) and kissed her on BOTH hands.

Mother said that the holiday had been 'absolutely magnificent', and that it was like a 'second honeymoon' (which was a bit odd, as she never actually had a first honeymoon, due to Father slipping his disc on their wedding night).

Gerald showed us the new video camera that Mother had bought him, but as he hadn't properly worked out the power button (he'd thought 'on' was 'off' and 'off' was 'on'), most of the film was just of Gerald's feet, walking through Paris. He really does have very, very small feet for a man.

Anyway, just as we were about to sit down to dinner, Gerald suddenly announced that he had to go to an important meeting with his 'explorer's club'. And with that (well, after taking a piece of cake for the journey, and planting two more kisses on Rita's hands), he left. Naturally he took Mother's car.

The cheek!

Tried to think of something to say to Mother during our meal, as I could tell she was secretly upset but I didn't really know what to say, so just ended up talking about what I was physically putting into my mouth at the time (i.e. soup, beef, potatoes, peas etc.).

Drove Mother home at about 11:15. Noticed that Gerald hadn't returned her car.

Saturday June 25th

Spoke to Mother this morning. She said that 'Gerryboo' had got back very late last night, as he'd had a 'meet and groot' with a group of tribal elders from Malawi (apparently there were a lot of them). Anyway, she seemed back to her usual self, so I felt a little better after that.

Had lunch (chicken and mustard sandwiches, crisps, 2 fried eggs and a bun), and then went to the library to see what I could find out about wood-pigeon gestation.

What I found out (about wood-pigeon gestation):

1) Wood-pigeon eggs are just called 'wood-pigeon eggs' (i.e. they don't have a special name, such as 'eggus pigeonius bosculatus').
2) Wood-pigeon eggs hatch on the 17th or 18th day after the physical laying.
3) Thus Smithie's egg/eggs will physically hatch on July 4th (American Independence Day) or July 5th (Canadian Independence Day?)
4) Gulp . . .

Sunday June 26th

After 8 hours in the shed, and with a little help from Tony (who moved back in again this morning with Susan-related black eye), my plan to catch the dastardly office pen-thief is finally ready. Make way for . . .

Cooper's Pen Thief Directional Detection Transmitting Device (or 'CPTDDTD') – designed to catch international office pen swipers:*

The 'CPTDDTD' by Robin Cooper:

1) Silver foil fitted to base of pen.

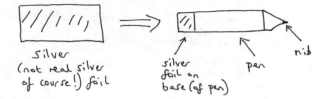

2) Pen is placed in pen holder. Base of pen holder also fitted with silver foil.

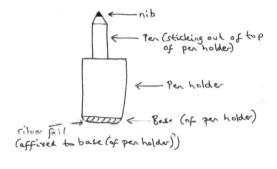

3) Underneath of pen holder fitted with (discreet) transmitting device (from old electronic garage door remote control unit).

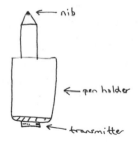

4) Receiver unit (made from old doorbell and television remote control) tuned to frequence of transmitter (594 Hz).

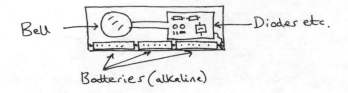

Bell → [diagram] ← Diodes etc.

Batteries (alkaline)

5) As soon as thief removes pen from pen holder, the circuit is broken, the transmitter sends an urgent message to the receiver unit, and the bell sounds.

Bell → " ( ) " Ring, Ring!

6) The thief is caught!

O‿‿‿O ← Handcuffs

By the way, Tony was so impressed with my device (and so full of Pennyfeather's) that he asked if I could make one that detected when Susan was just about to throw something at him!

I'm rather fond of initials at the moment! (Or 'IRFOIATM!')

Monday June 27th

Got up super early ('GUSE'), took my morning bath ('TMMB'), then stuck the receiver/bell unit to my chest with masking tape

('TSTR/BUTMCWMT' – I will stop that now!), before putting my shirt on over it ('BPMSOOI' – sorry I couldn't resist!). When Rita asked me why I was taking so long in the bathroom, I told her I was still 'dealing with the earwigs' (oh, if only she knew . . .).

Then, perfectly disguised, I went to work, set up my detection device under my pen-holder, and waited. My plan was to spend as much time away from my workstation as possible, in the hope that the culprit (i.e. Patel) would seize his opportunity and strike.

At about 3:00, while I was hiding out in the unisex toilet (that tomato perfume is ever so acrid), my alarm bell suddenly went off. I tried to stop it, but I couldn't unclip the battery. It was completely stuck!

The bell kept ringing and ringing. It was ever so loud and, after a while, there was a commotion from outside the door. No doubt my colleagues were curious as to why a bell should be ringing inside a toilet. Then the banging started.

'Open up!'
  It was Henderson.
  I told him I wouldn't be long.
  'What's all that ringing?' he asked.
  I didn't know what to say.
  'My mobular phone,' I said.

By now I had stripped down to my bare chest, and was frantically trying to remove the wretched device. It just wouldn't come off – all the tape was stuck to my skin!

'I'm giving you 5 seconds then I'm kicking that door down,' bellowed Henderson.

At once all my colleagues started counting down '5-4-3-2 . . .'

I had no choice. I opened the door.

As soon as she saw me, the red-haired tomato-perfume-wearing lady from workstation 1 screamed, 'He's got a bomb! He's got a bomb!' Everyone went running.

Within a second, Henderson wrestled me to the floor, Watkins from Delineation piled in on top, and horrid Corville sat right on my head.

Oh the indignity!

Once it was established that the device wasn't a bomb, and the bell had been switched off (or rather 'smashed off' by horrid Corville's boot), Henderson led me into his office.

'What on earth was that thing you were wearing?' he asked.

I'm ashamed to say, Dear Diary, that I lied for England (and Wales, and Scotland and Ireland) (and also the Isle of Man). I told Henderson that I was wearing a special 'hi-tech blood-pressure monitor' that was on trial from the 'University of Physical Sciences of the United States of America'.

I also explained that I suffered from high blood pressure (worries re wife's ankle etc.), and that the unit – which I called a 'Blood-Pressure Belling Machine' (only thing I could think of at the time) – transmitted data all the way from my body, to a professional professor, who was sitting in a high-blood-pressure laboratory in Michigan City, the home of 'international high blood-pressure research'.

Henderson listened intently, but then his mobular phone went off, and he reached into his desk drawer to get it.

I couldn't believe my eyes.

Inside were at least a dozen pens, all with the distinctive, sparkly 'Linegan's Luck' logo on them. Henderson was the culprit!

Our eyes met. He knew that I knew . . .

Henderson switched off his phone, slowly closed his drawer, then leaned forward and said: 'Cooper. How would you like a pay rise?'

I didn't know what to say (apart from 'yes'!) And thus, I am now £19.50 a week richer! Or to put it another way – 5.46 × one litre tubs of rum 'n' raisin ice cream extra per week! Hoorah! Crime DOES pay!

Tuesday June 28th

Despite the embarrassmentizations of yesterday, I'm already reaping the benefits of my pay rise. On my way home this evening, I bought 2 tubs of rum 'n' raisin ice cream and ate both of them on the bus. What a terrific journey!

Later, Linda and Ian came over for dinner, but Ian sat on Rita's glasses and broke them. If that wasn't enough, I had to help Linda physically pick the glass out of his bottom with a pair of tweezers. I can safely say that I know that bottom better than mine!

Wednesday June 29th

Tony and I have lost our only customer. Philip Teff is now officially on a diet.

His aim is to lose 5 stone (and 4 chins) by December 31st (ultimatum from thin wife) and so he's now strictly 'off the chocolate'. Offered to make him a diet version ('Aqua Choc Lite'), but he politely declined, before biting into a carrot.

Tony – who's been with us for 4 days now – was so annoyed when he heard the news, that he voluntarily packed his bag and went back home. I'd never seen him do that before!

Then things got worse . . .

Mother phoned this evening with something very important to say. Gerald Hale was moving in with her.

Words cannot describe how lost for words I was.

When I put the phone down, Rita asked me what was the matter, as I'd apparently gone white.

I told her the news, my voice literally a-trembling with every syllable, and then Rita sat me down, looked me in the eye and said: 'Robin, if your mother is happy, then you should be happy for her.'

I thought about what she'd said for a bit, then excused myself and went off to the shed. On my way out, I took the framed photo of Father (the one with him holding a giant umbrella) from the hallway.

Lay down in shed, looking at Father's photo, wondering what he would say if he were here today (apart from 'What is that man doing in my house?' and 'Get out!?'). Never really realized what sad eyes he had.

My head was swimming. I felt confused about everything (also couldn't understand why Father needed such a big umbrella for such a small head). Did Mother know what she was doing? Was this Gerald chap really right for her? And why was his safari suit always so tight? Oh Dear Diary, there was just so much to think about.

Then there was a knock at the shed door. It was Rita. She'd brought me a nice cup of tea and a lovely butter sandwich.

I suppose, if Gerald Hale can make my mother half as happy as Rita makes me, then there's really nothing to worry about.

Thursday June 30th

Perhaps there really is nothing to worry about . . .

Hark! Hoorah! Tony and I are one step closer to becoming confectionary millionaires!

British Chocolate Conglomerates
De Vere House
14 Parsons Hill Road
London WC2

27th June

Cooper & Sutton Chocolatiers
Brondesbury Villas
London

Dear Messieurs Cooper and Sutton,

Thank you for you letter dated 23rd June. Please accept my apologies for not replying any sooner.

Your product sounds very interesting, as none of my colleagues at BCC have ever heard of a chocolate bar with a water centre.

We are always on the look-out for new and exciting ideas, so perhaps you would like to call my office next week to arrange a meeting.

I look forward to hearing from you.

Yours sincerely,

Alan Towning
Product Manager
British Chocolate Conglomerates

Invited Tony round, and we celebrated with ale and toffees (Tony had the ale, I had the toffees. Tony also had some toffees).

Make way for the British Chocolate Conglomerates Brothers! Or to give us our full names: Mr Robin British Chocolate Conglomerates and Mr Tony British Chocolate Conglomerates!

P.S. – Have just realized that I am officially halfway through my diary! What an achievement my dear Robin, (i.e. I) and what an achievement, Dear Diary (i.e. you!).

July

Friday July 1st

Lovely hot sunny day. Perfect for the start of July . . .

Birds singing, bees buzzing, leaves crinkling. In fact it was so hot, I even made some ice cubes in the freezer. I love ice cubes!

Telephone rang precisely 9 times this evening (well, 9 different phone calls, but 37 individual rings), with all sorts of people calling about Rita's advert for her new 'Happy Scribbling' calligraphy group.

One lady wanted to know if she could bring along her cats (I said 'no' of course), and this afternoon I spoke to a man whose voice was so posh, I honestly couldn't work out if his name was 'Charles Giles' or 'Giles Charles'!

P.S. – Very warm evening. Think I might sleep in my pants tonight.

Saturday July 2nd

Slept in pants, but changed to pyjamas halfway through the night. Somehow it just didn't feel right.

Another hot day again, so for breakfast I had a cup of cold tea, four pieces of cold toast, a cold apple and a cold egg. Finally, to finish off, I ate up all the ice cubes. They were delicious!

3:00 driving lesson with Miss Marsh. Her nose was so runny, that I made the following calculations:

1) Miss Marsh got through 10 tissues (10 of MY tissues) today.
2) With each tissue valued at 0.4p (there are 200 in a box, and the box price is 80p), this works out at 4p in total.
3) Thus, if we continue at the current rate of tissue usage, then by the year 482774 (not taking into account the rate of inflation/life spans etc.), I will have spent exactly £1 million on tissues for Miss Marsh.

What an expensive nose!

Sunday July 3rd

Gerald moved into Mother's this morning.

I don't think I can write any more today.

Oh Mother . . .

Monday July 4th – American Independence Day

Woke up feeling a little strange due to the above, but Rita made me a nice omelette for breakfast, which cheered me up a little. She then made me another nice omelette, which cheered me up even more.

Phoned British Chocolate Conglomerates' Alan Towning at lunchtime today (from a phone box of course: external calls are prohibited on pain of dismissal). He seemed pleased to hear from me, and Tony and I have an official meeting with BCC re AC (British Chocolate Conglomerates regarding Aqua Choc) on F22NDJ (Friday 22nd July).

H! (Hoorah!)

Called Tony at work to tell him the good news. Am sure I heard him opening a can of ale in celebration. How DOES that man stay in full employment?

Tuesday July 5th – Canadian Independence Day?

It's happened . . .

Eggs hatched. Smithie has two baby birds. Two beautiful little Smithlings.

Oh dear.

Oh dear oh dear.

Oh dear oh dear oh dear.

Oh dear × infinity . . .

Wednesday July 6th

Rita was not happy.

'What do you mean I'm now a grandmother?' (It was the best way, I felt, to break the news).

Followed by . . .

'What do you mean there's a family of wood-pigeons living in the loft?'

Followed by . . .

'You mean to tell me that all this time, you've been pretending to varnish the beams in the loft?'

Followed by . . .

'Those birds have to go. Now!'

I tried to reason with her but she would not have it. In fact, Rita was so angry, she went straight over to Linda's, leaving me to make my own dinner (luckily there was some left-over chicken, a few potatoes, a bit of beef, some carrots, and a couple of slices of apple pie).

Sat in shed for an hour, trying to think of what to do.

I think I have a plan.

Thursday July 7th

Rita came back very late last night. She was still livid with me, although silently livid I should add as she was refusing to talk to me again.

I don't know if I did the right thing, Dear Diary, but I told Rita (via the easy-wipe message board on the fridge) that Tony had agreed to take the birds off our hands, and that he was now looking after them over at his house.

Of course I'd done no such thing, but I made certain that Tony knew his side of the story beforehand. He swore that he wouldn't tell Rita the truth (although am slightly concerned as he swore 'on Susan's life').

Lord only knows what Rita would do if she found out I was lying.

The Smithie Cooper Family!

Birdling 1

worm

Smithie
(formerly 'Smithy')

Birdling 2

(NB: Not to Scale)

Friday July 8th

I'm living in a veritable spider's nest of lies at the moment, and I keep digging myself deeper and deeper (into the nest).

Have had to find an excuse as to why I still need to go up to the loft, so have told Rita (again via easy-wipe board writation) that this time I really and truly am going to be varnishing the beams, and not just pretending to. Rita's response was written in rather ominous capitals: 'YOU BETTER NOT BE LYING.'

Lucky she can't walk up that ladder.

Rita's 'Happy Scribbling' calligraphy group got off to a good start this evening – not that I was allowed in the house at the time. I was made to stay in the shed. Fortunately, Tony came over to keep me company, and together we watched the proceedings via my binoculars.

In total we counted 8 calligraphizers (4 women, 1 man, plus Rita, Linda and depressed/depressing Mary). Am pretty sure the man must have been the incredibly posh chap I spoke to on the telephone (Charles Giles or Giles Charles) as he was wearing a bow-tie and monocle.

When we were eventually allowed back inside – just in time to help clear up, I should add – Rita made a big point of thanking Tony for taking the birds off our hands. I knew what she was up to . . .

Without even blinking, and remaining as cool as a refrigerated cucumber, Tony replied, 'No problem Rita. Just please don't tell Susan. I don't think she'd be very happy with me.'

Good old Anthony Lewis Sutton!

Saturday July 9th

Miss Marsh has now perfected changing gears, but not perfected not stalling. She caused a bit of a scene in front of the hospital today (blocked three ambulances), and then stalled on – literally ON – a traffic island. Tissue consumption now at roughly 15 t/ph (tissues per hour).

Came back and did a bit of 'real varnishing' (i.e. pretend varnishing).

I must say Smithie makes a fabulous mother, but then I always knew that she would (except for when I thought she was a 'he'). Every few minutes she flew out through the little gap in the roof, only to return with some tasty morsel for her birdlings (moth wing, beetle head, worm torso etc.). She must have been exhausted, but she never complained (i.e. squawked in a negative tone).

Watching the birdlings gulp down mouthful after mouthful of mashed invertebrates soon made me feel quite hungry, so went down to kitchen to get a spot of lunch. Thought about offering them a bit of chicken, but concluded it wouldn't really be right.

Sunday July 10th

Very odd dream last night: Tony was rushing down the high street, as if he were late for something really important. Nothing too strange about that I suppose – except that that he was pregnant!

This afternoon, Rita and I popped over to see Mother and her new 'live-in lover' (as Mother called Gerald the other day), but he was out. Mother said that Gerald had been called away to another 'emergency' meeting at his explorer's club. (Apparently the Malawians were back.)

Anyway, when the women were in the kitchen, I had a quick look in Mother's bedroom, to see if I could find out a bit more about this Gerald chap. I must say, for someone who'd just moved into a new home, he hadn't brought a lot of things with him . . .

Gerald's things:

1) 1 × hat (brown)
2) Slippers (also brown)
3) Pyjamas (not brown)
4) Pair of shoes (size 6!)
5) 2 × shirts
6) 4 × socks (i.e. 2 × pairs) (i.e. 4 × socks)
7) Packet of toffees (well I suppose, we're all human)
8) 1 × jumper (brown again)
9) Wash bag (didn't open it for hygiene reasons)
10) Book on antiques ('Antiques')
11) Box of assorted watches (how strange!)

Was just about to help myself to one of his toffees, when Rita suddenly walked in.
   'What are you doing in your mother's bedroom?' she asked.
   I had to think fast.
   'I got a bit lost looking for the loo.'

Rita gave me a look, which clearly meant 'I don't believe you', but I pretended it meant 'I do believe you', and calmly walked out and went into the toilet (where I pretended to 'go').

Where are the rest of Gerald's belongings . . .?

Monday July 11th

I think Rita may be on to me re Smithie and co.

I was coming down from the loft this evening, holding my trusty (but secretly never used) tin of varnish, when Rita was standing at the foot of the ladder. I tried not to act surprised.

'Robin,' she said, 'do you mind if I have a little look inside your tin?'

'Why do you want to do that?' I replied.

'No reason really,' she said, all innocently. 'It's just that I've always wondered what varnish actually looks like.'

That Rita is a very clever woman!

But luckily, I am a very clever man! Two weeks ago, I poured half of the varnish down the drain.

I opened up the tin, and Rita had a look inside, made some 'ooh' and 'ahh' noises, and then went back downstairs again.

I'm safe for the moment, but just how long will this safeness last?

It's no good – all my guilty secrets and treacherous bird/birdling-related deeds are here in black and white for all to read. I've had to make a drastic decision. I am going to physically hide my diary, so that no one will possibly find it.

Monday July 18th

I haven't written in my diary for the past 7 days because . . .

I couldn't find it. In fact, I'd completely forgotten where I'd hidden it! I looked everywhere: in the loft, in the garden and in the shed. I searched the boot of the car, the boot of Rita's car, and the boot of Tony's car (in which I found that shirt I'd lent him some five months ago). I even, rather daringly, had a peek inside Henderson's workstation.

In the end, it was found by the one person I'd hidden it from – Rita! She found it in a plastic bag, underneath a brick, underneath another brick, which in turn was underneath my upturned wheel-barrow (covered in a black plastic sheet), right at the back of the garden, amongst the stinging nettles.

The funny thing is, I had no recollection of putting it there at all!

When Rita handed it back to me, she said: 'I don't know who you've been hiding it from, but you do know I would never dream of looking at your diary.'

I didn't know what to say. How could I even think that Rita would even consider reading one letter, one syllable of my diary? My very own wife! My (almost) flesh and blood! Oh what have I become . . .?

Sat in shed for a while, feeling pretty ashamed with myself. But life, as they say, 'simply has to continue going on'. So, after removing a rather stubborn woodlouse from the centre pages, it was time to get back to proper diarying again . . .

So here is all the Cooper-related action from the past week:

1) Have named Smithie's offspring 'Binky' and 'Alfredo'. Binky, because he blinks a lot (and because I don't like the name 'Blinky'), and Alfredo (after Signor Alfredo Pantini) because he has such a high 'tweet'.
2) Rita and I have booked our summer holiday. We're going to Bournemouth in August. Hoorah! We just love Bournemouth! (Looking forward to the crazy golf – and all those ice creams – already!)
3) The makers of Mentathon 3000 have brought out an exciting new toothpaste, called 'Mentathon 4000'. It's even mintier!
4) Saw two people on the bus yesterday wearing t-shirts with the slogan 'Alright My Lover!' Couldn't work out what on earth it meant (a song in the hit parade? A thing that computers say to you in the morning?). Very odd.
5) Miss Marsh had a 'summer cold' last week. What a nose!

6) Michael rang from Sydney. Told him about Gerald moving in with his grandmother, but all he said was 'fab!' (have noticed he uses that word a lot these days).

7) Tony and I have set a date for 'The Parmaynu International Ping-Pong Masters' – our annual five day Cooper-Sutton outdoor table tennis championship, named after my jolly table tennis bat character, Parmaynu. The games commence on July 25th. Last year Tony beat me 110 games to 108, but this year I shall have my revenge. I wish myself luck!

8) Mother lost her gold necklace – the one that Father gave her when I was born. She was very upset. Gerald thinks she probably lost it down the sink, when she was doing the washing-up.

9) Ian showed us a new scar on his bottom (sat on plug).

Tuesday July 19th

Exciting times . . .

With The Parmaynu International Ping-Pong Masters looming, I've converted my table tennis table into a fully-functional and fully-functioning practise (table tennis) table (see diagram).

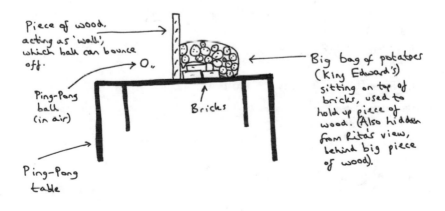

Robin Cooper's Practice Ping-Pong Table:

Piece of wood, acting as 'wall', which ball can bounce off.

O"

Ping-Pong ball (in air)

Bricks

Ping-Pong table

Big bag of potatoes (King Edward's) sitting on top of bricks, used to hold up piece of wood. (Also hidden from Rita's view, behind big piece of wood).

After work, I spent all evening playing against myself in the garden. Actually, I wasn't really playing against myself. I was really playing against my imaginary opponent, Uckob. I've been competing against Uckob (in my head) for years, even though Uckob is quite an erratic player, rather temperamental, and, in fact, not a very nice man.

Today's scores:

COOPER   UCKOB
21   9
21   4
14   3   (Match postponed after Uckob threw his bat)

Hoorah for Cooper!

Wednesday July 20th

Couldn't concentrate at work at all today. Think I've gone ping-pong mad!

Here's how my day was spent (all times are approximate):

6:00am Rise (i.e. get up)
6:03 Shower
6:12 Get dressed
6:17 Breakfast (toast, tea, eggs, cereal, apples etc.)
6:40 Go out to garden
6:41 Wipe table tennis table (bird mess/spiders/mites etc.) with damp cloth
6:42 Start playing (against Uckob)
8:00 Leave for work
6:15pm Return from work. Go to toilet then to garden
6:35 Re-wipe table
6:36 Start playing again
7:15 Light dinner (i.e. chicken and potatoes/sausages and potatoes, peas, carrots, ice cream)
9:00 Argument (in head) with Uckob

9:15 Chase Mr Alfonso's cat, Monty, away from ball
10:00 Snack (biscuits, cup of tea, bit of cake, ice cream)
10:15 Put torch on table for extra visibility
10:17 Put additional torch on table for additional extra visibility
10:20 Final game (Uckob storms off in a mood)
10:45 Check on Smithie, Binky and Alfredo in loft (i.e. 'varnish beams'!)
10:55 Clean teeth/blow nose etc.
11:00 Bed

Thursday July 21st

After a day's resolutioning (only 63 data forms – couldn't stop thinking of ping-pong), I sat with Tony in the shed, drafting our 'plan of attack' for our big Aqua Choc meeting with British Chocolate Conglomerates tomorrow:

Our plan (of attack):

1) To arrive on time (this includes T. Sutton)
2) To be dressed smartly (see above)
3) To be professional (see above, again)
4) To SUCCEED (see us in five years when we're both millionaires!)

I wish myself and my colleague, Tony Sutton, luck! Even Rita (begrudgingly) wished us luck!

P.S. – Cooper beat Uckob 4 games to nil today, and Uckob stormed off again. He is such a bad loser!

Friday July 22nd – official Aqua Choc 'pitching' day

Despite the fact that Tony was late for the meeting (18 minutes), looked a total scruff (sockless, tieless), was completely unprofessional (he winked at the receptionist), we still SUCCEEDED!

They loved it! Yes, British Chocolate Conglomerates loved Aqua Choc!

Well, when I say 'loved it', the man we were supposed to meet (Alan Towning) was away, so instead we met a nice young trainee named Oliver, who, whilst he didn't actually taste our bar of Aqua Choc himself (Oliver has diabetes), said that he would 'make sure' someone else in the company would – and that he was sure 'they would love it'.

His very words: 'they would love it.'

Fingers crossed, but this surely bodes very well indeed.

Saturday July 23rd

Couldn't sleep at all last night. Kept thinking about our FANTAS-TIC meeting yesterday. Spoke to Tony this morning, and he said that he couldn't get to sleep either (although I think it was more to do with the 9 cans of Pennyfeather's he'd consumed in celebration).

Driving lesson with Miss Marsh. Emergency stops today, or rather 'emergency stalls'. Noticed her hair was up in 'bun formation' again. In total, I counted 25 separate bun 'units'!

Monday July 25th

Da-da-da-da-da-daaaaaa! The official opening of The Parmaynu International Ping-Pong Masters.

But first, Dear Diary, a quick note about our rules.

Tony and I play a slight variation on standard table tennis rules, known as 'Sydney Bellingham rules'. Quite who Sydney Bellingham is neither of us can ever remember, although Tony seems to think that Sydney Bellingham might have been related to Fred Astaire (himself a keen table tennis player, apparently).

The Sydney Bellingham Rules:

1) The winner is the first to reach 15 (not 21, as in standard games. This makes the games faster and more exciting)
2) Players play ten games per day

3) The championship lasts for 5 days
4) No games may be played at the weekend (I do not know why this rule is in place. It seems so impractical – but rules are rules. I suspect this came via Susan Sutton originally)
5) Volleys are permitted
6) Players are only allowed to spin the ball three times per game (this often leads to arguments, as it is quite a vague rule)
7) Players must never aim for the eyes – even out of anger
8) No uncouthities (i.e. foul language)
9) No spitting

And so, at 6:00 this evening, after sounding our ceremonial bugle (Tony whistling quite loudly down a tube of cardboard, painted with the Union Jack flag, and the cheerful face of ping-pong character, Parmaynu), we were off . . .

Even Rita had come out to watch (and cheer Tony along I should add), and so, at the end of an exciting day's play, the final scores were:

COOPER	SUTTON	
15	9	
15	10	
10	15	
4	15	(Couldn't concentrate – Monty kept trying to run off with ball)
11	15	
13	15	
15	11	
3	15	(Smithie flies out of roof of house while Rita outside)
9	15	(Smithie and Rita go indoors halfway through game)
15	13	(Concentration back on!)

Tony leads 6 games to 4. The rotter!

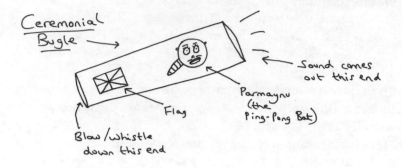

Ceremonial Bugle →

Sound comes out this end ←

Parmaynu (the Ping-Pong Bat)

Flag

Blow/whistle down this end

Tuesday July 26th

Did an hour's ping-ponging at quarter past 6 this morning. Spotted Mr Alfonso watching me from his kitchen in his pyjamas (he's always been a bit envious of my table). Pretty sure I also saw him kissing Monty on his nose and paws.

Mother came to watch today (Gerald dropped her off, as he had another one of his 'meetings'). Don't think she quite understood the game, though, as she kept shouting out 'catch!'

COOPER	SUTTON	
12	15	(Mother shouting out 'catch!)
15	11	
10	15	(Mother continues to shout out 'catch!')
15	4	(Tony has phone call from Susan)
15	14	(Mother stops shouting out 'catch!')
15	5	(Susan phones back)
9	9	(Game abandoned. Monty bit ball)

That wretched Monty! I was doing so well!

Cooper and Sutton now level at 8 games each. Must buy new ball.

Wednesday July 27th

Saw the ex-chocolate-eater, Philip Teff, on the bus this morning. He's still on his diet and looked a little slimmer (i.e. 3 chins). Today he was eating a raw onion. The lady next to him moved.

Then, at work, I gave Patel an update on our table tennis tournament. He's quite a fan of ping-pong, actually, and has even started writing down our scores in his British Airways notebook. Have invited him over on Friday to watch. He is ever so excited.

By the way, Mr Alfonso coughed up the money for our replacement ball today (80p), and so, as a mark of gratitude, I allowed him to sit in our garden and physically spectate.

COOPER	SUTTON	
15	14	(Rita and Mr Alfonso cheering me quite loudly)
15	8	
11	15	(Mr Alfonso switches allegiances)
12	15	
9	15	(Rita joins Mr Alfonso and cheers Tony. The cheek!)
4	15	(Smithie flying in and out of roof)
15	6	(Tony gets phone call from Susan. Good old Susan!)
15	9	
15	10	(Rita cheering me again)
15	8	(Mr Alfonso cheering me as well!)

Cooper leads competition 14 games to 12. Hoorah!

Thursday July 28th

Ping-pong postponed all day due to the below . . .

British Chocolate Conglomerates
De Vere House
14 Parsons Hill Road
London WC2

25th July

Cooper & Sutton Chocolatiers
Brondesbury Villas
London

Dear Messieurs Cooper and Sutton,

I am terribly sorry that I was unable to attend our meeting re Aqua Choc last week. Unfortunately I was called away to an urgent cocoa conference in Swindon.

My colleagues and I have now had a proper chance to sample your product, and we were all in agreement about one thing: instead of using water in the middle, we thought that you might want to consider trying a different ingredient, such as caramel, or even nougat. It may prove to be a more popular centre.

I am sorry that Aqua Choc is not something for us, but I would like to wish you all the best with your product for the future.

Yours sincerely,

Alan Towning
Product Manager
British Chocolate Conglomerates

Friday July 29th

Rather dramatic events at the Parmaynu International Ping-Pong Masters . . .

Tony and I had our biggest crowd to date: Rita, Mr Alfonso, and special guest, Patel, who was wearing a 'limited edition' Spitfire baseball cap and business class Air France socks.

All was going well: Rita was serving sandwiches (egg, turkey, butter, jam etc.), Mr Alfonso was keeping score, Patel was noting down planes as they passed overhead (luckily he didn't spot Smithie flying in and out of loft), and I was leading by four games to three.

Then suddenly, just as I was in the middle of my serve (and using up my third and final regulatory spin), Tony suggested that we should put caramel and nougat in our chocolate bar, and 'be done with the water centre'.

I couldn't believe my ears.

When I told him that this would 'just be a Mars Bar', Tony replied sharply, 'Well, we'll call it a Venus Bar, then.' Naturally Rita got involved, and said how much she loved the new name, which then prompted Mr Alfonso to add, 'It's an excellent name – and did you know that Venus is also the goddess of love?' (That's the last time I ever allow a headmaster to sit in our garden.)

Tony then said, 'All those who think that a chocolate bar containing nougat and caramel, called Venus Bar, is a good idea, raise your hands.'

I was outvoted 4-1.

Well, Dear Diary, I was so angry that I stormed off to the shed, and slammed the door behind me. I had expected Rita to follow, but instead she picked up my bat, teamed up with Mr Alfonso, and proceeded to play doubles against Tony and

Patel. This carried on for at least an hour, and when they'd finished no one even bothered to see how I was.

Remained seething in shed till 10pm, and when I went back into the house Rita was already fast asleep in bed.

P.S. – It has now just gone midnight. Have just had a rather aggressive phone call from Tony, in which he claimed to have won the tournament. When I told him that we hadn't even finished playing all our games, he grew very abusive and called me a 'stupid b**tard head' and a 'bl**dy table tennis moron'.

I told him I would not talk to him until he apologized, to which he replied 'ping-pong off!' and then hung up on me.

What a lousy day.

Saturday July 30th

Woke up in a lousy mood, and then had a lousy argument with Rita over a no-less lousy breakfast re her similarly lousy table-tennis treachery. However, I think I won as Rita ended up giving me three extra pieces of (non lousy) toast.

Driving lesson with Miss Marsh. It seems that Miss Marsh is finally beginning to gain some form of control over the vehicle, as we are now down to just 7 stalls per lesson. However, she still really struggles with reverse gear. According to Miss Marsh, it makes her nose run.

Anyway, I told Miss Marsh that I thought she was ready to sit her written driving theory test, since she seems to know her Highway Code pretty much off by heart (apart from the section on 'Horses/protective headgear for young riders').

Miss Marsh agreed that it was a good idea, although she did say that she's always sick before, during and after every exam she ever takes.

Well, I suppose that's something to look forward to!

Sunday July 31st

The woman on the radio said it was the hottest day of the year today, and a man from Surrey phoned in to say that his wife had tried frying eggs on the bonnet of his car (but it didn't work).

Mother's for tea. Noticed her car was looking particularly grubby in the driveway. Why doesn't that man (i.e. Gerald Hale) ever bother cleaning it?!

Gerald was actually there this time, but I must say he was in a very 'casual' mood indeed. When we walked in, he was casually sucking an ice lolly (strawberry Mivvi), while wearing nothing but a casual shirt and an extremely casual pair of swimming trunks.

'Sorry all,' he said, 'I'm just very hot,' before wandering off to the kitchen and returning with another lolly (another Mivvi).

And do you know what, Dear Diary . . .?

He didn't even offer me one – and I LOVE lollies/Mivvis.

The cheek!

August

Monday August 1st

I am in shock.

Found out today that Tony and Patel went to an air show together on Sunday.

According to Patel, they had a 'fabulous' time, and Tony met a real-life fighter pilot, had his photo taken in the cockpit of a MiG-25 jet, and was even interviewed live on local radio.

Why wasn't I invited?

Tuesday August 2nd

Another letter from Gunter. But strangely, no sign of the mysterious 'house handles' . . .

Landsberger Strasse 60
CH-8006
Zürich
SWITZERLAND

Wednesday the July [27]st

My dear friendly Robin,

It has been a long time since I have before written but now I am here. I am sending my sorries to you.

Once again Heidi and I had such great enjoyment with the stay in your beatiful country, and we have been liking the photo images that we have been making of. Did you return to Critter Land?

Since we are returned, Heidi has decided to be taking the England language lessons so we only have you to thank dear Robin! Of course this is a big committing for her, and she will need much steerung, but Professor Zemmel thinks that she is worthy of the troubles because of her alinements, but of course we do not no otherwise.

New electrik oven.

Robin, I have told my friend in the chockolat company about the Water Chock. His name is Ralf Buller. Ralf Buller thinks the Water Chock it is a good idea and will be happy to receive you when you visit in November, or do you no otherwise?

We are looking forward with impatience your arrival here in Zürich.

Your ever friendly,

Gunter Schwartz

Gunter Schwartz

SP - Please send my best regardements to the others (the Tony who is living in the little house in the garden).

Hoorah! A chocolate official from Switzerland – the country where chocolate was officially born – likes (the idea of) Aqua Choc. What higher praise do I need?!

Shame I can't tell Tony, on account of the fact that we're still not on speaking terms since our ping-pong dispute.

Oh well, Tony or no Tony (and at the moment it's definitely 'no Tony'), I shall have to start physically preparing my presentation. Perhaps I shall do it all in German. I'm sure that would impress them.

P.S. – Rita and I have been trying to work out what happened to Gunter's 'house handles'. Perhaps they (whatever they were) vanished/rotted/got blown up/were eaten/drunk/stolen/hidden/crushed/ frozen/liquidized/zapped – who knows?!

Wednesday August 3rd

Patel has a new hobby: Tony Sutton. When he's not talking about him at work, he's sending him blasted textual messages. Kept hearing mobular phone boepage noises coming from workstation 6 all day, followed by loud laughter.

Am not afraid to admit, Dear Diary, that I've become a little bit jealous. In fact it's been affecting me so much that I had a terrible tummy ache all afternoon, and had to keep running to the toilet. Very upsetting (i.e. Tony), and very embarrassing (i.e. toilet).

In the evening, Rita spent about an hour trying on her swimming costumes for our holiday on Saturday, but she got rather annoyed with me when I said that her green one made her look 'like a lizard' (it did, though). Tried to make up with Rita, so made her some soup (pea), which worked, luckily.

Good old soup!

Thursday August 4th

The now 3-chinned, Norfolk-promoting Philip Teff is still eating onions on the bus. No one dares sit anywhere near him.

Not much else happened today, although I did find 2 marbles in the shed. Where DO they come from?

Friday August 5th

Rita had another 'Happy Scribbling' meeting tonight. Here are the 'Happy Scribblers' as Rita calls them . . .

1) Sandra Bailey – early 60s, artistic type with slender, almost feline features. Looks not unlike Monty, but without paws and tail (although she does have a hint of whiskers).
2) Charles Giles/Giles Charles – definitely the poshest man I have ever met. He calls the ladies 'ma'am', and carries what I think is a snuffbox. Doesn't seem to use his pen much. (Rita and I now think he may even be called 'Charles Charles'.)
3) Margaret Flynne – mid 40s. Wears a lot of yellow and talks non-stop. Seemed to get on well with Linda. Has terrible handwriting and smudges everything.
4) Carol Barker – large lady (why are all Carols large?). Apparently a mother of 8 boys. Very good at underlining.
5) Doreen Hutch – thin woman, 50s. Drinks tea without milk, smokes a lot and generally quite 'moody'. Depressed/depressing Mary likes her.
6) Linda – (I know her.)
7) Depressed/depressing Mary – (I know her too.)
8) Rita – I most certainly know her!!!

The evening began with a round-up of calligraphy news – nib developments, ink availability etc. followed by an hour of intense 'copying out' (Rita hates it when I use that phrase).

The group has started making a giant facsimile of the Magna Carta in its original Latin, with each member writing one word at a time (surely there must be a quicker way). Did feel sorry for Doreen, as she kept getting the word 'et', and also for depressed/depressing Mary, whose role appeared to be 'Chief Blotter'.

My job was to take coats and hats, serve tea/wipe up tea (Margaret Flynne spilt hers all over the floor), and to administer biscuits (Carol Barker ate 6, and I ate 9 secretly in the kitchen).

To be honest, Dear Diary, the whole evening felt like watching paint (i.e. pen paint, i.e. ink) dry!

Saturday August 6th – the summer holidays cometh!

Our holiday didn't start fantastically . . .

Just as we were passing junction 4 of the M4 (signposted 'The West'), the piece of paper I'd written the route on got blown out of the window.

I'd warned Rita of the perils of open-window-motorway-driving but of course she wouldn't listen. To make things worse, she even refused to read from the map, citing 'bad ankle'. That woman and her ankle can be so stubborn sometimes.

After driving frice (i.e. five times) through Winchester, we finally arrived at our destination: the Bournemouth Corby House Hotel (3 official stars).* It's quite a nice place. There are 65 bedrooms, and 3 'suites', plus they even have an ice machine on every floor. However, the receptionist was a bit over-friendly, and kept calling me 'Robin' rather than 'Mr Cooper'/'Sir'/'Sire'. Actually, it was quite irritating.

We are in room 20. It has a mini-bar, a colour television set, a kettle, some tea bags, coffee sachets, mini milk cartons, biscuits, soaps, shampoos, and a framed photograph of Norman Lamont visiting the hotel ten years ago.

Relaxed by swimming pool with Rita. Rita swam 10 widths (her ankle seemed absolutely fine by the way), then lunched on beef sandwiches (a bit dry), had a bath (a bit wet!), followed by a traditional Bournemouthian dinner of fish, chips and ice cream. Yum!

Hoorah for the holidays! Hoorah!

We normally stay at the Royal Wessex, but after what happened last time (dead squirrels in jacuzzi) we decided it was time for a change.

Sunday August 7th

Dreamt about Tony again last night. He was pregnant again (just what is that supposed to mean?) and had locked himself away in my shed. I kept banging on the door, but he wouldn't let me in. Eventually it opened, but when I looked inside, Tony had been replaced by Fat Carol, who was eating a giant bowl of mashed potato and peas.

Woke up in a dreadful state, so when Rita was in the bath, I secretly dialled Tony's number. Unfortunately he was out and when I asked Susan where he was, she replied, 'At the RAF museum with his new friend.'

Tried to have a nice day with Rita, but felt terrible inside. How could Tony – my best friend – my confidant – my (sometime) business partner – get a new friend (i.e. Patel) without my permission?!

Sat on beach, ate a toffee apple, counted seagulls (52), played cards with Rita (same number of cards in pack as gulls, excluding jokers), had some fish and chips (2 portions), then bed.

Monday August 8th

'I am on holiday, and there is no point in me thinking about my one-time best friend and feeling all sorry for myself.' (I told myself this, this morning.)

That said (i.e. the above) Rita and I had a smashing day today. We played 'Crazy Golf' – or rather 'Krazy Golf' as it was spelt above the Crazy/Krazy Golf hut – and I thrashed Rita 4 games to nil. She was worse than Uckob!

Later, we sat on the beach, and watched the sunset together. Rita told me how much she loved me, and I reciprocated. It was most romantic.

Tuesday August 9th

Phoned Mother this morning to see how she was, but she didn't sound great as she'd lost another necklace. Then Gerald came to the phone and said that he was sure it had fallen down the plug-hole again, and that he was going to call a plumber to look inside the sink.

I told Rita that I thought it was a bit strange that Mother had lost two necklaces in one month, but Rita said 'That's what happens when you get old'. Poor Mother.

Afterwards I found a frog hopping around in our hotel bath-room. Didn't dare tell Rita, as she hates amphibians. Quietly christened him 'Froggles', then put him in my wash bag (he only ribbited a bit, luckily), and took him down to reception.

As soon as the overly-familiar receptionist saw him, he said, 'Chef will like that, Robin, he's French.' I enquired as to what he meant, and he replied, 'Well – frog's legs!' then burst into hys-terics. I didn't know what to say!

When we did sit down for lunch, I was dismayed to find that frog legs were actually on the menu. I do hope that Froggles hopped his way out of that kitchen alive. Couldn't eat much for obvious reasons (although I did manage to get down some beef sandwiches, some chicken sandwiches, and a couple of portions of trifle).

Went to the beach (think the sea air is really good for Rita's ankle), and bought a lovely shell necklace for Mother, from a shop called 'Shelly's Winkles' (although the owner was actually called Ruth).

P.S. – Someone keeps leaving little pyramid-shaped chocolates on our pillows every time we leave the room. I'd like to shake that person's hands. They're (not the hands, the chocolates) delicious!

Wednesday August 10th

It rained the whole day today. Rain, rain and then some more rain! Spent most of the afternoon sitting in lobby, crosswording, while Rita practised her Ms and Ns with one of her special calligraphy pens, called a 'de Montford Smooth Tip'. She also did a 'dot-to-dot'.

Rather small portions at dinner tonight, and when I complained, the waitress replied 'a portion is a portion'. Fancy that!

Met a nice couple in the bar afterwards. They're called Ron and Sandra (Ron is the man), and they're from Orpington in Kent. Ron is a mattress salesmen, and Sandra works for a company that sells seasonings. Ron made a funny joke about his job. He said, 'When people ask me what I do for a living, I say I have the best job in the world: I tell them I work from bed!'

Sandra didn't have a joke to match her occupation, but I've just thought of one now . . .

> What did the grain of salt say to the grain of sugar?
> – I don't know
> Hello sweety!

I will tell them my joke tomorrow.

Oh – I have just thought of another one (seen from the point of view of the grain of sugar) . . .

> What did the grain of sugar say to the grain of salt?
> – I don't know
> I have never met someone of your sort (i.e. 'salt')!

I don't think I should send them into the local newspaper here, just in case the dreaded Ted G. Fetfus is holidaying in Bournemouth.

Anyway, a bit about Ron and Sandra (by the way Dear Diary, I may be a little tipsy!):

1) They have been married for exactly the same amount of years as Rita and I (i.e. 23).
2) Sandra doesn't have a bad ankle.
3) They have 5 dogs, called 'Alaska', 'Bill', 'Spangle', and I don't remember the others.
4) Ron is quite hairy.
5) Sandra isn't! (Apologies Dear Diary – I couldn't resist!)
6) They used to live in a bungalow in Bedford.
7) Ron has quite a few tattoos.
8) Sandra can do an American accent better than Ron (we were all doing impressions – I can only do ones from mythology – i.e. Zeus).
9) Sandra calls Ron 'Kippy' – well at least it's not 'Kippyboo'!
10) Ron also has a shed (but doesn't use it much).
11) Sandra is allergic to grapefruits and avocados.

Who needs the sun when you've got (new) friends?!

Friday August 12th

The receptionist here is most annoying. He's started calling me 'Mr C'. Must have words with somebody in responsibility here.

Bumped into Ron and Sandra on the Crazy/Krazy golf course today. They challenged us to a game, and we proudly accepted. Unfortunately they beat us 13 holes to 5, mainly because Rita kept dropping her ball – and her club – into the fishpond. She's always had terrible grip.

Afterwards, we all had lunch at a local café. It was a 'light' meal (soup, bread, egg and chips, chocolate sponge, custard, tea, biscuits, an apple) but quite pleasant. I must say though, Ron didn't seem to stop talking (mainly about mattresses) and Sandra has probably the loudest laugh I have ever heard in my life. In fact, when I told her my two jokes from yesterday, she laughed so loudly that the manager actually came over and told her to be quiet!

Went back to the hotel (found a marble in the hallway – where DO they come from?), had a little lie-down (Rita had a headache), ate dinner, then watched a calypso band play in the lobby.

After about half an hour, Ron and Sandra joined us. Think they were a bit drunk. Sandra (who was wearing a sarong) laughed particularly loudly, then got up and did a slightly 'erotic' dance in front of the man playing the steel drum instrument. Ron didn't seem the least embarrassed.

Rita and I stayed for one more song ('Hey Big Spender') and left when Sandra started to remove her sarong.

Oh dear – not so sure about our new friends.

Saturday August 13th

Spent most of the day trying to avoid our new friends. Luckily it was raining again, so Rita and I sat in our room crosswording/calligraphizing/dot-to-dotting. I even made my own dot-to-dot, which I was quite proud of. (See picture which I am about to draw.)

Also came up with a new and exciting word game today. I have called it the 'Opposite Rhyming Animal Game', or 'Orag' for short. It's definitely a hit!

The idea of Orag is to work out what animal I'm thinking of. Here's how it works:

1) I think of an animal.
2) I do not tell you what it is, though.
3) Instead, I say a word, for example, 'thin'.
4) Now, you have to think of its opposite – i.e. 'fat'.
5) So the animal I was thinking of is the one that rhymes with the opposite (i.e. with 'fat').

6) So the answer is . . . 'cat'.

7) Well done!

Like all the best games it's simple but effective. Actually, that was quite a bad example, as it could have been 'rat'. Anyway, Rita and I played it for hours this afternoon (or 'bat') and I'm CONVINCED Orag could catch on (or 'gnat').

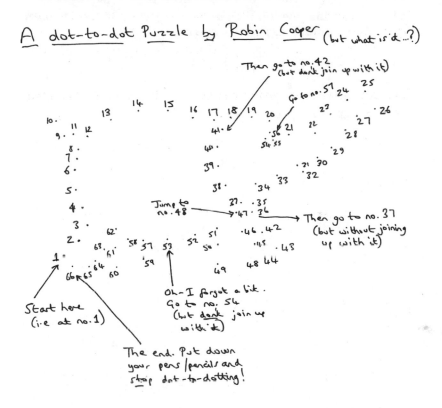

Spotted Ron and Sandra at dinner. They invited us to join them, but we politely declined, saying we were both very tired. I don't think Ron was very happy. Rita claimed he kept staring at us, while knocking back whiskeys, all through his main course.

Skipped dessert and went back up to bedroom. Tried not to look back at Ron on the way out. He really does have an awful lot of tattoos.

213

Sunday August 14th

Couldn't face seeing Ron and Sandra again, so got up super early this morning and drove a few miles out to a different beach. Our plan physically worked (i.e. they weren't physically there), but then worse things physically occurred . . .

Rita and I spent a lovely day on the sand (collecting shells, eating ice creams, avoiding crabs, playing Orag etc.), but then at about 5:00, we both fell asleep in the sun.

When we woke up, the whole beach was deserted, and Rita and I were completely scorched. Rita's ankle was red raw, and I'd even burnt my gums (I must have slept with my mouth open). It was most painful.

Worse still – when I went to the car park to get the car, I realized I'd lost my car keys. I searched everywhere, but couldn't find them. It was a real night (well, day) mare.

Luckily, a man in an ice cream van – called Alf – took pity on us (I got Rita to limp a bit for extra sympathy), and offered to take us back to the hotel. Unfortunately, the journey – which should have taken no more than fifteen minutes – took nearly two hours, as Alf insisted on travelling his normal working route, stopping off on the way to sell ice creams. What's more, I was made to help out!

What I had to do (in my capacity as an ice cream van vendor's unofficial assistant):

1) Fetch lollies from the freezer. (I wasn't even allowed to have any for myself.)
2) Rinse the scoop out in bowl of water. (The water was filthy, and there was even a bluebottle swimming about in it.)
3) Clean the ice cream nozzle with tissue paper. (I saw Alf use the same piece of tissue to blow his nose.)

When we finally got back to the hotel, who should be sitting in the lobby but Ron and Sandra. Ron commented that we resembled a

214

'pair of bl**dy lobsters', and Sandra laughed raucously, while swigging back what looked like a pint of port.

After waiting for three hours for a man to come and cut us a new car key (with a special cutting machine called 'The Vixen'), Rita and I eventually arrived home at 1:35 in the morning.

Oh Dear Diary, I think we both need a holiday . . .

Monday August 15th

Rita and I had a dreadful night of sunburnt (un)sleep. Rita kept complaining of a 'throbbing ankle', and I felt like someone was trying to barbecue my mouth.

Found a rather sweaty tortoise gallomphing around the garden this morning. Don't know what it was doing there, but it looked ever so hot, poor thing. Brought it a little bowl of water, and it lapped it all up. Never realized what nobbly tongues tortii have!

Then, back at work.

Noticed Patel wasn't being as friendly to me as usual, and was still sending mobular textual messages to Tony. It's obvious that Tony has been saying things about me during my absence, although what those things might be I can only guess.

Actually, thinking about it, I can't guess at all what those things might be!

Tuesday August 16th

That rather sweaty-looking tortoise in the garden has given me a new idea. Not literally of course (i.e. the tortoise didn't physically come up to me and tell me the idea), but what I mean is, my 'tortoise sighting' sparked off a new idea inside my head.

And it's a sure-fire billy-boy hit! So make way for the 'Tortimikeppi Tortoise Hat' . . .

The Tortimikeppi Tortoise Hat (see below) is designed to keep the tortoise's head nice and cool, whilst keeping flies away from head, eye and nasal areas.

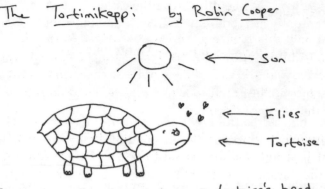

The Tortimikeppi   by Robin Cooper

It is hot. Sun bakes down on tortoise's head. Flies circle around tortoise, and nibble at eyes and nose, causing irritation. Tortoise is sad.

It is still hot. Tortoise now wears Tortimikeppi (tortoise hat). The menthol 'ridge' repels all pests, such as flies. Tortoise is happy.

Tomorrow morning, I shall physically produce my Tortimikeppi prototype, and once I've found that tortoise again (think it wandered off in the direction of the stinging nettles at the back of the garden), use it as my professional – and official – model.

216

Tony Sutton can keep his mashed potato and pea job if he wants, but I'm going off to become the world's first 'tortimillionaire'!

Wednesday August 17th

Got up at 5:00 this morning, and went straight to the shed to make my Tortimikeppi prototype. I used a piece of old curtain (well, I secretly cut a bit out of the curtain in the living room) for the actual tortoise hat, and some mentholated 'chestal rub' ointment for the menthol ridge bit.

Then searched everywhere for the actual tortoise (I tried toffee as bait at first but it didn't seem to work), before finding it right at the back of the garden (where I got badly stung by those wretched nettles). After a bit of a struggle (tortoise tried to bite me), I finally managed to get the Tortimikeppi on to its head.

It was an instant success. The hat shielded the tortoise's eyes from the glare of the sun, its head seemed nice and cool, and all flies/flying things left the immediate area, immediately.

But then something happened, which – in a stroke – consigned my Tortimikeppi to the bin of history.

The tortoise put its head back into its shell, and the hat fell off.

I hadn't thought about that!

Thursday August 18th

Got a bit of a shock today.

I bumped into Tony.

He was coming out of Mr Singh's shop, drinking a can of Pennyfeather's ale, whilst eating a Mars Bar ice cream (what a combination!). At first we just stood around in silence, looking at the ground. It really was most awkward, but I had to do something, so I put my hand out for him to shake. Tony didn't do anything for a good (or rather, bad) 20 seconds, then he too put out his hand, but stopped just before it met mine.

'I'll shake it, if you say I won,' he said.

'I beg your pardon,' I said. (I had heard him really, but was sort of stalling for time.)

'Say it!' he said. 'Say that I won at ping-pong!'

'No,' I replied. 'Never!'

And with that, Tony unleashed a barrage of 'b' and 's' words at me. He was so angry that Mr Singh had to come out of his shop, and physically move him off down the street. In fact, Tony caused such a scene, that even Old Milly (who's a habitual street-shouter herself) tutted.

Oh alas . . .

Friday August 19th

Woke up miserable. How could a simple game of table tennis lead to such total and utter devastation?

Then Michael phoned from Sydney, which cheered me up a little. He sounded quite happy and said that he was going to be putting on a 'live dancing show' with Simon. They must be very good by now.

Didn't speak to Michael for long, as he said he wanted to talk to his mother about something. Don't know what it was all about though, since Rita took the phone into the other room as usual, and all my 'listening devices' (i.e. wine glasses) were in the dishwasher.

By the way, noticed the traffic lights were causing chaos on the high street tonight. They seemed to have a new and very odd sequence:

1) Middle light flashes once
2) Top and bottom lights flash twice in unison
3) Top light flashes once

4) Bottom light flashes twice then stays on for approx 10 seconds
5) All lights flash on and off 15 times

Everyone was beeping their horns and shouting at each other. Sat on the bus for ages, not moving, then decided to get off and walk the rest of the way home. Just as I was leaving, I saw Old Milly wander into the middle of the road, and start directing the traffic. Then, a man in a removal's van threw an apple core right at her – which she promptly ate!

Saturday August 20th – Miss Marsh takes her (written theory) driving test

Miss Marsh kept to her word and was sick before, during and after her written theory driving test – but . . .

She passed!

She actually, physically passed!

To celebrate, I bought her a big box of toffees, and a bumper pack of tissues. Well done Miss Marsh! And well done I!

Hoorah!

Now all we have to do is get her to actually drive.

Sunday August 21st

A dark day today. A very dark day.

Gerald Hale drove off with Mother's car last night, and didn't come back. He also took her purse, her jewellery box, her collection of mini china and glass bells, and rather bizarrely, a roast chicken that was in her fridge.

What a scoundrel! How could that man do such a dreadful thing to my very own mother? I knew there was something wrong with him. Why didn't I SAY something? Why didn't I DO something? If I ever lay my eyes/hands on him, I swear,

Dear Diary, I shall not be responsible for my thoughts, or indeed my actions!

Oh if only I could turn back both hands of time . . .

Rita and I spent the day consoling Mother. She was completely distraught, poor thing, and kept wandering about in a daze, mumbling 'my Gerryboo, my Gerryboo' over and over again. It really was heartbreaking.

Later on, two police officers came and took some details. They were very pleasant, but did seem to spend an inordinate amount of time asking questions about the roast chicken ('How big was it?' 'Was it in a marinade?' etc.) but I suppose they know what they're doing.

Monday August 22nd

Popped round to Mother's on my own tonight. She was not in a good way at all, and her hair was in a terrible mess (it actually looked a bit mauve). Think she'd dyed it at home, which is never a good sign.

What made it even worse, though, was that today, August 22nd, was her birthday. Sadly, Mother didn't even have the strength to look at her presents, let alone open them. In fact, she even made me put them back in my car.

Made Mother a bowl of soup, which seemed to cheer her up a little, then watched a bit of (very loud) television. Put her to bed at 11, and kissed her goodnight. Just as I was leaving, she looked at me with tears in her eyes and said, 'Thank you, my little Robinboo'.

Oh Mother, poor, poor Mother . . .

Tuesday August 23rd

Put this letter through Tony's letterbox today. Didn't dare ring the bell (Susan does not allow visitors).

Robin Cooper
Brondesbury Villas
London

Tony Sutton
Heddon Road
London

23rd August

Dear Tony,

It is I, Robin, here.

I am writing to tell you how sad I am that we are no longer on speaking, or even seeing terms – and all as a result of a game of sport (ping-pong).

And so I ask you…

Is not sport meant to act as a unifying force in the world in general? Is not sport meant to symbolise the oneness of mankind? Is not sport meant to be a bringer-together of men (and women)? Just think of the 'Olympic spirit!'

I may have repeated myself somewhat, but I'm sure you understand what I am trying to say (you may need to read the above paragraph again if you don't).

Tony, we have been such wonderful friends for so many years. We've had good times (i.e. before our argument) and bad times (our argument and afterwards, i.e. now). It would be a terrible shame to throw it all away or discard it like some 'wanton beast'.

Thus, I say to you Anthony Lewis Sutton, please let the light of friendship shine 'pon the two of us, and please let us be friends once again.

Yours,

Robin (Cooper)

Wednesday August 24th

Tony responded to my letter this morning. When I say 'responded', what I actually mean was he dumped 5 empty cans of Pennyfeather's in our front garden, with my scrumpled-up letter poking out the top of one of them.

Is this what 14 years of friendship have come to?

Walked to bus stop feeling very low. Noticed they still hadn't repaired the traffic lights on the high street, and there were lots of men up ladders fiddling with bulbs, while angry motorists exchanged words with them from below. The atmosphere was very tense, so I decided to see if I could be of any help.

I stood at the base of one of the ladders and called up to a young man at the top.

'Good afternoon,' I said.

'Uh!' the man grunted back.

'I just wanted to let you know that if you need me, I used to be a full-time driving instructor.'

'If we need you?' Came the rather terse reply.

'Yes.'

'And why would we need you then?' he said.

'Well, as a former – and now part-time – driving instructor, I have a mass of experience on the roads, and hence, traffic systems.'

'Can you fix the lights?'

'No, not exactly,' I replied

'Well pi*s off then!'

What is wrong with the human race at the moment?

Thursday August 25th

Spoke to the police this morning. No new leads on Gerald Hale, although they did say that they'd spoken to a man at Sainsbury's regarding Mother's roast chicken. Anyway, they said they'd keep me updated.

Played Orag with Rita, Linda and Ian tonight. Here are some of the best ones:

Clues:

1) Short wasp
2) Didn't
3) Gloss
4) Pencil
5) Double Yellow Line

Answers at the bottom (not of Ian's, but of the page!).

Answers:

1) Donkey   (Opposite: Long Bee)
2) Squid   (Opposite: Did)
3) Camel   (Opposite: Enamel)
4) Wren   (Opposite: Pen)
5) Aardvark   (Opposite: Car Park)

It was a shame Tony wasn't there. He loves opposites. (Although he doesn't really like rhymes.)

Friday August 26th

Mother still in shock. When we went round to see her this evening, she was wearing her nightie, and a pair of Father's old leather gloves. What's more, the television was on at full volume, and when I tried to turn it off, she shouted, 'Leave it! It's the horse racing!'

Mother has never liked horse racing or even horses. In fact, Rita and I once took her on a day out to see a working farm, and she almost fainted when a pony sneezed on her.

'I have won every race,' she announced. 'I am now a rich woman!'
   'Really?' I said.
   'Yes, I have made lots of money.'
   'Have you been betting, Mum?' said Rita
   'Yes.'

'Have you been going to the betting shop?' I asked, now mildly concerned.

'No. I don't need to. They take my money through the television.'

'Do they really?' I asked, throwing Rita a look.

We then watched as Mother held up a 10p piece to one of the horse's mouths ('Sammy's Boy, 6-1') on screen.

'There we are,' she said in a slightly deeper voice. 'Bet accepted, Mrs Cooper.'

The journey home was pretty quiet.

Saturday August 27th

Driving lesson cancelled because . . .

Rita slipped on an apple (bramley) in the kitchen, and re-sprained her ankle again.

Oh sooth! What unhappy times!

Cue another frantic drive to the hospital. (I really think we should have our own lane by now.) Usual 5 hour wait in Accident and Emergency, but what was unusual was that we kept on seeing people we knew:

1) Mr Singh from the newsagents: he had swallowed a large ball of Blu Tack. How it got into his mouth in the first place, he wouldn't say.
2) Jimmy (Tony's 'friend' who used my garden for his 'business'): was being led away by two police officers, while shouting 'I'm not drunk!' (he was).
3) Lillian Driftnet (ex school friend of Rita's): had bit her own knee, while falling over.

Rita's now back on wretched 'ankle sticks'. Have also been given some cream, called 'Oxy-formulatis-bri-propus II', to rub into her ankle, thrice daily.

Poor Rita. Poor Mother. Poor Coopers.

Sunday August 28th

Despite her hobblements, Rita insisted that her calligraphy group went ahead today. She spent most of the time with her foot up on a stool, while the other 'Happy Scribblers' (apart from Charles Giles/Giles Charles/Charles Charles)* fussed around her (i.e. chocolate cake and chocolates).

The Magna Carta copying-out project is coming on nicely, it seems, although they still have a very long way to go. I'm sure there must be a more efficient way of working than to have each person writing one word at a time, although when I suggested they tried two words each, Rita literally hissed at me.

I'd never seen her do that before!

Spoke to Mother tonight. Think she must be a little better, as her friend-she-doesn't-like, Mrs Clarke, was there. Also, I didn't hear the word 'boo' (in its suffix form) once.

*Rita and I now suspect he may even be called 'Giles Giles'.

Monday August 29th – Bank Holiday

I don't know why I did it, but I did (it).

I wrote another joke and sent it off to the Brent Herald. It really is very, very good (although Rita didn't get it because she couldn't find her glasses), and this time I am POSITIVE that I'm BOUND to win!

How could Fetfus rear his ugly head again when faced with this corker . . . ?

> I say I say I say, what did the bank say to the holiday today?
> – I don't know, what did the bank say to the holiday today?
> Nothing, as they were both on holiday! (i.e. 'Bank Holiday'!)

The prize: a set of golf sticks (shame they weren't Crazy/Krazy golf sticks!) plus ten cartons of washing powder.

I also did something that took even greater braveness . . .

I telephoned Tony to tell him my joke.

Unfortunately he was out (Red Arrows show) and so I asked Susan to write it down for him. She agreed, begrudgingly, and after I'd finished saying it, she said, 'Which bit is the joke?'

I know Tony is going to call. He just LOVES my jokes.

Tuesday August 30th

Nothing from Tony. Did my joke not please him? Perhaps Susan wrote it down wrong, or missed out my fantastic punchline.

Dramatic times at work: the big plant in the middle of the office has got greenfly. It's literally caked in the beasts! The red-haired woman in workstation 1 sprayed it with her tomato-based perfume, but the only effect it had was to give 85-year-old Lewis an asthma attack, and he had to go and have a lie down behind the photocopier.

By the way, I don't think that cream from the hospital has been doing Rita's ankle any good at all. It's swollen up to the size of Fat Carol's fist.

Wednesday August 31st

Bumped into Patel at the tea and coffee machine at work today. I know I shouldn't have, but I asked him if Tony ever asks about me. Patel replied, 'Tony once asked me if I'd ever seen you blow your nose on your sleeve.'

The cheek! I have never done such a thing in my life!

September

Thursday September 1st

Another letter from Gunter. Again, no mention of the 'house handles', but at least it was reassuringly baffling . . .

Landsberger Strasse 60
CH-8006
Zürich
SWITZERLAND

Friday the August 26st

My dear friendly Robin,

I am hoping you are in good spirits and also is Rita. I am and also is Heidi, but then again we would not no otherwise!

A funny thing has been happening before a week. Heidi and I traveled to see our friends Hans and Lotte Schwimberg, but the autobus was so full up, that we continued with our feet. In the end we were walking with 1 hour but Heidi was losing one of her shoes. When we were arriving, Lotte Schwimberg said that it was all because of the needles that were pointing south! (I think this is how you say it in England). Did you ever hear such a thing?

Heidi is being good for the English language lessons. Now she is saying the gerunds and the words for "Hund" and "Warmwasserheizung" but is having the problems with the writing of your sayings, such as "good night" and "good knight". However, Professor Zemmel is content.

We are still all looking forwards to seeing you in November. The Schwimbergs are most exciting as well and I am sure we will be all be enjoying the famous Lozärner Chügelipaschtete! Also perhaps Herr Pohl will be in attendance with his sister Helga (head injury).

Your ever friendly,

Gunter Schwartz
Gunter Schwartz

Must admit, it was rather disappointing not to be able to write out one of our 'house handles' lists on the easy-wipe message board again.

What is currently written on the easy-wipe board:

- Take back cottage cheese
- Pay gas bill
- Thamat (I think it says 'Thamat'. Don't know what 'Thamat' is though)
- Linda owes Rita £1.40
- Buy ankle cream
- Check smell in bin

What a depressing read!

Friday September 2nd

Did something embarrassing at work today. I tripped over and fell into the big plant! I was literally covered in greenfly, and was still picking them out of my ears on the bus home! I do hope they're not the burrowing type.

When I got back, Rita told me that the police had called today with some news on Gerald Hale. Apparently they'd tracked down the roast chicken, and were 'taking it in for tests'. Good old police!

Sat with Smithie and co. this evening (have had to tell Rita that I'm now 'fixing the loft's inner guttering'). Was a bit naughty, as I fed Binky and Alfredo from my hand (chocolate buttons), but luckily Smithie didn't seem to mind. In fact, she tucked in as well!

Saturday September 3rd

Think those chocolate buttons from yesterday must have seeped into my self/un-conscious (I never know the right word for that), as I had another turquoise button dream last night.

Things zapped:

1) Smithie, Binky and Alfredo (their wings were no match for the powerful turquoise ray)
2) Gerald (hoorah!)
3) Tony (also hoorah!)
4) Mother (shame)
5) Roast chicken (also a shame as I was just about to eat it)
6) Plant with greenfly (good riddance!)
7) Me (certainly not good riddance!)

Think that is the last time I feed those birds chocolate buttons. (NB: buy Maltesers).

Had a pretty good driving lesson today. Miss Marsh even hooted her horn (Old Milly shaving legs in road), and did her three-point turn in only six. It's just a shame she didn't come to my rescue as Cardinal Wig-Wam Tommy last night.

By the way, noticed our loo was making a very strange 'gargling' sound today.

Sunday September 4th

I've been racking my brain (and my mind) to come up with a way of getting Tony and I to start communicating again. It's now been over a month since we've been friends – and enough is enough!

Well, I think I've come up with a solution . . .

It's a new alphabet!

Yes, I have invented an entirely new alphabet just for myself and Tony to use. It'll be our own private language, that we will learn, and then talk, and it will (hopefully) bring us closer together.

Here it (the new alphabet) is:

The New Millennium British Alphabet System
by Robin Cooper

Name (of letter)	Sound (letter makes)	Name (of letter)	Sound (letter makes)
Wilby	(as in 'willoughby')	Epson	(as in 'epsom')
Sveh	(as in 'sventy')	Fov	(as in 'fences')
Dlent	(as in 'dlent')	Rralve	(as in 'valve')
Naarnst	(as in 'nanny')	Ust	(as in 'crust')
Libby	(as in 'Llewellyn')	Tlin	(as in 'tin harry')
Onty	(as in 'opportunity')	Kibby	(as in 'kibby')
Psy	(as in 'silence')	Oob	(as in 'tube')
Mancharve	(as in 'mummy')	Ooob	(as in 'tubes')
Ibs	(as in 'infected')	Ibel	(as in 'libel')
Sharvu	(as in 'shandy')	————•	(Loud hissing sound)
Pfon	(as in 'pfennig')	Ffalf	(signifies a question)
	(silent sounding letter)	Pilfon	(as in 'plum')

Put a copy through Tony's letterbox, with a note attached, explaining usage.

I wish myself luck!

Or perhaps I should say . . .

Monday September 5th

Rita woke up in a lot of pain this morning. Her ankle was as big as an ostrich egg! Rushed round to Doctor Margolis, who took one look at the cream we'd been using, and told us we'd been given the wrong stuff. Apparently it's meant for nappy rash!

P.S. – Think my new alphabet system idea is already over. This was Tony's reply:

Charming!

Tuesday September 6th

General Incorporated Business Solutions' greenfly problem continues. There were greenfly everywhere in the office today. My workstation was literally crawling with them. From my countation, there were:

1) 6 in my pen-holder (three alive, three sadly deceased)
2) 12 in my waste-paper basket (all deceased)
3) 1 in my other waste-paper basket (alive – it obviously made the right choice vis-à-vis which waste-paper basket to sit in)
4) 9 on my computer screen (all alive and hopping about)
5) 3 on my pile of incoming data forms (hard to tell: may have been sleeping/playing dead)

6) 1 on my chin (very much alive – horrid Corville pointed it out of course)

When no one was looking, I gathered up all the dead greenflies (15) into an envelope, and then put it away in my trouser pocket. I think they'll make a well-deserved treat for Smithie, Binky and Alfredo. (Potentially) lucky birds!

P.S. Gargling loo getting louder and louder. Must fix.

Wednesday September 7th

Oh sooth . . .

2-9 Lyndhurst Road, London NW4

5th September

From: Local Follies Department, The Brent Herald.

To: Robin Cooper
Brondesbury Villas, London

Dear Mr Cooper,

I say I say I say,
What's this, another joke?
I say I say I say,
From that really stupid bloke?

I say I say I say,
It really was insane,
I say I say I say
I doubt he has a brain!

Yours sincerely,

Ted G Fettus

Words cannot describe the anger, the rage, the fury, the sheer irateness, the utter and total enragement, the anger, the annoyance, the complete rage, and the anger I felt when I read this.

In fact, I think it's better if I sum up my mood in numbers: 9999999999.99999999999999999999999999999.999999999999 999999999999

I called Tony at once. Whatever had happened between us, he was still my friend – my best friend – and thus HAD to know.

In the end I left a message on his mobular telephone (actually quite an easy operation, I just had to talk AFTER the beepage), and read out Fetfus's letter in its full unglory, my voice a-quivering with every despicable word.

O' Tony, O' Anthony Lewis Sutton, if you have a heart, if you have a soul, I beseech thee – put down your Pennyfeather's and pick up your phone, for together we can defeat this aberration of man, this blight 'pon mankind, this thorn in humanity's kidney – the accursed Ted G. Fetfus . . .

Thursday September 8th

Got a very dramatic phone call early this morning, which led to a series of other (equally) dramatic phone calls. I jotted them all down as soon as they were over:

'Mr Cooper?'
　'Speaking.'
　'Gary H. Meadows, the editor of Brent Herald here.'
　'Oh, Mr Meadows, I've been meaning to speak to you.'
　'I bet you have, Mr Cooper, I bet you have.'
　'I'm sorry, I don't quite know what you are talking about.'
　'You know very well what I'm talking about, Mr Cooper.'
　'Do I?'
　'Yes. And what on earth are you going to do about it?'
　'About what?'

'Well, where do I start? Perhaps I should start by telling you that I've spent the last three hours scraping mashed potato off every surface in my office, while wading through thousands of frozen peas.'

Oh dear. Mashed potatoes and peas. I wonder who could have done that . . .

'Are you trying to accuse me of dumping food in your workplace?' I said.

'Not accuse you, Mr Cooper, I'm telling you it was you.'

'Is that so? And what may I ask is your proof?'

'How about the words "get stuffed" written in three-foot-high potato letters on top of my filing cabinet?'

'And what do the words "get stuffed" have to do with anything?'

'I asked myself that very same thing, Mr Cooper, until I realized that "get stuffed" was a perfect anagram of Ted G. Fetfus . . .'

I performed a quick anagramization. He was right! Why hadn't I spotted that earlier? I'm normally so good with jumbled-up wrods.

Mr Meadows went on . . .

'So – are you going to come clean, or am I going to have to call the police?'

'Give me five minutes,' I said. 'I'll call you straight back.'

Immediately I dialled Tony's number. I woke him up. He didn't sound too fresh. Our conversation went thusly:

'Tony.'

'Yes.'

'It's me.'

'Oh hello.'

'Hello.'

'Hello.'

'Tony?'

'Yes.'

'Was it you who . . .?'
'Yes, it was. It was me.'
'Oh.'
'Yes.'
'I see.'
'Yes.'

There was a pause.

'Why did you do it, Tony?'

There was a long pause.

'Do you really want to know?'
   'I do, Tony. I really do.'

There was a longer pause.

'Well . . . I did it for you, Robin. I did it for our friendship.'

Tony sounded choked up, and I'm sure I heard him blow his nose
(by the way he's the one that normally uses his sleeve, not me).
   'Well, what are we going to do now, Tony?'
   'Leave it with me, Robin.'

Tony hung up.

Five minutes later, the phone rang again. It was Gary H.
Meadows. The conversation went thusly:
   'Mr Cooper?'
   'Speaking.'
   'Gary H. Meadows here, Brent Herald.'
   'Hello, Mr Meadows.'
   'I've just been speaking to your colleague.'
   'Oh yes.'
   'The one that works at the canning factory.'
   'Oh him, yes.'

There was a pause.

'All right, I'll come clean. I'm sorry. It was my son who'd been sending you those letters. I didn't know how to stop him. He's only been here on work experience, just to keep him out of trouble. He's a good lad really but this time he's gone too far. I'm really sorry.'

'Oh I see.'

'Yes. I promise it won't happen again.'

'So you won't be pressing charges then?'

'Oh no. And you won't be pressing charges against my son?'

'No. You don't need to worry about that. I have a son too you know!' (Although Michael would never DREAM of doing such a thing!)

'So would you perhaps consider this matter closed now, Mr Cooper?'

'Yes, I think that would be a good idea, Mr Meadows.'

'Oh thank you, Mr Cooper.'

'Not at all. Goodbye then.'

'Goodbye.'

'Oh – Mr Meadows?'

'Yes, Mr Cooper?'

'Does that mean I've won the golf sticks?'

'No, I'm sorry, that prize has already been sent out . . .'

'Oh can't you get it back from—'

'. . . to a man who's in hospital at the moment.'

'Oh I see. Well, thank you.'

'Goodbye, Mr Cooper.'

'Goodbye Mr Meadows.'

I phoned Tony.

'Hello, Tony.'

'Oh hello, Robin.'

'So you spoke to Mr Meadows?'

'Yes I did.'

'And what did you say to him?'

'Oh nothing much.'

'I see.'

'Well, I did say something.'

'And what was that?'

'I told him that if he went to the police, I'd tell them exactly what I found in his office drawer.'

'Oh dear. And what was that?'

'Nothing. I didn't even look in his drawer. But it always works!'

Good old Tony!

Happy days are here again!

Friday September 9th

It is now 3:22 in the morning (strictly speaking it is really Saturday) and I am writing this bit rather worse for wear – and tear!

Indeed, Dear Diary, it could be said that I, Robin Cooper, am slightly tipsy. In fact, I'll be honest with thee – I am completely betipsied!!!

Yea, 'tis true, I have bedrunk 4 full (but now empty) cans of Premium Strength Pennyfeather's ale, with my best and favourite friend in the world, Tony Sutton. And what exactly is wrong with that, I ask you?

Nothing! Nothing at all!

HOORAH! HOORAH TO ONE AND ALL!

HOORAH!!!

Saturday September 10th

Woke up in a terrible state. It felt like someone had been moving a cupboard about in my head all night. I swear, Dear Diary, I am never EVER going to touch a drop/dropette/dram/dramini of alcohol again in my life.

Driving lesson was a bit of a blur to be honest. All I can remember was Miss Marsh stalling on the dual carriageway, wiping her nose, starting the car again, then stalling again. (All this × 2.)

Was really not in the mood, but went to the cinema tonight to see a film called 'Decisive Actions' (another recommendation from Linda). It was all about an older woman who had to decide whether to marry a rather unsuitable man (a former wrestler) or to continue living life as a spinster.

Not quite sure what the woman decided to do in the end, because Rita and I were fast asleep within fifteen minutes. However, I did manage to wake up and catch the final 30 seconds, in which the woman appeared to be sitting alone in her living room, sobbing into a cushion, so I presume:

1) She didn't marry the man in the end.
2) She did marry the man, but he:
     a) died b) ran away c) had an important 'come back' wrestling match, which he lost.

P.S. – Our gargling loo has been getting worse. I just flushed it tonight and it sounded as if it was talking to me. In fact, I could have sworn it said, 'I wish you well.'

Sunday September 11th

Rita was just about to put the washing machine on this morning when she came into the living room holding a pair of my work trousers.

'Robin?' she said. 'Why have you got an envelope full of dead greenflies in your pocket?'

Oh dear! I knew there was something I'd forgotten.

'For research purposes,' I replied. (I didn't know what else to say.)

'Research into what?' she asked

'Greenflies,' I mumbled.

'Greenflies that have done what?'

I thought about this for a few seconds.

'Died,' I said.

'Well, why are they in an envelope then?' she asked.

'Because I was going to send them off,' I replied.

'To where?'

This was a very good question, which required a very good answer . . .

'I can't remember,' I said. 'That's why the envelope's blank.' (That was definitely a very good answer.)

Rita gave me a look, as if to say 'there better not be something going on', and then said, 'There better not be something going on.'

Later, when she was doing one of her dot-to-dots, I quietly retrieved the envelope from the bin, crept up to the loft, and offered the contents to my feathered friends.

After all that fuss, they didn't touch a single greenfly, and just gobbled up the envelope instead.

That's gratitude for you!

Monday September 12th

Tony must have spoken to Patel, because when I got into work this morning, there was this sticky note stuck to my computer screen:

Dear Cooper

I am sorry if I have upset you. I really do like you as a friend and colleague. I also enjoyed watching you play table tennis in the garden in the summer. I think you should have won really, but please don't tell Tony.

From Patel

PS - Look inside your desk.

I did what Patel's 'PS' ordered, and there, inside my desk, was a ticket to the 'Shuttleworth Autumn Air Display' in Bedfordshire, on Sunday October 2nd (ticket price: £16). Patel had invited me to an air show! My very first air show! What an honour!

I thanked Patel heartily (multiple hand-shaking), and told him how delighted I was. He was delighted too, and told me that I would only need to pay for half my ticket.

Hoorah for Cooper! Hoorah for Patel! Hoorah for Shuttleworth Autumn Air Display! (My actual ticket price: £8.)

Tuesday September 13th

Gargling loo spoke to me again today. Pretty sure it said, 'cinnamon sausages Swansea', although when I flushed it again, it sounded more like 'civic hostages Humphrey'. Rita keeps nagging me to get it fixed (apparently it called her a 'silly horse' this morning) but I rather like having a talking toilet. In fact, I told Rita it was a 'talking point'! (She didn't see the funny side, though.)

Tony popped over tonight, and together we had a couple of late night butter sandwiches in the shed. It was just like old times.

He told me that the day after our ping-pong disagreement, he'd had a terrible row with Susan all about their anniversary. When I asked him if it was because he'd forgotten it again (Tony forgets every year), he replied, 'No, I remembered – but on the wrong day.'

Tony ended up sleeping in his car for a week, and then, when Susan hid his car keys, had to bed down in his garden, and sleep underneath a sheet of tarpaulin. Poor Tony.

Afterwards, I told him he was always welcome to stay over at our house – to which Tony replied, 'Thanks Robin, you're a great mate.'

And with that, he left the shed, walked into the house, went up to Michael's bedroom, and shut the door behind him.

The (good old Tony Sutton) cheek!

Wednesday September 14th

Henderson handed round the following note this morning:

General Incorporated Business Solutions

Workers of General Incorporated Business Solutions

FROM: HENDERSON

14th Sep.

Re: "Economy Drive"

Due to various complicated business matters, I regret to inform you that we have had to make the following financial cutbacks:

1)   Tea and coffee machine: This has been returned to it's suppliers ('Thomson & gray electricals Inc') due to high rental charges.

2)   plastic Cups. We will no longer provide these, so please bring in youre own mug (one per person) if you want to make a hot drink.

3)   Tea And coffee: Please supply your'e own.

4)   Toaster – this is being returned to Mrs Henderson, as it was hers.

5)   Bread for toaster – see point 4.

6)   Toilet rolls – somcone has been using far too much toilet paper. Please can we **ALL** make an effort to cut down.

Much murmuring in the office, and everyone gossiping.

I do hope everything's going to be all right. And who could Henderson be referring to in point 6? It can't be me. I only ever do a wee at work.

Thursday September 15th

Linda and Ian's for dinner tonight (one piece of lamb, four roast potatoes, 30 peas, and just two helpings of cake – how DOES Ian cope?).

Mother was there too, but thankfully she looked a little better, even though she was still wearing gloves indoors and her hair was still mauveish.

After our 'meal', I played a few rounds of Orag with Ian, while Rita and Linda discussed astrology/nibs etc. Ian absolutely loves Orag (it also appears to keep his trousers and pants from coming off), and is now rather good at it. His best clue – in my opinion – was 'upstanding citizen'.* Mine – also in my opinion – was 'nurse pup'.**

By the way, Linda told Rita that she thought she saw that scoundrel Gerald Hale driving down the high street in Mother's car yesterday. Obviously no one dared breathe a word to Mother. Will have to keep a good look-out for that scallywag . . .

*Answer: 'Trout' (Opposite: 'lout')
**Answer: 'Octopus' (Opposite: 'doctor puss')

Friday September 16th

Some sad commuter-related information: Philip Teff (now down to just 2 chins) will no longer be travelling on the same bus as me in the morning, as he's moving to York on Monday to start a new job promoting Bristol.

And so, with the bus driver and passengers' prior permission, Teff put away his carrot for the last time, reached into his carrier bag, and pulled out an onion, which he bit into with a solemnitude that I have rarely seen (of an onion eater).

I am not ashamed to say, Dear Diary, that I was not the only one on the bus who had tears in my eyes. However, whether this was from emotion, or onion fumes, I may never know.

Saturday September 17th

What a horrible way to start the weekend. This morning our gargling loo called me a 'selfish swine', and a 'saucy swindler'. Something must be done.

Three o'clock driving lesson: Miss Marsh was almost physically sick when I told her the date of her driving test. It's Thursday the 22nd – just 5 days to go! Anyway, here – in figures – are the results of today's lesson:

1) Stalling: 6
2) 3-point turn: 8 (i.e. it was done in 8 turns)
3) Parking: 0 (just couldn't do it)
4) Emergency stops: 1
5) Real emergency stops: 1
6) Horn hooted (by her): 2
7) Horn hooted (at her): 9
7) Sneezing: 5
8) Tissues: 10

TOTAL: 45 (I'm not sure why I just added up all the figures.)

Anyway, fingers (and figures) crossed!

Sunday September 18th

Our abusive toilet is no more.

This morning I took some drastic action, and bought a toilet plunger. Unfortunately the man in the hardware shop had run out of plastic bags, which made the walk home extremely embarrassing. I just didn't know what to do with the thing. At first I held it by my side but people kept catching sight of it.

Finally I settled on a sort of 'sergeant major' look, holding the plunger under my arm, with the stick end pointing outwards. But just as I was passing the newsagent's, Mr Singh (who has clearly recovered since his Blu Tack swallowing incident) rushed out of his shop and called out, 'Morning Mr Mainwaring, from Dad's Army!'

This caused a nasty group of girls to fall about laughing, and when I remonstrated with them, they started making obscene 'toilet' noises behind my back, and then followed me all the way back home.

Luckily Mr Alfonso from next door saved the day. He recognized a few of the girls from his school, and gave them on-the-spot detentions. Good old Mr Alfonso!

Anyway, gargling loo silent once again – although I shall miss our little 'chats'.

Monday September 19th

Woke up today to find our doorstep sprayed with the word 'grass' in red capital letters (i.e. 'GRASS') (but in red).

This is insolence of the highest kind! In fact it's insolence of the lowest kind! It's even worse than that wretched Monty and that accursed Fetfus put together! How dare they?! How DARE they?!

Had strong words with Mr Alfonso, who assured me that he would take the necessary action, as soon as he got into school. Offered to build him a set of stocks to put in the playground, but he politely declined.

Spent all morning repainting step, which made me very late for work. Henderson was not happy (he tapped on his window with one of his – i.e. my – pens), and horrid Corville sniggered loudly behind my back.

I am surrounded by impertinence whe'er I go.

P.S. – Some good news: Binky and Alfredo have sprouted feathers. They've become little 'boy birds' – unless they're actually little 'girl birds'!

Tuesday September 20th

Terrible night's sleep. For some reason I just couldn't stop wondering whether you could boil an egg in a kettle. I wonder if you can?

Office greenfly situation is now almost totally out of control. Yesterday Henderson found one of them up his nose, so this morning the red-haired woman in workstation 1 was dispatched to fetch some ladybirds (keen greenfly-eaters) from outside.

About an hour later she returned with four ladybirds (no doubt they'd been attracted to her tomato 'scent') and then placed them on the big plant – the centre of greenfly production. Hopefully they'll soon get chomping, and we'll all be able to blow our noses with confidence once again.

By the way, the 'grass' spraying culprit wouldn't own up from amongst the group of girls, so Mr Alfonso put their entire year in detention. What power!

Wednesday September 21st

It IS possible to boil an egg in a kettle!

The secret is to leave the egg in the water – after the kettle has boiled – for 6 minutes (soft), or 8 minutes (firm). For hard-boiled, merely leave the cooked egg in the water for about an hour afterwards.

Had a bit of a panic when one of the eggs broke inside the kettle

(Rita would have gone berserk), but managed to clean the albumen off the filament just before she hobbled into the kitchen.

P.S. – Ladybirds doing a grand job re greenfly removance, although they do seem to be mating at quite a rate. Henderson seemed happy (he bought biscuits for all), and red-haired lady in workstation 1 was wearing a double helping of her tomato perfume today – presumably in celebration.

Thursday September 22nd – Miss Marsh's driving test

What a day.

Had set off for the test centre in Hendon, with Miss Marsh driving/stalling/tissuing, and we were just passing Old Milly on her bench (she gave me a 'wink'), when suddenly I spotted a very familiar vehicle right in front of us.

It was Mother's car – driven by the dastardly Gerald Hale.

I couldn't believe it!

'Follow that car, Miss Marsh,' I shouted, 'and fast!'

Miss Marsh put her foot down on the accelerator, and instantly stalled.

I explained the situation as quickly as possible, but there was no time for me to take over the wheel so, instead, I offered to do the gears. However, Miss Marsh refused:

'Mr Cooper,' she said, 'it is time I learnt to drive all by myself. You can rely on me this time.'

And with that, she glanced in her mirror, put the car into gear, stepped on the gas, and zoomed off after him. Hoorah for Miss Marsh!

By now, the scallywag-of-the-century (i.e. Gerald Hale) was three cars in front of us but, breaking all the rules of the Highway Code (in particular, section 112: 'Lane discipline'), Miss Marsh pulled out on to the other side of the road and

250

weaved between the traffic, until we were right behind him once again.

I'd never seen her drive like that before! I'm sure Cardinal Wig-Wam Tommy would have been most proud!

Gerald knew we were on to him, and began to wave his arms at us to 'go away'. I responded by hooting my horn several times and throwing toffees at him. One of them hit his aerial, which would have definitely interfered with his AM/FM reception, had he been listening (which I hope he had!).

Miraculously, Miss Marsh kept on Gerald's tail. Wherever he went, Miss Marsh followed. She was literally driving as if she was possessed (i.e. by the ghost of an ex-getaway driver).

But suddenly, Gerald spun his car around and sped off down a narrow side street. There was nothing for it. I pulled on the handbrake and as we skidded right round, I bellowed at Miss Marsh to 'bl**dy step on it!' (adrenalin can do terrible things to a man, Dear Diary). Miss Marsh slammed on the accelerator, and we raced off after him. She even let out a 'whoop' of joy!

Then, just as Gerald turned off into an industrial estate, a huge lorry pulled out in front of his vehicle, and Gerald slammed on his brakes. He tried to reverse, but Miss Marsh drove right up to him, until we were bumper-to-bumper. Gerald Hale was trapped.

I leapt out of my car, opened Gerald's door and wrestled him to the ground (he wasn't very strong for an explorer). Then I called out to Miss Marsh to telephone the police ('999'), and she got dialing, mobular-wise. It was like in that film (I can't remember the name, though).

Meanwhile, Gerald started to protest loudly. 'There's been a terrible mistake,' he said, 'I was just taking your mother's car in for its MOT.'

The cheek!

When the police arrived, they questioned us a little (further interrogation re the roast chicken etc.), then handcuffed Gerald, put him in the back of the car, and drove off. And thus, Dear Diary, justice was done. Or as they say in the law courts these days – 'justinium finalium'!

Unfortunately, Miss Marsh had missed her driving test, but she really didn't seem that concerned. In fact, she told me she'd 'loved every minute', and that it had all been 'just like a film'. (I really wish I could remember the name.) She then let out another 'whoop'!

I couldn't believe it. Was it really Miss Marsh who had been driving my car? When did she suddenly get so good/dangerous?

Got home, and told Rita what had happened, and I'm delighted to say that she called me her 'hero', and instantly awarded me a thrice-a-decadon of kisses (i.e. 13). Now that's got to be better than getting a bravery award from the Queen!

Popped up to loft to tell Smithie and co. (I mimed the action but I don't think they totally understood), then made myself a nice cup of tea, and – when Rita wasn't looking – two 'kettle eggs' to celebrate!

Hoorah!

P.S. – Actually, I wonder if I will get a bravery award from the Queen . . .?

P.P.S. – I think the name of the film was 'The Car Chase'.

Friday September 23rd

Rita and I went round to Mother's this evening to break the news about Gerald Hale.

She listened quietly throughout, and then, when we'd finished, took a deep breath, removed her gloves (at last!), and without saying a word, went off to the kitchen. Rita and I looked at each, not knowing what to do.

A minute later, Mother came back into the room holding a bottle of champagne.

'I saved this bottle especially,' she said. 'I had a feeling Gerald wasn't right when I saw him take his shirt off.'

'Really?' asked Rita. 'Why was that?'

'He was wearing a gentleman's corset!' she replied.

And thus we drank to Mother, to merriment and to male corsetry. It was truly wonderful, Dear Diary, to see Mrs Hilary Cooper back to her old self once again.

We finished off the afternoon (after we'd finished off the bottle!) by watching some good old-fashioned (and extremely loud) 'Songs of Praise'. Rita remarked that the vicar looked like a young Princess Anne (he did actually), and we all had a jolly sing-song, while Mother danced the foxtrot to 'Morning Has Broken'.

Happy days . . .

Saturday September 24th

I have a new idea!

It's a hit! A sure-fire, billy-boy hit! In fact, I think it may even have the word 'hit' physically written all over it – in every language known to man! (i.e. infinity languages.)

But before I could make a start, I decided it was time to complete my Shed Inventory, which I noticed has been left unfinished since March:

Shed Inventory (No. 19 still contd.) as at 6:45pm, Saturday September 24th by Robin Cooper

Radio

3 × milk bottles

Box of porridge oats (Best Before: 6th June 1997. NB: must throw away.)

1 × bottle of washing up liquid (empty)

Lavender tablets

Lincoln powder

Costumes of King Henry VIII and Anne Boleyn (from 1996 (cancelled) Tudor Festival)

Emergency sewing kit (for repairing emergency clothes?)

8 × scythes

1 × hat box

6 × cans of Pennyfeather's ale (empty) (NB: This has GOT to stop!)

Brake fluid

Putty

4 × bulbs (60W bayonets)

12 × bulbs (60W small screw caps)

3 × bulbs (not for lights, but for plants)

Nail scissors

Kettle

The other pruning glove (found it at last!)

15 bars of chocolate

1 × pipette

1 × burette

1 × marble (think someone is playing a cruel joke on me)

Half packet lemon wipes

Table salt

Bottle of ketchup

1 × red onion (farewell gift from Philip Teff)

Didn't quite finish inventory (manure bag too soft), or get round to the actual physical inventing bit, but will reveal all about my new idea, Dear Diary, tomorrow.

All I can say is that this idea has been 'brewing away' for some time, and it is now ready to 'hatch' . . .

Sunday September 25th

Thus . . .

Robin Cooper
Brondesbury Villas
London

The Chairman
Morphy Richards Kettles (and similar appliances)
Talbot Road
Mexborough
S Yorks
S64 8AJ

September 24th

Dear Sir/Madam

A revolution in kettling (i.e. the use of kettles) is upon us!

And I - the revoultionaire – am here to tell you all about it…

The 'Nest Egg' Kettle is the world's first kettle designed for:

1) Making tea (as per usual)
2) Making coffee (again as per usual)
3) Other sundry boiling uses (once again as per usual)
4) Boiling eggs (certainly NOT as per usual!)

Yes it is point 4 that I wish to draw your ATTENTION to – for the 'Nest Egg' Kettle is the only kettle designed to make hot drinks and boiled eggs at once.

'So how does it work?' I hear you ask (in my head). Well, simple. Inside the top of the kettle is a mini sort of bowl device (the 'nest' bit), in which the egg eater carefully places his or her (women eat almost as many eggs as men do these days, apparently) egg.

Then, simply boil the kettle, and leave the egg in the water for the following times (for the following sort of eggs):

TIME (IN MINS) LEFT IN WATER AFTER BOILAGE	TYPE OF BOILED EGG
1	Nearly raw
2	Still basically nearly raw
3	A bit more cooked but inedible
4	Much too runny to eat
5	Almost edible
6	Nice and soft (i.e. edible)
7	Haven't tried this timing
8	Firm (some people like their eggs like this but I prefer my eggs soft)

9	Firmer
10	Very hard but NOT hard boiled
	(I wouldn't eat it, but others, such as your
	good self might)

So, when the time's up (see above), you can enjoy a perfect egg with an equally perfect cup of tea or coffee. Now that's gotta be a winner!

I have included a diagram, which I hope will assist you, visually.

So, do we have a deal?

I look forward to hearing from you. After all – time (i.e. egg time, i.e. an egg timer) is running out!

Best wishes,

Robin Cooper

PS – Poached eggs can also be made by simply cracking the egg into the kettle, but it's usually best to use the kettle to make your hot drink first (i.e. to prevent eggy water).

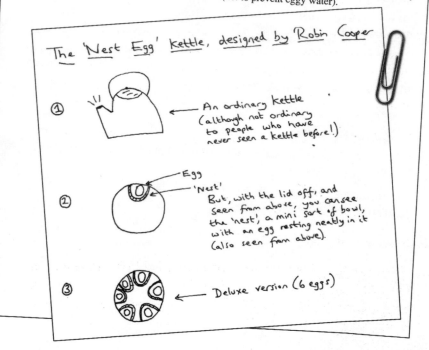

The 'Nest Egg' Kettle, designed by Robin Cooper

① An ordinary kettle (although not ordinary to people who have never seen a kettle before!)

② Egg — 'Nest'
But, with the lid off, and seen from above, you can see the 'nest', a mini sort of bowl, with an egg resting neatly in it (also seen from above).

③ Deluxe version (6 eggs)

Monday September 26th

My once bitter and deadly enemy, the Brent Herald newspaper, telephoned this morning (well, not the actual newspaper, but a lady from it) to ask me all about last Thursday's car-chase shenn-a-nanigans (MUST look that word up in dictionary) with Gerald Hale. Apparently they're thinking of printing the story. Fancy that!

Naturally I put on my best speaking voice, and explained everything that happened in sheer and utter detail. Surely, now, fame and fortune beckon . . .

I wish myself luck!

Meanwhile, back in the offices of General Incorporated Business Solutions, there's now an infestation of ladybirds.

I don't know what the little blighters got up to with each other at the weekend (well, I can guess!) but there were literally swarms of them everywhere. They'd clogged up the fax machine, blocked the sink in the unisex toilet, and even got into poor Lewis's beard. It was like Critter Land all over again! Spent most of the morning collecting the winged beasts with Patel (we filled up half a bucket), and then freeing them outside by the skip.

Office eventually back to normal. However I did notice a distinct 'crunch' to my butter sandwich at lunchtime, so closed my eyes and tried not to think of the worst.

Tuesday September 27th

Spoke to the police tonight.

Gerald Hale has come clean. Or rather, Bobby McPherson has clean. That's because Gerald Hale does not exist (although I'm sure there is another Gerald Hale somewhere else in the world), as he is really called 'Mr Bobby McPherson'.

Apparently, McPherson is originally from Edinburgh, a carpenter by trade – and thus not an explorer (I thought as much) – has a wife and three children (the swine!) and is a 'serial cheat' with a criminal record stretching back to February 1979, when he conned a farmer in Fife out of an ox, two rabbits, and a wife.

McPherson's trial looks likely to occur in the new year, and the police think he'll probably end up physically in prison. Serves him right! Did offer to build them a set of stocks, in the meantime, but my offer was politely declined.

Don't know what to say to Mother about all of this. She'll be heartbroken.

Driving student thwarts career criminal

Driving lesson turns into high-speed car chase

by **PETER BENSON**

A LOCAL WOMAN was branded a 'hero' this week by police officers.

Miss Geraldine Marsh, 40, of Elmsworthy Gardens, was taking a driving lesson on Saturday afternoon, when she spotted career criminal, Bobby McPherson, driving in a stolen vehicle along the Kilburn High Road.

Miss Marsh began to follow McPherson, but this soon escalated into a high speed car chase that took in Fryent Way, Wyre Grove and the premises of Glebes' Soaps.

Eventually, Miss Marsh, who is yet to gain her driving license, managed to block McPherson's vehicle in with her own, before calling the police, who promptly arrested the man.

Miss Marsh was also assisted by her driving instructor, Mr Robin Pooper, 63, of Brondesbury Villas. According to one eyewitness, Pooper helped restrain McPherson by "sitting on his head and pinching him repeatedly".

Ironically, Miss Marsh was on her way to her driving test at the time of the incident. "It all happened very fast," said Miss Marsh, a part-time bookkeeper, "I think I just went into overdrive."

DCI Brown, who attended the scene, said, "Miss Marsh acted extremely bravely, with very little consideration for her own safety.

"I have no doubt, that without Miss Marsh's quick-thinking and clever driving, this repeat offender would have certainly got away.

McPherson, 65, of no fixed abode, had been wanted by police for a number of years in connection with identity fraud, vehicle and oxen theft.

Don't forget: if you would like to nominate Miss Marsh or anyone else for this year's 'Brent Herald Local Hero' Awards, please contact the newspaper at our usual postal or email address (see page 52 for details). Voting ends on November 1st.

Robin Pooper?
  Pooper?!
  63?
  Pinching? (Well, I might have given him a couple of pinches.)
  Miss Marsh – up for a bravery award? What about me?!
The cheek!

Thursday September 29th

Mother saw the newspaper article, but took it much better than I'd anticipated.

'I hope you gave that man a big pinch from me!' she said.

Good old Mother!

Unfortunately, quite a lot of other people had also seen the article:

1) Tony – phoned to ask for the 'Pooper residence'
2) Horrid Corville – called me a 'Pooper Scooper'
3) Henderson – also called me a 'Pooper Scooper'
4) Mr Singh – ditto
5) Old Milly – just shouted 'Pooper! Pooper!' quite loudly and drunkenly from bench.

Anyway, the good news is that Mother has now got most of her things back, and last night the police returned her car all wrapped up with a ribbon and bow, made out of 'Police – Do Not Cross' tape! She was delighted.

The even better news is that Rita gave me a double helping of a thrice-a-decadon of kisses tonight (i.e. 26), before calling me her 'Super dooper Pooper'!

Such is love . . .

Friday September 30th

Spoke to Michael this morning. Think he'd been practising his dancing with Simon when I called, as he sounded particularly out of breath. Anyway, told him all about his grandmother/ Gerald Hale/Bobby McPherson. Michael said 'fab' again.

By the way, General Incorporated Business Solutions is now a ladybird/greenfly-free zone, but the economy drive continues at work. Under Henderson's orders, the radiators are now only switched on for one hour a day, and the office has started to get very chilly indeed. This afternoon I had to rub 85-year-old Lewis's legs (poor circulation) for ages. We got through a whole tub of Vick's!

Came home, had dinner (lamb, mashed potatoes, roast potatoes, peas, a bit of beef, and some ice cream and also some biscuits and two cups of tea), and then Fat Carol popped over.

We are now the proud owners of Samuel Johnson – the inventor of the English dictionary – as a beige Burmese!

P.S. – Tried to make a boiled egg in the dishwasher tonight.

P.P.S. It didn't work.

October

Saturday October 1st – 'Pinch punch, the very first day of the month!'

Tony let himself in this morning. Apparently he'd had an argument with Susan all about their dustbin (i.e. Tony's non-emptying of).

Made him a (secret) kettle egg to cheer him up, and played Orag for a bit, but I don't think Tony really understood the game, as he kept saying capital cities instead of animals (plus he hated the rhyming bit).

Then it was time for my first driving lesson with Miss Marsh since our high-speed car-chase incident.

I was shocked.

Miss Marsh has changed.

Dramatically.

The tears, the stallings, the nasal snivellings – these were all replaced by horn-honking, 'whooping', and repetitive Highway Code breakage (in particular, sections 138–145: 'Overtaking'). Miss Marsh even put on a cassette of a pop song, which she listened to at full blast. Think it was 'Satisfaction' by the Beatles

I'm already missing the old Miss Marsh . . .

Sunday October 2nd – my first ever air show!

What a day! Went to the Shuttleworth Autumn Air Display with Patel, and together we saw the following air vehicles (i.e. planes):

1) A big red one with yellow stripes on it (can't remember the name).
2) A blue one with green wings (think it was some form of 'Moth' – but certainly not the insect!).
3) A few small old ones.

4) A 'Wetland Wasp' – (I remembered its name, because Patel knew the owner, who everyone seemed to call 'Motorway Bill' for some reason).

5) Some newish looking planes – but not ones I've ever been in.

6) 2 × helicopters. Patel refused to even look at them. He really hates helicopters.

7) A very noisy plane that was a bit annoying as it kept doing 'loop the loops' and making more noise, and just wouldn't get out of the air and stop flying. Tried putting pieces of tissue in my ears, but it didn't really help (also, couldn't get the piece out of my left ear for ages).

8) Other miscellaneous planes (including a 'fat' orange one).

9) An old Second World War plane (Spitfire?) driven by a man – well probably two men – dressed as a pantomime horse. (Apparently it's a tradition.)

The best bit – apart from the planes of course – was the grub! I had some delicious chicken sandwiches, some lovely beef sandwiches, some smashing cheese sandwiches, and I also had two hot dogs (with mustard), a beef burger (with ketchup), a packet of nuts, an apple, an ice cream (3 scoops vanilla) and a piece of lemon cake – shaped like a jumbo jet!

Patel was really in his element, and when he wasn't bumping into people he knew, (including a man with a wooden leg who had lost his real one in a shipping accident, ironically) he was writing down all the aircraft in his British Airways notebook. He'd even brought along his notes from last year's show, so he could 'compare and contrast' as he put it.

At the end of the day, Patel totted up his marks and announced that his final score was 56 out of 85, beating last year's tally of 47 out of 82. Although to be honest, I didn't really understand his marking system.

My only regret was that we hadn't really had a chance to chat. Patel had been practically silent on the drive there (he was clearly 'psyching himself up' for the event), and once we'd arrived he was just too busy with all his plane notation. However, during the journey home, Patel turned to me and said something absolutely incredible . . .

'Cooper?' he said.

'Yes,' I replied.

'Can I ask you something secret?'

'Of course you can,' I said.

'Do you promise not to tell anyone?' he asked

'I promise.'

'What does the company we work for actually do?'

I couldn't believe it! There was I thinking that I was the only employee baffled by General Incorporated Business Solutions, but now I had a co-baffledee!

'Patel,' I said, 'I have absolutely no idea!'

And with that, we burst into utter hystericments, and spent the next 20 minutes laughing uncontrollably. In fact, we laughed so much that we missed our turning on the motorway and got completely lost.

Hoorah! I am not alone!

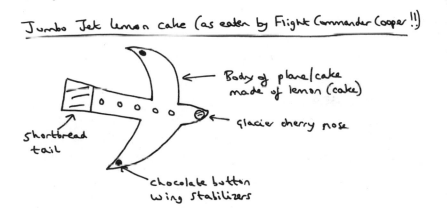

Jumbo Jet lemon cake (as eaten by Flight Commander Cooper !!)

Body of plane/cake made of lemon (cake)

glacier cherry nose

Shortbread tail

chocolate button wing stabilizers

Monday October 3rd

Patel and I have agreed never to mention our little chat again. It's our 'secret', our 'bond'. Think it's for the best.

Tuesday October 4th

Surely I'm set for a promotion!

I have come up with an ingenious, money-saving idea for General Incorporated Business Solutions, which will keep their heating costs to a minimum, while keeping all the workers nice and warm at the same time.

And it's called . . .

'The Tabiator'.

But before the Tabiator can be used (and also explained) here are a few things that need to be done:

1) Henderson to sell off all of the company's desks (at a market, or in a shop that buys desks, such as 'International Desk World')
2) All workers of General Incorporated Business Solutions then instructed to use the radiators in their workstations as their new desks.
3) But how . . .?
4) Well, just see opposite . . .

THE TABIATOR (In action!)

The Tabiator looks like any ordinary radiator, i.e it is physically affixed to the wall like a normal radiator that people have

BUT... The Tabiator flips up from the wall to become a horizontal table/radiator combo device - hence the name (Tabiator).

As this also works with desks,⊕ workers can then work in comfort - and warmth!

*By which I mean, the Tabiator doubles up as a desk, because you actually have no physical need for existing desks when you have Tabiators.

Thus, the money saved from the sale of the office desks can then be ploughed back into office heating costs (plus a small fee for Robin Cooper's inventing services) – and everyone wins!

I can't wait to show my fantastic Tabiator idea to Henderson. I'll be climbing the General Incorporated Business Solutions ladder in no time.

I wish myself luck!

Wednesday October 5th

Typed up my Tabiator idea last night, and put it on Henderson's desk this morning. Fingers crossed . . .

Rita held another 'Happy Scribbling' meeting tonight:

Depressed/depressing Mary was in a particularly depressed/depressing mood all evening, and announced that she was fed up blotting all the time. After a show of hands, it was agreed that Mary would also be allowed to rinse nibs and do up ink bottles. Think she seemed happier (reduction of depression and depressingness by about 5%).

The group are now almost a third of the way through the Magna Carta. Still don't know why they don't just photocopy the original.

P.S. – Rejection from Morphy Richards re 'Nest Egg' Kettle. Oh well, it's their loss! I'm sure there are dozens of other kettle conglomerates I could write to. Perhaps I could also contact chicken farmers re possible 'tie-ins'.

Thursday October 6th

Newsflash! Newsflash! (said in an American accent!) The 'house handles' are back!

Landsberger Strasse 60
CH-8006
Zürich
SWITZERLAND

Sunday the October ¹th

My dear friendly Robin,

The house handles situation is now returned and we do not no what to do otherwise.

When we are first finding it we were in gross schocken. I was telephoning the Central Platz on repeated times and Heidi was looking everywhere for the stoffen and knepplung. We have now tried with blast and waterings but nothing is seems to be working. Heidi was so unhappy, that she now has to sleep with Hans and Lotte Schwimberg. Lotte was also unhappy, but Hans was happy.

So when will you be coming to see us? We are free between the datum of 10st – 25rd of November. Can you be doing on these days? Also do not be forgetting your chockolat meeting with the Herr Buller.

I do hopes the situation will be good for when you are arriving, for we do not want it to be so that you are not able to do it with impossibility because of what is happening now as a result of the house handles, but then again, we do not no otherwise.

Finally, Heidi's English lessons is getting better. She writes this now:

I am Heidi Schwartz. I can be writing. Thanks you.

It is Gunter again. Yes, Professor Zemmel is content with the teaching of Heidi. He makes his English in the John Lewis in 1971. Do you no him?

Your ever friendly,

Gunter Schwartz
Gunter Schwartz

At last, the depressing list on the easy-wipe board (which had become even more depressing with the recent inclusion of 'Doctor re bunions') has been wiped clean. And thus:

'House handles' might be:

1) A fungus that grows in the walls that can't be removed by 'blast and waterings'.
2) Giant fleas?
3) Rats? (Do the Swiss have rats? Or just chocolate mice?!)
4) Something that reacts badly with 'stoffen' and 'kepplung' (NB must buy German dictionary)
5) Something that is only ever used by Swiss Germans and no one else in the world.

We think it's probably number 5, but all shall finally – and at lastedly – become clear in 43 days' time.

We leave for Zurich on November 18th. Hoorah!

P.S. – Still haven't heard anything from Henderson re my Tabiator idea.

Friday October 7th

Oh alas . . .

Something AWFUL has happened. Something truly AWFUL.

I can't write any more today.

Saturday October 8th

Am still too upset to write.

Sunday October 9th

Ditto.

Monday October 10th

Ditto ditto.

Tuesday October 11th

It is no good, I must be brave. Here is what happened:

On Friday morning, at precisely 10:00, Henderson

It's no good. I can't go on. O' forgive me, Dear Diary.

Wednesday October 12th

Called everyone out of their workstations to say

Thursday October 13th

the following:

Friday October 14th

Here goes, Dear Diary . . .

'I have some very bad news. Due to various complicated business matters, I regret to inform you that I am going to have to make further cutbacks. In this case, I am sorry to say that we will be losing one member of staff.'

Immediately there were gasps all around. Then Henderson went on:

'I will be speaking personally to that individual later on in the day. You may now go back to your duties.'

One hour later, Patel came into my workstation with his briefcase, looking shocked.

'It's me, Cooper. I'm the one. I've been dismissed.'

Words could not convey my total and utter be-stunnedment. Not Patel! How could they?! We were like brothers. We had a bond – a secret bond (of ignorance) that could never be broken. It wasn't fair! And I was having none of it . . .

I grabbed Patel's arm, marched into Henderson's office, and announced, 'If he goes, I go!'

As soon as I'd said those words, I couldn't believe they'd actually come out of my mouth.

'I beg your pardon?' said Henderson.

I said them again. What was I doing . . .?

Henderson got up from his desk, and looked at me hard in the eyes. 'Are you sure you know what you're saying, Cooper?'

'I don't think you should be saying that,' said Patel.

'I know very well what I'm doing,' I said (I didn't really). 'And I think it's very wrong that you're getting rid of Patel. And if he goes, I go!'

'Is that really how you feel?' asked Henderson. 'Because I'm prepared to give you one last chance to take back your words.'

'Be careful, Cooper,' added Patel.

But by now it was too late. I couldn't go back. My entire reputation was at stake.

'Yes,' I said. 'That is how I feel.'

I was given one month's paid notice, but decided – for the sake of Cooper honour – to take my leave there and then. (Henderson also returned my Tabiator designs, which he described as 'impractical'.)

And thus endeth my career as an Above-the-line Resolutions Officer at General Incorporated Business Solutions.

It was only once I'd stepped outside, that I realized I might have made a very big mistake.

So farewell General Incorporated Business Solutions.

Farewell.

Whatever it is you do . . .

Sunday October 16th

A gloom has descended 'pon the Cooper household. 'Tis a gloom worse than any other gloom this household has ever known (including the silent gloom we had back in March). I really don't know what to do with myself, and have been moping about the house (and shed) all weekend. I feel useless and all 'used up' (if such a feeling is psychologically/grammatically possible).

What am I to do? Will I ever find a job again? And will this mean horrible margarine for the rest of my life . . .?

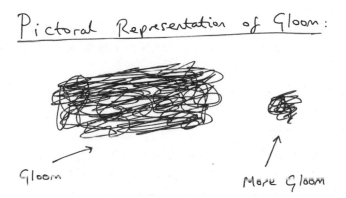

Pictoral Representation of Gloom:

Gloom

More Gloom

Monday October 17th

This morning I told Rita what had really happened (i.e. the bit about me offering to be sacked), as opposed to the 'sanitized' version I'd first told her (i.e. that I was the one that was to be made redundant in the first place).

She turned white with rage.

Gone was all the sympathy, soup and ice cream, and in their place came the shouting, the separate rooms, and finally the silence.

To make things worse, Patel popped over this evening to thank me for my loyalty, and Rita called me 'a big idiot' right in front of him (the only two words she'd said to me all night).

Anyway, Patel said that I should ask Henderson for my job back, but I told him that I couldn't possibly do such a thing, because of 'Cooper pride'. He thought about what I'd said for a while, nodded gently, then gave me a Lufthansa pillow as a 'gift of gratitude', before leaving.

I really have to face up to facts: I've let everybody down. I've let Rita down, I've let Mother down (sort of), I've let Michael down (again, sort of), I've let Smithie, Binky and Alfredo down (well, not really, actually), and I've let myself down (definitely).

Oh, what have I done . . .?

Tuesday October 18th

Spent most of the day sitting in shed, just staring at things.

What I stared at:

1) An ant carrying half a cornflake.
2) A piece of grit lodged in the criss-cross groove of a Phillips screw in my nail scissors.
3) An extremely transparent marble (it gave me a bit of headache when I tried looking through it).
4) Monty in garden (more furball emittance).
5) Feisil Powder bottle (just what is it meant for?).
6) The little finger on my left hand (am sure it's bigger than the one on my right hand).

Tony popped into see me this evening, but he got a bit annoyed when I started staring at him (I couldn't help it – it was like I was addicted), and left after just one can of Pennyfeather's.

Had a couple of late night butter sandwiches (how long will this luxury last?), then bed.

Being unemployed is absolutely exhausting.

Wednesday October 19th

Found 40p in the street today. I know it's not a lot of money but it's a start, and every little bit helps I suppose.

Also found another marble in the shed. This isn't a start at all, and no bit of it helps me in any way whatsoever!

Thursday October 20th

Moved back to bedroom last night, but Rita kicked me so hard in her sleep ('accidentally' she claimed) that I now have a bruise on my shin in the shape of the United States of America (i.e. v. large).

Then, when I woke up, Rita said that I should do what Patel suggested and 'go and beg' for my job back. Of course I refused, and told her – in no uncertain terms – that I would never 'stoop so low'. This then escalated into a row about Linda and Ian's Halloween party at the end of the month, with Rita informing me that she would now be going on her own.

'Fine!' I said (I didn't really think it was fine).

Spoke to Mother tonight – and guess what , , ,?

She offered me a job! When I asked her, 'As what?' Mother replied, 'As my little Robin.'

I tell you, Dear Diary, a tear almost came to my eye.

Friday October 21st

Good news – Michael telephoned from Sydney this morning. His dancing show with Simon was a great success, and the men have asked them to do another one next week. Hoorah! Michael said he would 'e-mail' me some photos, but unfortunately I don't have an e-mail (I don't think I do anyway), so I can't look at them (NB – must buy an e-mail).

Popped into job centre in afternoon. Looked around/did a bit of coughing, then came back and stared at Smithie and the birdlings. Think I must have frightened them a little, as Smithie flew right at me and tried to bite me on the nose. Wish I could stop all this staring business – but what else is there to do?

Saturday October 22nd

Miss Marsh drove quite recklessly again today. She let out a 'whoop' of joy when she went over a speed bump at 50mph, and even tried to run over a crow in the road. Hair full of buns again. Cassette still on. Think the whole Gerald Hale/Bobby McPherson incident has really gone to her head.

New test scheduled for November 5th. I do hope she doesn't try to run over the examiner!

Sunday October 23rd

Foggy morning. Visibility poor. Tripped over Monty in the drive-way when I was getting into the car, and almost poked my eye out on the aerial. Wretched cat!

Rest of day no better (but a bit less foggy). Had a bitter row with Rita re job situation (i.e. non job situation) and she even mentioned the dreaded 'm' word . . .

Margarine.

I absolutely HATE margarine.

It was no good. I had to succumb. I promised Rita that I would go and ask for my job back tomorrow morning.

Oh sooth . . .

Monday October 24th

Were it not for the fact that this diary is probably the only thing keeping me from losing my marbles at the moment (and incidentally, I found another one in the shed yesterday), I really do not know how I would have coped with what happened today.

This day – Monday October 24th – will surely go down in history as a day of sheer and utter infamy.

At 10:10 this morning, after taking three toffees (to calm my nerves) and a lick of Mentathon 4000 (for mental/mintal sharpening), I entered the offices of General Incorporated Business Solutions.

Neither looking left nor right, I strode up to Henderson's office, and, without knocking, walked straight in.

To my surprise, there was a thin, bald man in glasses (i.e. a different man) sitting at his desk.
'Can I help you?' he said.
'Yes,' I replied. 'I've come to see Henderson.'
'I'm afraid Henderson left on Friday,' said the man. 'I'm Collins, his replacement.'
'Replacement?' I asked.
'Yes,' he said. 'How can I help?'
I looked at him, blinking, my head fizzing with confusement.
'No, it's OK,' I replied. 'I think I've made a mistake. Goodbye'

I walked out and shut the door. I was completely stunned. But now for the sheer and utter infamy bit . . .

As I was leaving the office, I glanced towards my old workstation. There was someone else in it, sitting in my chair. It was Patel.

Yes – Patel!

'What are you doing here?' I asked, my voice a-trembling.
'I'm very sorry,' he said (his voice also a-trembling), 'but I came to ask for my job back, and they offered me your old job instead.'
'And you took it?' I asked, aghast.
Patel looked at me sadly. 'What could I do Cooper? I needed

the money. It's the Milan International Air Show in November . . .'

He'd said enough. It was over. Our bond – our secret bond – had been broken forever.

I left the building at once, drove straight home, went to the shed, looked behind the table tennis table, found an unopened can of Pennyfeather's, and took an enormous glug.

It tasted horrible.

Tuesday October 25th

Rita and I are (just about) on speaking terms again.

When I told her all about my day of sheer and utter infamy, she hobbled over to me, gave me a hug, and then planted a quadrant (i.e. 4) of kisses on my forehead. She also made me some soup (onion).

Dear Diary, I really owe it to my darling Rita to make things better (and butter!) again. If I can't find a new job, then I'm jolly well going to invent something that will finally make us our fortune.

I wish myself luck!

P.S. Good news – we are now going to Linda and Ian's Halloween party together. Hoorah! But what to wear . . .?

Friday October 28th

Scoured the paper for jobs this morning (but being Friday, it was 'Opportunities within the Oil Industry'), then went up to loft. Think I'm back in Smithie's good books again, as I was up there for at least half an hour and didn't stare at her once (although I couldn't help noticing that Smithie appeared to be staring at me).

Rita said a funny joke while she was doing one of her dot-to-dots tonight. She said that she hoped it (i.e. the dot-to-dot) wouldn't make her go 'all dotty'! I tell you, Dear Diary, we laughed so much, that we both had water coming out of our noses!

Of course, it's possible that some of our laughter may have been 'stress-related', but still – what a witty wife!

Saturday October 29th

Miss Marsh's pop cassette got all mangled up in my car cassette-playing machine this afternoon. She was most upset (I was most pleased!). Didn't seem to make her drive any safer though: she did 54mph though a width restriction, and a 3-point turn in about 1½ (turns).

Driving test next week.

Gulp . . .

Monday October 31st – Halloween

Have just got back from Linda and Ian's Halloween party, and it is now . . . wait for it . . . wait for it . . . exactly midnight!

W-H-O-O-A-H-H! (The sound of ghosts – because it is Halloween!)

(I am a little tipsy by the way.)

In the end, Rita went as Anne Boleyn and wore the old costume I had in the shed. For the 'headless' bit, I painted a suitably Elizabethan face on a melon, which Rita carried under her arm (although this did mean that she effectively had two heads – one being her own, and the other the melon's/Boleyn's). Anyway, she looked fantastic, and got a lot of comments ('you look fantastic' etc.).

I, myself, went as 'Earl Horror', a fictional figure I'd invented especially for the occasion. My outfit was thus:

'EARL HORROR'
(The outfit)

Black trousers
(the reason they
appear striped here, is
that I couldn't be
bothered to colour them
in, although I would
have probably finished
them off by the time
I'd written all this!)

Black shoes
(I coloured
them in but
only drew one
to save time)

White shirt
(no need to
colour in!!)

Green wig
(made from
left-over
carpet pieces—
don't have
green
pen!)

Crown
with flashing
LED bulb

Large letter 'E'
worn around neck
(to symbolize 'Earl')
(Didn't have time to
make large letter 'H'
for 'Horror')

Feisil Powder —
used to whiten face
(I knew it would come
in handy one day!!)

Bottle of ketchup
(used on shirt to
simulate blood)

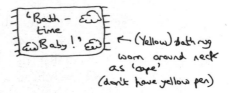

← (Yellow) bathing
worn around neck
as 'cape'
(don't have yellow pen)

I also caused a bit of a stir (although quite a lot of people thought I was someone from 'The King And I'), and when it came to them announcing the winner for best costume, I was sure I'd win.

I couldn't believe my ears: first prize went to depressed/depressing Mary, who had come as, what looked like, her mother in, what also looked like, her mother's clothes. Surely that was nothing but a 'sympathy' vote.

But worse followed . . .

In second place came Ian's brother – i.e. the HOST'S brother – as 'Dracula'. And in third place came Linda, yes Linda – i.e. the wife of the actual HOST (but also a HOST in her own right) – as a 'wicked nurse'.

This was vote rigging of the lowest kind! It was an outrage!

As soon as I got home, I went straight into the shed and typed out a letter to Linda and Ian, expressing my views in the STRONGEST terms possible (I didn't dare tell Rita what I was doing of course). I then went round the corner and popped the letter into the postbox.

That'll teach them!

November

Tuesday November 1st

Woke up with a terrible hangover, and a dreadful rash all over my face. Must have been that wretched 'Feisil Powder'. Rita had to rub cream everywhere.

Then, at about lunchtime, I suddenly remembered the angry, be-drunken letter I'd sent to Linda and Ian last night.

I do hope I haven't gone too far.

Wednesday November 2nd

Very odd thing happened today during my six-monthly check-up at the (dreaded) dentist's.

I was lying back in the chair, and Dr Davis was poking my teeth about, when suddenly I felt something fall into my mouth. I tell you, I almost choked to death!

When Dr Davis investigated (after shouting 'lie still'), he discovered that the offending item was actually a tooth. But it wasn't one of mine – it was one of his! Apparently Dr Davis' left molar had fallen out of his mouth, into mine!

'That's the second time that's happened to me this month,' he laughed, and then carried on with his work.

I MUST get a new dentist!

Thursday November 3rd

Linda and Ian got the letter.

They didn't like it.

Not one bit.

What they specifically objected to:

1) Being called the following:
   a) Cheats

b) Swindlers
c) Rotters
d) Fixers
ei) Conmen
eii) Conwomen
f) Second-and-third-prize-hoggers
g) No good 'Henry Hamptons' (I don't actually remember calling them this, as I have no idea who Henry Hampton is)

2) My drawing (picture of scales of justice being trampled on by Linda and Ian's feet).

3) Linda's feet (apparently I'd only given her four toes).

Rita went mad! Absolutely mad! And as soon as she'd put the phone down, she sent me round to Linda and Ian's to apologize. She literally pushed me out the door!

Linda and Ian were not pleased to see me at all. Linda had her arms folded (which is apparently a 'negative body language sign', according to a picture I once saw in a book), and Ian used several strong words (similar to ones that Tony uses, beginning with 'b' and 's').

They didn't even let me in.

Returned to an empty house. Rita had gone out with depressed/depressing Mary. Phoned Mother for a bit of company, but she said she was 'a little busy with the television', so went up to loft to see Smithie and co. (Binky was in my pyjamas). Then had a lie-down in shed, and when I woke up, it was 10:30pm. Rita hadn't even called me in for dinner.

Bedroom door locked (I never even knew we had a lock!), so back to Michael's room again.

Oh alas . . .

Friday November 4th

Tried to patch things up with Rita today (flowers and soup), but it didn't work. The flowers went straight out the window (well at least they'll get some fresh air) and the soup went down the sink (the soup will probably drown though).

Just what am I supposed to do?

Saturday November 5th – Sir Guy Fawkes, and also Fireworks Night

Miss Marsh took her driving test this afternoon.

She drove 45 in a 30 zone, 55 in a 40 zone, and 65 in a 50 zone (why did she keep adding 15 to all the numbers?), then reversed into a hot dog stand (fried onions all over back window) and got her three-point turn mixed up with her emergency stop (examiner 'cricked' his neck).

Result: fail.

Miss Marsh was inconsolable and inconsobbable (i.e. she sobbed a lot). Luckily I'd bought a new box of tissues just in case, and she got through at least 20 (I didn't mention the cost). Tried to cheer her up with toffees, and even offered her some of my Mentathon 4000 toothpaste, but to no avail.

Drove Miss Marsh home while she lay in the back of the car, and when I let her out, I noticed there were tears all over the seat. Poor Miss Marsh. Poor seat. Felt pretty low after that, but was rather glad that Rita was out when I got back.

Sat in shed, and then Tony popped round with a big bag of very dangerous-looking fireworks (including one called 'The Hexacutioner' which was shaped like a six-sided guillotine). Fortunately none of them would light, as they'd all got soaked in his bag (ale spillage), and so we just waved a couple of damp, unlit sparklers about, pretending to spell our names in the air.

After that, Tony drank a whole can of Pennyfeather's while standing on his head (his new trick) and then went home. Still, it was company, I suppose.

Rita got back late (calligraphizing at depressed/depressing Mary's), and went straight up to bed, without saying a word to me. Sat in kitchen on my own for a while, ate quite a large apple, then tried to get into bedroom, but it was locked again.

I tell you Dear Diary, there were definitely no 'fireworks' for me tonight.

Sunday November 6th

Tried the following 11 (verbal) methods of getting into my own bedroom tonight:

1) I am sorry 2) I really do apologize 3) Please forgive me 4) I really am regretful 5) I promise I won't write a letter to Linda and Ian ever again complaining about their lack of fairness 6) How could I have done such a thing? 7) What a fool was I 8) I rue the day I ever did such a thing 9) I am very sorry 10) I really am very, very sorry 11) Please let me in now.

Result: fail.

Monday November 7th

This morning Rita caught me trying to make a cast of the lock on our bedroom door.

She was not happy.

'Hand over that putty!' she snapped.

Naturally I refused, but then Rita went all sort of 'dramatic', shouting, 'I can't believe you were thinking of burgling your way into my heart!'

Well, Dear Diary, I didn't know what to say to that (she really must be under a lot of stress at the moment), and I soon found myself handing over the putty (plus Tony's 'Do-It-Yourself Key-Making Kit').

Oh the shame!

Didn't really know what to do with myself, so popped over to Mother's. Alone.

As usual the television set was on. Ended up watching a programme about the Norfolk Broads. Apparently, some of the banks (not money banks, but mud ones) were being eroded due to the affect of boating. What happens is when a boat goes along, the water bounces off it at a faster rate than the speed of a normal piece of water that would be in the water if there wasn't a boat there in the first place. Thus, this bit of (faster moving) water then hits the bank with a more powerful force than the normal piece of water as mentioned before, causing erosion.

Anyway, it all was very interesting, although now, when I think about it, it wasn't.

Tuesday November 8th

Michael's birthday today! 22 today!

Happy birthday Son!

Sang Michael happy birthday this morning (see June 2nd for full, official word list) but when I finished, he went all quiet and then burst out crying. Naturally Rita grabbed the phone off me and went into the other room. Tried to listen at door with wine glass, but all I could make out was something about a friend of Simon's, called Jeremy, who was flying over to see him in Sydney. Afterwards, when I asked Rita what was the matter, she just said it was 'general growing pains'.

Poor Michael.

After that, saw an intriguing advert in the local paper, for a

'Constructive Guidance Administrator' for a company called 'A.D.L.H & M. Holdings Inc'. Had to stop myself from responding (my CV was already in the envelope), as I have resolved never, ever to apply again for a job that I don't understand.

I suppose you could call that my 'November 8th Resolution'!

Wednesday November 9th

Brought Rita breakfast in bed this morning, but she made me leave the tray outside her door and go back into Michael's bedroom, while she took it inside.

I waited 15 minutes, and then Rita came out and thanked me for the breakfast (although she did say that 4 boiled eggs were a 'little too much'), and said that she'd allow me to move back into our room – provided that I don't 'slip up again'.

I promised Rita most severely, but when I went to give her a kiss I noticed that she moved away from me.

I think I will have to tread/kiss very carefully indeed . . .

Thursday November 10th

Looked in Mr Singh's shop window this morning, but there was only one job going – for a 'part-time yoghurt salesman'. Didn't apply (don't like yoghurts). Then saw Old Milly on her bench, and gave her my customary 50p (total trampal donation: I've forgotten) but when she took it, she looked at me and said, 'Haven't you heard of inflation?'.

The cheek!

Ended up giving her an additional 10p (taking my total trampal donation up to: I've forgotten + 10p).

Tony popped round later on, and we discussed our strategy re my big Aqua Choc meeting in Zurich. Unfortunately, things got a bit heated when we moved on to 'financial terms', as I wanted a 70-30 split in my favour, and Tony wanted a 60-40 split in his favour.

In the end we sort of half settled on a potentially fluctuating system of 45-55 in both of our favours, depending on a variety of, as yet, undefined factors. It was all a bit vague really, as Tony was quite muddled by then (Pennyfeather's) and had started standing on his head again.

I do hope my meeting in Zurich goes well. The entire future of Cooperdom rests upon it.

Friday November 11th

Tony must have let himself into the house very early on today, because when I went to the bathroom this morning, I met him on the hallway coming out of Michael's room. He looked awful and had a big bruise above his left eye.

Tried to find out what his latest squabble with Susan was all about, but all he would say, was 'something to do with British Steel'. In all my 23 years of marriage, I don't think I've ever had an argument with Rita about a former metal alloy conglomerate (although we did once have a row about silver foil).

Spent most of the day in the shed with Tony (he 'threw a sickie' as he called it), and together we prepared some new bars of Aqua Choc for my meeting. Naturally, I did most of the work and Tony did most of the drinking. Also tried to think of some other ideas for inventions together, but neither of us had any brainwaves really. The best Tony could come up with was a 'bath plug that dissolves'.

When Rita came home, Tony stuck around for dinner (typical) and then, when it was time for us to go to bed (and Rita and I hinting that he should probably go home), Tony wished us a pleasant night, then sunk back into the armchair and switched on the TV (also typical). Think I heard him stumbling up the stairs and into Michael's room at about 2:00 in the morning.

How does Susan put up with him?

Answer: she doesn't. We do!!!

Saturday November 12th

Miss Marsh has taken a 2 week 'sabbatical' from driving lessons. Think it's a good idea – for the both of us.

After lunch, went shopping with Rita for our trip to Zurich. We split up into two groups (i.e. two groups of 1), with Rita in charge of clothing and I/me in charge of 'travel essentials'. However, when we met up later, Rita got very annoyed when she found out how many things I'd bought in 'travel form'.

'Travel form' items:

1) 'Travel' plug (for plugging in things whilst travelling)
2) 'Travel' toothbrush (for me)
3) 'Travel' toothbrush (for Rita)
4) 'Travel' wash (i.e. washing powder but in liquid and also 'travel' form)
5) 'Travel' soap (bar of soap in handy 'travel' container)
6) 'Travel' socks (to protect Rita's ankle against thromboculosis (or whatever it's called) which occurs on flights when your legs go all sort of itchy, and then you wobble about when you get up, and then you fall over, and then everyone panics on the plane)
7) 'Travel' teapot (Rita made me take this back immediately)
8) 'Travel' toffees (I refused to take these back!)

Saw Linda and Ian tonight. A slightly stilted evening, as they still hadn't fully forgiven me for my Halloween letter misdemeanour. Luckily Ian sat on Rita's hairbrush and we all ended up inspecting Ian's bottom for scratches, which seemed to break the ice a little.

Sunday November 13th

Gunter telephoned from Switzerland today to discuss our travel arrangements. This time he remembered the word for 'hello', but forgot the word for 'goodbye' (which is 'goodbye').

And so it's official – Rita and I arrive in Zurich at precisely 3:15pm* on Friday 18th November, and my Aqua Choc meeting with Herr Buller, of Buller und Bleicher Schockolade GmbH (whatever GmbH stands for) is at precisely 10:00am* on Monday 21st November.

Hoorah!

What's also (hopefully) official is that Rita and I will also (hopefully) know the meaning of 'house handles' in exactly 5 days.

(Hopefully) hoorah again!

*All times are Swiss times.

Monday November 14th

I was struggling to fit a parcel into the postbox this morning (Rita wanted me to return the Christmas pudding she'd bought from a catalogue, that had 'leaked' sultanas) when I suddenly came up with a new and FANTASTIC idea . . .

It's a hit! A sure-fire, cotton-bottomed (think that's the right expression), billy-boy hit!

My idea is for an entirely NEW and much BETTER British postbox – one that will bring British postboxes, and indeed the entire British postal system, into complete and utter modernity – for complete and utter eternity!

Here it is . . .

Robin Cooper's (new) British Royal Mail Postal Box

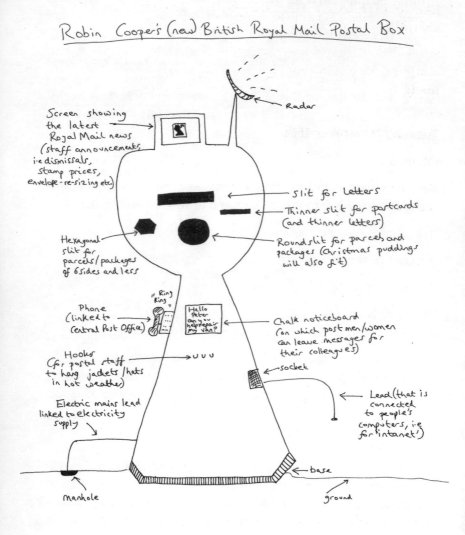

Radar

Screen showing the latest Royal Mail news (staff announcements, i.e dismissals, stamp prices, envelope-re-sizing etc.)

slit for Letters

Thinner slit for postcards (and thinner letters)

Hexagonal slit for parcels/packages of 6 sides and less

Round slit for parcels and packages (Christmas puddings will also fit)

Phone (linked to central Post Office)

"Ring Ring"

Hello Peter can you help repair my van?

Chalk noticeboard (on which postmen/women can leave messages for their colleagues)

Hooks (for postal staff to hang jackets/hats in hot weather)

socket

Electric mains lead linked to electricity supply

Lead (that is connected to people's computers, i.e for 'intranet')

manhole

base

ground

I suppose if Aqua Choc fails in Zurich (and I'm sure it won't), I'll always have this idea to fall back on (although I wouldn't really like to LITERALLY fall back on it – that radar looks very sharp!!!)

P.S. – Tony finally went back home tonight. But just what could he have said about British Steel to have made Susan so mad?

Tuesday November 15th

Oh dear . . .

Fat Carol came over for dinner this evening, so beforehand I went up to the loft to bring down her historic cat paintings.

But what I saw came as something of a shock. A big shock.

A very big shock.

All the paintings had been attacked by Smithie and her birdlings. They were ruined!

Birdal damage to Fat Carol's historic cat paintings:

1) Napoleon: damage to left eye, lips, and tail.
2) Lord Nelson: damage to left eye, and tear in sling.
3) Sir Winston Churchill: damage to right eye, and rip in cigar (how could they?!).
4) Harold Wilson: damage to right eye, and evidence of scratching to pipe.
5) Beethoven: damage to left eye (why do birds always go for the eyes?), tearing of ruffles, hole in quill.
6) Richard Nixon: damage to right eye, rip in presidential desk.
7) Mary Shelley: damage to left eye, tearing of whiskers, and hole in bubbling beaker of dry ice.
8) Florence Nightingale: damage to right eye, tear on dress and tail (lamp untouched).
9) Frank Sinatra: damage to right eye, microphone torn.

10) Charles de Gaulle: damage to both eyes, mouth, moustache, nose, ears, hat, tear in chin, multiple holes in medals, and bird droppings all over uniform.
11) 'Princess Fifi de Mer': damage to eye (think she was meant to be some form of Cyclops originally), and tear in tiara.
12) Henry VIII: damage to right eye, rip in beard, and evidence of pecking to tabby wives.
13) Samuel Johnson: damage to left eye (they really hate eyes!), and words 'English Dictionary' reduced by tearing to 'glish icti'.

Rita was not happy.

'What am I going to say to Fat Carol?' she screamed. 'It's those wood-pigeons isn't it?! You lied to me!'
I tried to convince her that I'd had them removed ages ago (oh sooth!), and that it must have been a 'rogue crow' that had somehow flown in, done some pecking, and then flown out again, but Rita was having none of it . . .

She started to climb the ladder up to the loft.

I begged her to cease, but she wouldn't listen. She just kept on climbing, each rung bringing her closer and closer to the truth.

But then, just before she reached the top (well, actually she was only 3 rungs from the bottom), Rita stopped (vertigo/slight ankle twistage).

'If I find out that you've been lying to me all along about those bl**dy wood pigeons,' she screamed, 'I promise you will live to regret this day to the end of your life, Robin Cooper!'

Gulp!

When Fat Carol arrived – and noticed the house was bereft of her cat paintings – she went completely white (and that's a lot of white!).

'Don't worry, Carol,' said Rita, 'Robin's just been polishing the frames up in the loft.'

'Yes I have,' I added, for realism.

298

Fat Carol's natural colour returned (a lot of pink).

'Thank heavens!' she replied. 'For a moment I thought that maybe you'd gone off my cats.'

Rita and I laughed nervously, while Fat Carol handed over her latest offering: President Franklin D. Roosevelt as a short-eared tomcat.

As soon as Fat Carol had gone home, Rita went straight up to bed, shut the door, and locked it.

I'm back in the doghouse (i.e. Michael's room) again.

Wednesday November 16th

Silent breakfast with Rita this morning. Had to use mime to ask for a simple bowl of Rice Krispies, but Rita gave me Cornflakes (already with the milk and sugar on them) instead. Am sure she did this on purpose.

Nothing exciting in job centre – just lots of computers/coughing etc. – so stuck a new advert in Mr Singh's window for driving lessons. Drew a bit of tinsel to make it look a bit 'season-y' (i.e. Christmassy), and added the words 'Free travel toffees'. Hopefully this will be an extra selling point.

Spoke to Tony after dinner. He practically begged me to take him along to the Aqua Choc meeting in Zurich, but I had to say no. Felt a bit bad, but I really can't afford any more 'slip ups' at the moment. Needless to say he wasn't too pleased, and called me a 'bl**dy b*mface traitor' before hanging up.

Finished off the evening with a bit of (silent) packing with Rita, then back to Michael's bedroom again.

Hopefully Rita won't ask Gunter if we can sleep in separate rooms . . .

Thursday November 17th

More silence at home. We've gone back to using the easy-wipe message board on the fridge as our means of communication. This morning I awoke to find the words 'I really do hope you are not lying' written in capitals, with the word 'really' underlined frice.

Oh dear.

Showed the postman my new postbox design today, and he took one look at it and said, 'Is it supposed to be a dalek?' The cheek! Oh well, perhaps it was just a bit too ahead of its time.

Afterwards, spent several hours in the shed practising my Aqua Choc 'pitch'. I bought a German phrase book from the charity shop (£1.10) last week, and I've now learnt the following phrases, which may come in useful:

1) 'Guten Morgen' – Good morning (when I enter the office)
2) 'Ich bin von England' – I am from England (as I sit down)
3) 'Dass ist es' – This is it (and then I will point at the bar of Aqua Choc)
4) 'Es Schmeckt gut!' – It tastes nice! (I will then point at his mouth)
5) 'Ich bin mude' – I am tired (just in case I yawn)
6) 'Wo ist die Toilette bitte?' – Where is the toilet please? (To be used only in an emergency)
7) 'Herzlichen Gluckwunsch!' – Congratulations! (When we sign the Aqua Choc deal)
8) 'Auf Wiedersehen' – Goodbye (when I leave)

I wish myself luck! Or as they say in German . . .

Oh, they don't have it in the phrase book.

Friday November 18th – we go to Zurich!

We have arrived! Hoorah!

When Gunter saw us at the airport, he shouted out 'Welcome from the Switzerland!', kissed us both three times on both cheeks (i.e. 6 times on 4 cheeks), and presented us with an oversized Emmenthal! It was great to see him again.

However, when we got into his car (orange Citroën with orange seats) Gunter said something rather disappointing:

'Do not be worrying. The house handles they are gone now forever, and you will never be seeing them.'

At that moment, Rita and I – having just spent 105 silent, grumpy minutes on the plane – were instantly reunited via our shared sense of disappointment. How would we ever find out what 'house handles' were – and would we ever know the truth . . .?

We tried to pry a little but Gunter got quite irritable, and told us, 'I cannot talk about the house handles. This is my holiday also!' His driving then grew erratic, and rather fast (which reminded me a little of Miss Marsh) so we decided to keep quiet.

I suppose we shall have to try a different approach.

Gunter lives all the way up a hill overlooking Lake Zurich (could just about make out some swans and a couple of nesting herons). His house is roughly the same size as ours, although there's a bit more wood in it (i.e. sort of stuck to the sides), and the front garden has a bench in it 'for the sitting', as Gunter explained.

Heidi wasn't at home when we walked in, and when we asked where she was, Gunter replied – in true Gunter fashion – 'She will follow.'

We didn't ask again.

He then took us to our room (even more orange than the car), and gave us a quick guided tour of the house.

Six things I noticed during Gunter's guided tour:

1) Everything is very neat. For example, no soapy water in soap dishes causing soaps to de-soap, and no errant crumbs behind/beneath/beyond toaster. Also, when I asked Gunter to show me my letters, he said, 'Oh no, I throw them because of the untidiness. They are all in the fire.' The cheek!

2) There are two toilets (I would love to have two toilets) and a rather mysterious room on the first floor, which appeared to be just for batteries and plastic bags (wouldn't really want one of these rooms).

3) There are photos of Gunter everywhere – but none of Heidi. One of them featured Gunter patting a seal on the head, while dressed in a tuxedo. When Rita asked him to tell us a bit about it, he replied, 'It is me and the water dog. It was the good times!' We nodded politely.

4) On the living room floor, there's a huge half-finished 'map of the world' jigsaw, which belonged to Heidi. Actually it was more like 'twelfth-finished', as I could only make out the Poles, parts of New Zealand, and what I think was Alaska. Anyway, it took up so much of the carpet that Rita and I had to practically hold on to the walls just to get round the room. It's a death trap!

5) Apart from the jigsaw, the only real evidence of Heidi actually living in the house was her enormous collection of mini shoes. According to Gunter, Heidi had 305 mini shoe ornaments (not including mini boots) all around the house. Rita loved them. I absolutely didn't!

6) The downstairs smells of apples. (The upstairs doesn't have a smell.)

After the tour, Gunter announced that it was time for dinner, but it was only 5:15 in the afternoon! We had cold ham and cheese sandwiches, a small bowl of crisps each (a strange Swiss flavour) and an apple cut into segments (perhaps that explained the downstairs smell).

What was really odd was that the entire 'meal' was served on paper plates with plastic cutlery, but when I asked Gunter if this was how people in Switzerland ate at home, Gunter replied:

'No, not the others. It is for much ease, and you can just throw them away after, without the obligatory washing up. Ja!'

After we'd finished, Gunter threw our plates and cutlery into the dustbin, and announced, 'Now, if you would be excusing me.' He then left the room, and went upstairs. We heard a door being shut.

Rita and I sat at the table for a while, just looking at each other, not really knowing what to do. At about 6:45 Rita suggested I go and checked on Gunter, just in case something had happened to him. I went upstairs and knocked gently on his bedroom door but there was no reply, so I opened it a little, and peered inside. Gunter was fast asleep in bed!

I went back down to tell Rita. Should we wake him? Should we not wake him? After discussing the matter, we decided it was probably best to wait and see what happened.

Tried to watch some television, but couldn't work the remote control (very complicated, and sort of shaped like a cup) so in the end – and against Rita's wishes – I did a bit of Heidi's jigsaw (most of Italy) and then ate a piece of our Emmenthal.

By 10:45, when it was absolutely clear that Gunter wasn't going to get up again, Rita and I were left with no other option: we walked upstairs to our bedroom, got undressed, and went to bed.

What a strange start to our holiday.

Saturday November 19th

Gunter was up bright and early this morning (no wonder – he must have slept at least 12 hours!) and as soon as he saw us, he asked if we'd 'had a nice evening?' Rita and I didn't want to be rude, so we just said 'yes, it was very nice, thank you.'

After breakfast (Swiss cheese – nice, Swiss bread – quite nice, Swiss tea – not nice), the front door opened and Heidi walked in. She DID follow! But where had she been all night?!

Anyway, Heidi said hello/performed multiple cheek-kissing and told us that she wanted to 'be practise in the English'. She then picked up an exercise book, and started to read to us.

Heidi's English phrases:

1) 'We are in the house' (Rita and I agreed)
2) 'Where is the man?' (we pointed at Gunter, but Heidi shook her head and then scribbled something in her book)
3) 'Did you be seeing the lion?' (didn't really know what to say to this)
4) 'I am from the Sainsbury's' (ditto)

When she finished, Rita and I clapped a little. Heidi curtsied, put away her book and then went to have a look at her jigsaw. However, as soon as she noticed that someone had finished off a bit for her, she started shouting at Gunter. At first, Rita and I just stood there watching, not knowing what to do, and then Rita went over to apologize, but – horror of horrors – she stepped on a piece of the jigsaw (my bit of Italy), and slipped right over.

Half an hour later we were all sitting in the Accident and Emergency ward of Zurich's University Hospital.

Rita is on (Swiss) crutches again.

Oh alas . . .

Spent the rest of the day back at Gunter's house, sitting in the living room, while Rita lay in bed. Fed her some cheese, and tried to cheer her up (i.e. told her she could raise a lot of money by doing a sponsored 'hobblethon'!), but nothing really worked.

'Why couldn't you have done Australia?' Rita said, angrily. 'Why did you have to do a country that was right in the middle?'

Bed at 7:00 (half an hour after Gunter and Heidi).

Oh, to be back home . . .

Sunday November 20th

Crack open the trumpets . . .

I know what 'house handles' are! (And so will you, very soon, my dearest of diaries!)

While Heidi was helping Rita with some pre-lunch leg exercises (knee bends/ankle distentions etc.), Gunter said to me: 'Now we will be taking a nice walking to see the Hans and Lotte Schwimberg.' He then put on his walking boots (orange) and we left the house.

Hans and Lotte Schwimberg lived precisely three doors away, so our 'nice walking' took precisely 44 seconds!

Hans and Lotte Schwimberg spoke pretty good English but they didn't actually speak much, so there wasn't much for me to do or say. I smiled a lot (they weren't big smilers though), and sat and watched the television (a programme about a forest in Sweden I think), while Gunter ate cheese next to me.

Suddenly, Gunter shouted out, 'Ach! No! Schrecklich! Schrecklich!' at the top of his voice. I asked him what was wrong (Gunter was literally maroon with anger), but he kept repeating 'Schrecklich! Schrecklich!'. Hans and Lotte Schwimberg then joined in with him.

Finally Gunter took a deep breath, pointed at the screen, and said, 'Look Robin, the house handles!'

I looked at the screen. In a clearing amongst the trees, by a patch of dry mud, was a hamster.

House handles = hamsters! House handles = hamsters!!!!!!!!

The mystery of the millennium was over!

When Gunter finally regained his composure, he talked to me for the first time about the whole 'house handles' saga . . .

The Whole 'House Handles' Saga:

1) About a year ago, Gunter and I spoke on the telephone.
2) Apparently I told Gunter about our hamster, Hambles, who (until the set of encyclopedias fell on top of him) kept nibbling Rita.
3) To Gunter's untrained and un-anglicized ear, 'Hambles' sounded like 'handles'.
4) As Hambles (or 'handles') lived in our house, Gunter assumed the correct English term for a hamster was therefore 'house handle'.

Then . . .

5) Shortly after our telephone conversation, Gunter bought himself a pair of 'house handles'.
6) The pair soon mated, producing an additional 6 'house handles'.
7) The additional 'house handles' also mated, producing an additional, additional 18 'house handles'.
8) One night, Heidi accidentally left the cages open, and all 26 'house handles' escaped.
9) The 'house handles' started hiding in the house (burrowing under the floorboards, and into the walls), chewing through electrical cords, nibbling guests (particularly the Schwimbergs) and generally causing havoc and smells.
10) The man from 'Central Platz' (I never quite worked out who he was), finally managed to catch them all (didn't understand how, either, as Gunter appeared to be miming 'swallowing a fridge') before taking them all away.
11) That is it!

During our 44-second walk back, Gunter asked me, 'So what did you think I am talking about, when I am saying the house handles?'

It was a good question.

I thought about it for a moment, and then chose what I felt to be the most diplomatic answer possible.

'Gerbils.'

Gunter nodded thoughtfully, although I doubt he understood. It really didn't matter though. All that mattered was that this saga – the saga of the humble 'house handle' and the humble hamster – was now over, and through it all an Englishman (me) and a Swiss Germanman (he) had grown closer together.

Thank you 'house handles'. Thy work hast been done.

Monday November 21st – Aqua Choc pitching day

Terrible night's sleep. Turquoise button returned, zapping me, Rita, Gunter, Heidi, jigsaw (which was now of a hamster eating pasta), and most of Zurich. Eventually Cardinal Wig-Wam Tommy appeared but just sat around reading the Highway Code booklet, without even firing any missiles. (Must have words with Miss Marsh when I get back.) Woke up incredibly nervous for my big Aqua Choc 'pitch' day.

But then things got worse . . .

When Gunter and I arrived at the offices of Buller und Bleicher Schockolade GmbH (never found out what that bit stood for by the way), Gunter just followed me straight into the building. I asked him where he was going, and he said 'to the meeting'. I then asked why, and he replied, 'For the translating purposes.'

There was nothing much I could say to that!

We sat in an orange waiting room for about 20 minutes (why is everything in Zurich orange?), before being led into Herr Buller's office. It was a very impressive room, with lots of confectionary awards on the walls and a life-size grandfather clock modelled entirely from chocolate (and a clock).

Then, Herr Buller – a fair-haired man in his 60s, with a surprising amount of freckles – entered, shook my hand, and exchanged 6 kisses with Gunter (i.e. 3 per person per every other cheek). Suddenly I was very nervous but I took a deep breath, said 'Go on Cooper,' (not out loud but in my head) and began to pitch.

I started well – outlining the glorious history of Aqua Choc (i.e. established April), and explaining its various health properties (i.e. water). Luckily Herr Buller spoke very good English, although this did mean that he had to keep re-translating things back into German for Gunter, who really did get in the way.

But then, Dear Diary, Gunter REALLY did get in the way . . .

Just as I was about to get to the important bit (i.e. getting Herr Buller to physically taste Aqua Choc), Gunter – unexpectedly and uninvitedly – took a bite out of one of my chocolate bars and suddenly had the worst choking fit I have ever seen. He went from white to yellow to orange (yes orange!), red, more red, redder still, burgundy and then, when he got to purple, Herr Buller was forced to get down and give him the 'kiss of life'.

There was nothing more to be said. The meeting was over. Everything was ruined.

Drove a semi-conscious Gunter back home in his car, while he (semi-consciously) directed, then dragged him up to his bed, and watched Heidi perform the kiss of life on him again (I think it was the kiss of life).

Later Heidi drove Rita and I to the airport, while Gunter nursed his throat at home. We then flew back to England in almost total silence, Rita wincing at her ankle twinges and me wincing at Gunter, Zurich, and life in general.

Oh woe . . .

Tuesday November 22nd

Rita took the day off work and spent most of the day hobbling between sofa and bed. I stayed mainly in the shed, hobbling between manure bag and floor. I don't think I've ever felt more disappointed in my life.

Tony popped round in the evening, and when I told him all about my disastrous meeting he literally exploded, and threw his six-pack of Pennyfeather's against the wall. He also called Gunter a 'bl**dy Zurich fool' and a 'shi**ing dumbface'.

Oh woe . . .

Woe, woe, woe . . .

Wednesday November 23rd

Telephoned Gunter tonight.

I was sort of dreading it, but I have to say that despite everything it was actually rather comforting to hear his (now rather hoarse) voice again.

Gunter apologized for the Aqua Choc incident (he was almost crying with sorrow) and also the accident with the jigsaw (which, by the way, Heidi has finished, apart from bits of Chile and Japan). Finally, Gunter invited us over again 'for a better times' next year. I thanked him, and said that Rita and I would definitely 'think about it'.

Thursday November 24th

Tony moved in again this morning. Back to his 'old room' as he calls it (i.e. Michael's). Found a couple of cans of ale under the bed. Must have words.

Rather annoyingly, Tony mentioned a new job at his work ('mashed potato supervisor') right in front of Rita this morning. When I told him that I 'didn't like the sound of it', Rita hissed at me (that's the second hissing I've had this year) and then marched (i.e. limped) out of the room.

Told Tony he should probably think about going back to Susan, but he pointed to the fresh bruise below his left eye and said, 'When this goes, I go.'

Unfortunately, it was quite a big bruise.

Friday November 25th

Promised Rita I would try a little harder in my job-searching (she told me to try 'a lot' harder), and so looked through the paper for jobs. Unfortunately, being Friday, it was 'Opportunities Within The Oil Industry' so, again, largely irrelevant.

No replies to my latest advert for driving lessons as yet. I do hope my offer of 'free travel toffees' hasn't put customers off. Times change I suppose – perhaps people don't chew and drive these days.

P.S. – Spoke to Michael this morning. Don't think he's been getting on too well with Simon lately. Apparently Simon's friend, Jeremy, has been in Sydney for the past two weeks and Simon has completely neglected his dancing practice.

Saturday November 26th

My first driving lesson with Miss Marsh after her driving test 'sabbatical'.

It was as if we'd gone back in time . . .

Miss Marsh's hair was all 'limp' again, her nose was all drippy, and she hardly said a word. Managed to get her in the driver's seat after much persuading (tissues and toffees), and then she drove particularly slowly (average speed: 12mph) before stalling in front of the fire station – during one of their emergencies.

Her new test is scheduled for December 15th.

Gulp!

Mother came over for dinner this evening, and Rita and I had a big row right in front of her. It began when I asked Rita – very politely – to fetch me some ketchup, to which she replied, 'What did your last servant die of?!' I told her that I knew times were hard at the moment, but that there was 'no need for that!' Rita then got up and shouted, 'I'm sick of working 8 hours a day for a man who spends his time stuffing his face with toffees and dreaming of becoming the next Leonardo da Vinci!'

Naturally she stormed (i.e. hobbled) out.

I sat there eating my second portion of roast potatoes for a while, and then Mother turned to me and said, 'She's right, you know'.

Why are women ALWAYS right?

Sunday November 27th

It's official.

We are back to margarine.

I see dark days ahead. Very dark days . . .

Monday November 28th

Tony's bruise went down sufficiently enough for him to go back home this morning. He cursed his 'self-repairing skin' as he left. House pretty quiet again.

Wednesday November 30th

I was right.

The dark days have arrived. The very dark days . . .

Rita and the 'Happy Scribblers' were calligraphizing in the living room tonight, putting the finishing touches to their Magna Carta ('copying-out') project.

After helping with coats, and the serverance of tea, I went up to the loft to 're-insulate the central partition slats', but unfortunately I forgot to close the hatch.

While I was approaching Binky and Alfredo with a handful of cake crumbs, Smithie, who was sitting on one of the beams above, suddenly – and without warning – dived straight at me. Luckily, I managed to move out of the way just in time, but unluckily Smithie flew straight through the open hatch, and right into the house.

I hurried down the ladder as fast as I could and spotted Smithie in the middle of the hallway, just feet away from the open living room door – and Rita.

Slowly, very slowly, I crept downstairs. Smithie didn't move. I reached the bottom, and cautiously removed a coat that was draped over the banister. Smithie still didn't move. Taking careful aim, I raised the coat above my head, took a deep breath, and threw it towards Smithie.

Smithie moved.

I missed.

Smithie let out an enormous squawk, and flew straight into the living room. At first there was silence, but then approximately 1.6 seconds later, there was utter non-silence . . .

Screams.

I rushed inside to find Smithie causing havoc. She flew into the mantelpiece, and smashed Rita's favourite vase, and then dive-bombed depressed/depressing Mary's head. I tried to free Smithie from Mary's hair, but she was all tangled up. Everyone was shrieking and running about. Rita was hysterical. It was chaos.

312

Eventually I freed Smithie, but she flew straight for the living room table, on which sat the precious Magna Carta manuscript.

Then everything went into slow motion . . .

Smithie crashed into the ink bottles, spilling them all over the paper, then grabbed the manuscript with her claws and flew around the room with it, squawking loudly. Finally, she perched at the top of the curtains and proceeded to rip the paper up into shreds with her beak.

Linda fainted. Rita slapped me in the face. Linda was revived (Charles Giles'/Giles Charles'/Giles Giles'/Charles Charles' snuff). Depressed/depressing Mary rubbed Savlon into her bleeding head, and then Linda slapped me in the face.

Eventually, I caught Smithie (I put her in the laundry basket) before being made to fetch Binky and Alfredo down from the loft and take them – and myself – off to the shed.

And that, Dear Diary, is where I am right now. In the shed. Rita has locked me out of the house, and so I have no choice but to 'bed down' for the night.

Oh alas . . .

Oh alas, alas . . .

December

Thursday December 1st

Very cold night last night. Almost froze to death. Had to sleep with the plastic table tennis cover over me, which couldn't have added any more than about 0.5 of a degree (Fahrenheit) heat. On top of that, Smithie and the birdlings, who are now on a shelf in a makeshift nest (plastic pot full of pencil shavings), kept shuffling about and tweeting noisily.

Woke up to find a small suitcase outside the shed door, with this letter attached:

Robin,
Last night was the final straw.
I have never been so embarrassed in all my life.
But what is worse, is that you lied to me. Again. How could you? After everything you said.
I really don't know what to do anymore.
I think it's best if you remain in your shed (after all, that's where you seem to be your happiest), until, well until whenever.
Perhaps now you will have a long hard think about what you have done.

Rita

P.S. Mary had to have three stitches in her head.

Inside the case were some of my clothes, my wash bag, my wallet, and a small framed photograph of Rita and I from our wedding. Oh predicamentus terribulum!

Tried to reason with Rita (by bellowing through the letterbox) but she sneaked out of the back and drove off to work without me even realizing.

Sat in shed for a bit thinking about what I was going to do. What would I eat? Where would I wash? Where would I toilet? Thought about going round to Mother's, but Cooper pride prevented me. Tony's was a possibility, but unfortunately Susan forbids guests – upon pain of bruising (to Tony).

In the end, Mr Alfonso from next door kindly said I could use his facilities in the mornings and evenings.

I'd never been inside a real-life headmaster's house before, but I must say it was as neat and tidy as I'd expected. Mr Alfonso even had a noticeboard up in his hallway, with a chart detailing Monty's feeding times. Noticed Monty had a piece of mackerel at 7:45 this morning, and was due salmon at 1:15. Lucky (wretched) cat.

Did my business and went back to shed. Then, in the evening, I went back to Mr Alfonso's and did my business again.

What an existence.

Friday December 2nd – Day 2 in shed

Tony gave me his spare set of keys to our house last night, but Rita had already changed the locks. She'd also got a man to fill in the hole in the loft, so the birds wouldn't try to fly back inside again. That woman is always thinking!

In the meantime, I've had to make a little opening in the shed wall so Smithie and the birdlings can come and go as they please. Unfortunately it's made the shed even colder. Today I woke up with a blue nose. In fact, it was almost navy!

Used Mr Alfonso's bathroom before he went off to school (Monty was having sardines), and when I came back to the shed I realized I needed to 'go' again. Went off to nettles in back of garden, and ended up stinging myself in quite an unfortunate place. Oh the indignity!

When Rita came home from work I tried to reason with her through the back window, but she just pulled the curtains shut. I really am in a pickle.

Speaking of pickles, here is my list of food and drink items I currently have in the shed:

Pickles
2 × bags of carrots
4 × apples
Block of Cheddar
Block of Emmenthal (not as nice as Gunter's though, and I never know if you can eat the rind)
Block of Brie
1 × bag walnuts
2 × bags peanuts
Bottle of tomato ketchup (a must!)
Turkey slices (× 10)
Chicken slices (× 16)
Beef slices (× 16)
Sausages (× 24)
Gravy powder
Cereals
1 × loaf of bread
4 × bottles of water
Crackers (as 'treats' for Smithie and co.)
2 × tubs of butter (I keep them outside to remain fresh)
1 × onion (don't really know why I bought this)
1 × sprig of parsley (ditto)
2 × sponge cakes
1 × chocolate cake

½ dozen eggs (NB – hide from Smithie and co. due to feelings)
Tea bags
Carton of milk
4 × bags of toffees
Saffron ('impulse' buy)

I do hope this paltry larder will last me the weekend.

Saturday December 3rd – Day 3 in shed

Had a visit from Mother today. She brought along a flask of meatballs for my dinner. I was very pleased to see her (and the meatballs).

Mother suggested that I should stay with her for a while, but I told her I was worried that Rita might forget all about me if I moved away from the shed. Think Mother understood. Anyway, she didn't stay for too long as she got a bit frightened when Smithie looked like she was going to 'dive-bomb' again, but did say she'd visit again soon. Felt quite sad when she left.

After that, gave Miss Marsh a driving lesson. She seemed a little better since last week (noticed a few hair buns on left side of head), and said that she was 'determined to pass' this time. Tissue consumption down to just 5 t/ph, so fingers crossed . . .

Came home, sat on back step feeling rotten for about twenty minutes, and then when it started to rain went over to Mr Alfonso's for a wee.

Oh meatballs of mine,
That I eat from this flask,
Is it too much to beg,
Is it too much to ask?

To somehow convince,
My wife, Rita Cooper,
To take me back home,
Oh that would be super!

320

Sunday December 4th – Day 4 in shed

Tony has moved in.

I repeat. Tony has moved in.

To the shed.

Apparently his 'British Steel' argument with Susan had been intensifying for weeks, culminating in a massive shouting (and throwing) match during which Tony received two direct hits from a metal spoon and one indirect hit (rebounded off radiator) from a very large baked potato.

Tony was in a terrible state, Pennyfeather's-wise. Tried to tell him it was impossible for both of us to stay in the shed, but he wouldn't listen. He didn't even seem to care that his former nemesis, Smithie, was perched just 18 inches above his head with two other potential nemeses.

Instead, he finished off his can, chucked it behind the table tennis table, threw off his shoes, and lay face down on the floor. He was out cold within 5 seconds!

Tony is now snoring like a bus. How on earth am I going to sleep tonight?

Monday December 5th – Day 5 in shed

In answer to my previous question (i.e. 'How on earth am I going to sleep tonight?'), the answer is: 'You won't' (i.e. I didn't).

Not only did Tony snore, he also talked in his sleep. At one point I could have sworn I heard him say, 'I'm at the rabbit festival' (although it may have been 'Aim at the Abbot Percival'). Had to keep prodding him, but nothing seemed to work.

Breakfasted on kettle eggs (what a marvellous invention!), while Tony had his trademark cup of tea and cup of coffee. Birds had a few crumbs of sponge cake, plus a nibble of parsley.

Since Tony seemed bent on staying for the immediate future (and with Mr Alfonso now away on a school skiing trip for 2 weeks), we were presented with a major problem: where would we wash/toilet?

Places we discussed using:

1) Mr Alfonso's: Tony suggested we just 'broke in'.
2) Mother's: Never! (Cooper pride etc.)
3) Tony's mother's: Tony said he was sure she would oblige, but unfortunately she lives 200 miles away.
4) A skip: Tony's suggestion – which I ignored.
5) Mr Singh's newsagent's: probably doesn't have a bath or shower, being a newsagent's.
6) The washrooms at the pub: I would never lower myself to do such a thing!

What we agreed on using:

1) Our bathroom: the bit of the garden behind the shed.
2) Our shower: garden hose.
3) Our washbasin: wheelbarrow.
4) Our toilet: latrine in back of garden (which we will have to dig)

Neither of us could quite face taking a cold shower, or digging a latrine straight away, so instead we washed with the old kettle water, and then took turns amongst the stinging nettles. (Tony stung himself in the same unfortunate place as me!)

Tony then went off to work (what a professional!) and when he came back, we just sat around doing very little. Cooked a few turkey slices in the kettle, while Tony sang some of his 'blue' songs (until Smithie 'dive-bombed' again), then put plaster on Tony's eye and went to bed.

He's snoring again.

Tuesday December 6th – Day 6 in shed

Dug the latrine today.

I really don't think I need to say any more.

Wednesday December 7th – Day 7 in shed

Tony threw one of his 'sickies' this morning. He told his boss that he had inflammation of the 'clanartis gland' and that he'd probably be off all week. I didn't approve.

Think Tony's actually enjoying being in the shed. Wish I felt the same. It's cold, damp, and uncomfortable. There's barely enough room for both of us to sit in there, let alone sleep (which we do wedged together on the floor). To make things worse, when Tony's not snoring (or muttering about rabbits/abbots), he's hogging all the pillow (bag of manure).

Went into town this afternoon to get some supplies. Christmas decorations up everywhere. Lots of couples shopping. Felt a little lonely. Also, I can't be sure but I think people were crossing the road when we walked towards them.

Anyway, Tony bought 20 cans of Pennyfeather's (he really is planning a long stay), while I stocked up on essentials (biscuits, cakes, parsley etc.).

By the way, I think the shed is beginning to pong a little.

Thursday December 8th – Day 8 in shed

Day 8 in shed! Day 8!

Well, that's it . . .

If Rita won't let me back in again, then it's really not my fault any more. I have tried my hardest to speak to her. I've phoned her. I've written her notes. I've banged on the windows. Yesterday, I even decorated a hard-boiled egg with love-hearts

323

(drawn in gravy), as a symbol of my affection, but it was still sitting on our front doorstep this morning. Think Monty had taken a little bite out of it.

I've given up trying. There's simply no point. From now on I am going to follow my good friend, Tony Sutton's advice, and play 'hard to get'. If it works for the ladies, then I'm sure it'll work for me.

Had half a can of Pennyfeather's tonight, and do you know what, Dear Diary?

It tasted great!

Friday December 9th – Day 9 in shed

Haven't had a proper wash for 5 days now. Haven't shaved either. I now have a bit of a beard, which, when I looked at myself in the mirror, is full of bits. The funny thing is, I don't really care!

Tony doesn't seem bothered either, but then again he's never really been one for personal hygiene. He's still 'off sick' by the way ('clanartis gland'), and seems to be having the time of his life. To be honest, I feel quite happy too. So what if Rita doesn't take me back? I've got my shed, I've got my Smithie, and I've got my (well, not really my) Tony.

By the way, we've finally got a bit of heating for the shed: Tony bought a paraffin heater today. Don't know where he got it from but he assured me it was the 'latest model', although it didn't look very 'latest' to me. Actually, I do hope it's OK.

Our 'new' Paraffin Heater:

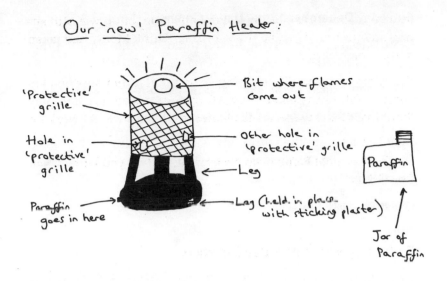

'Protective' grille → [diagram]

Hole in 'protective' grille →

Paraffin goes in here →

← Bit where flames come out

← Other hole in 'protective' grille

← Leg

← Leg (held in place with sticking plaster)

Paraffin

Jar of Paraffin

Anyway, dined on kettle turkey slices, then had a couple of cans of Pennyfeather's (it's definitely growing on me). Afterwards, Tony and I sat in front of the paraffin heater, singing a few songs. We even made one up:

> *We are the men,*
> *We are the men,*
> *The men in the shed,*
> *The men in the shed!*
>
> *We live in the shed,*
> *We live in the shed.*
> *We are the men.*
> *In the bl**dy shed!*

I think we sang this about 50 times! Even Smithie and co. seemed to sing (i.e. tweet) along.

Roll on the good times!

Saturday December 10th – Day 10 in shed

Gave Miss Marsh a driving lesson today. She commented that she could smell 'dung'.

Then came back to the shed for some super, terrific, great times . . .

It was Tony's birthday today. Happy birthday Tony Sutton!

Spent practically the entire day eating, drinking and singing. Sang our funny 'shed song' about 100 times today. It just gets funnier and funnier!

Am now particularly be-tipsied.

But . . .

Life is great!

I am great!

Tony is great! We're ALL great!

Hoorah for greatness!!!!!!!!!!!!!!!!!!!!!!!!!!

Hoorah for Pennyfeather's!!!

P.S. – Rita has just shouted at us through the back window to 'shut up!'

So, she's finally spoken to me. My 'playing hard to get' plan is working . . .!

P.P.S. – HOORAH AGAIN!!!

Sunday December 11th – Day 11 in shed

Woke up with the worst headache I have ever had in my life. I'm sure there were men in my head doing some drilling.

Not sure Smithie, Binky and Alfredo were feeling too good either (think I overdid the parsley), as they'd left quite a lot of 'bird deposit' all over Tony's face in the night. Spent about 15 minutes cleaning him up with a damp cloth. Bird stains can be very stubborn indeed.

Joined Tony in his trademark cup of tea and coffee 'hangover cure', although it only made my head feel more confused. Tried a quick 'shower' with the garden hose, but nearly froze to death. Had to sit under a blanket by the paraffin heater (which now leaks by the way), and shivered myself back to warmth.

There must be more to life than this.

Thought about ringing Rita's doorbell, but decided against it. Saw Linda's car outside. Wonder what they were saying about me? Perhaps they weren't saying anything about me? Perhaps everyone's forgotten about me already.

Went into town – alone – for a walk. People were definitely crossing the road. It wasn't a nice feeling. Even Old Milly looked shocked when she saw me, so I sat down on her bench and told her all about my row with Rita, the shed, and my general woeful predicament. When I'd finished, Old Milly looked at me and said, 'Robin, I'm sure your wife really loves you, but if you ever change your mind, you could always come and live with me on my bench.'

She then gave me a little kiss on the cheek – and do you know what? I gave her one back!

Yes, Dear Diary, I, Robin Cooper, have kissed a trampette! (Her cheek tasted a bit like an onion.)

Monday December 12th – Day 12 in shed

Old Milly has moved in.

I repeat. Old Milly has moved in.

To the shed.

This evening at about 7:00, while Tony and I were gorging on kettle sausages, the shed door suddenly burst open, and Old Milly – who was as drunk as a Lordess – came a-bundling in.

Tony was not very happy. Neither was I. Nor were the birds (v. odour-sensitive). We tried protesting, but we couldn't push her out really: it was bitterly cold outside, plus she was just too heavy.

Old Milly soon got comfortable (several cans of Tony's Pennyfeather's) and even described the shed as a 'palace'. She also commented on the wonderful 'toilet facilities' (i.e. the latrine). Strangely I felt rather proud.

Spent the evening listening to Old Milly's tales of the road (she once walked all the way from Chichester to Glasgow just to punch her sister), watching her eat (she took her ketchup straight from the bottle) and then Tony and I taught her our shed song, which we all sang until the early hours.

Am now bedding down for the night, squashed in between Tony and Old Milly. Really am exhausted, but am also sort of dreading going to sleep.

P.S. – Shed definitely pongs.

Tuesday December 13th – Day 13 in shed

Hardly slept at all! Had Old Milly and Tony snoring and muttering in my ears all night long. Tony was back to his rabbits/abbots again, while Old Milly just kept repeating the phrase 'them belts, them belts', and then laughing very loudly. Also think she might have tried to kiss me in the night, as my face definitely smells of onions.

When Tony woke up this morning he said he was 'really missing Susan' (although I noticed he only said this when he realized Old Milly had finished off all his Pennyfeather's). Anyway, he packed his bag (and swiped half of my chocolate cake) then said goodbye, leaving me all alone with Old Milly.

Thanks a lot Anthony Lewis Sutton!

Sat for a while thinking about my predicament. And what a predicament . . .

There I was, lying on the floor in nothing but my pyjamas, while a strange female lady lay snoring beside me. I was effectively 'living in sin' . . .

Oh, Dear Diary, how did it all come to this? How could I win my Rita back? And what if I didn't? Would I be spending Christmas all alone in the shed? Or would it be me and Old Milly sitting there eating nothing but turkey slices straight out of the kettle?

Depressed myself to sleep for a couple of hours, before I was woken by a knock at the door. It was Mother.

'Oh I didn't know you had – company' she said, seeing Old Milly stretched out on her back.

I tried to explain.

'I can see it's not the best time,' she said, 'but I've just come to wish you a happy anniversary.'

Oh alas . . .

I'd completely forgotten.

In all our years of marriage, I have NEVER, EVER forgotten our anniversary.

Banged on front door, and apologized loudly through the letterbox, but Rita shouted back at the top of her voice – 'I don't want to know any more! That's the last straw!'

I tried to reason with her, but Rita replied – in the severest of tones – 'Why don't you go back to your girlfriend?!'

I told her I didn't know what she meant, and she said, 'I saw that bag lady letting herself in last night! How could you?!'

Finally, she opened the door and, with her eyes streaming, looked at me and said, 'I have decided that I don't want you living in the garden any more, Robin. Tomorrow, you move out completely.'

Rita slowly shut the door.

I stood there all alone for a while, then went back to the shed. Old Milly had gone.

And so as I sit here, shivering in front of a rickety old paraffin heater, with nothing but this diary, and a plastic pot of birds for company, I really have to face up to facts . . .

For the first time in 24 years, my marriage to the love of my life, the petal of my blossom, the pearl of my wisdom – my darling Rita Cooper – may well and truly be over.

Sunday December 18th

I write these words with an a-trembling hand.

There was a fire.

A terrible fire.

Monday December 19th

It is no exaggeration to say that were it not for my brave lady wife, Rita, then I, Robin Cooper, would have physically perished for ever and ever.

From what I can recall, I woke up on Tuesday morning to find huge flames (of fire) all around me and Rita dragging me out of the shed, while I scrabbled to save my precious diary.

The next thing I remember was coming to in a light-green room, and gazing up at the face of a nurse – a lady nurse – with a moustache.

I spent the following two days in hospital, recovering from shock and smoke inhalation (although I did have to eat a lot of ice cream for my throat, which was nice), and then returned home – yes, HOME – to my safe, warm bed.

Here at Cooper mansions, I'm relieved to say, the bickerings, argumentations and wars of silence have been replaced by love, affection, and soup. Yes, Dear Diary, this horrendous (un)natural disaster seems to have brought Rita and I closer than ever before, and only this morning she gave me a quattro do-decimalium of kisses (i.e. 24) on the forehead.

To think – I could have lost my darling Rita forever.

I have also received several 'Get Well Soon' cards from various get-well-soon-wishers:

1) Miss Marsh – card featured a picture of a rose 'crying'. (Rita kept quiet about the 3 Xs she'd put inside). Miss Marsh also added that she'd failed her second driving test ('because I was sick on the man').
2) Mother – enclosed a cheque for £10. (I think she thought it was my birthday again.)
3) Mr Singh – I don't know how he knew, but he wrote 'I will give you a free newspaper and a packet of crisps the next time you come in.'
4) Mr Alfonso – sent me a card from his hospital bed (he'd skied into a lake).
5) Old Milly – a torn piece of cardboard, with the words 'Thank you Robin' written in lipstick (plus a few twigs left in the envelope). Rita put it in the bin.
6) A card from someone called 'Don Mapesbury' sending 'best wishes', which was very thoughtful, except I've never heard of him!
7) Tony – wrote the words, 'Sorry about the paraffin heater, mate' – as a 'P.S.'.

Tomorrow I am finally allowed to get out of my bed (I've been in it for exactly 92 hours). But what will confront me when I step into the garden and survey the damage to my beloved shed? And what o' what has happened to dear Smithie, Binky and Alfredo . . .?

I fear the worst.

Tuesday December 20th

My beloved shed is now a blackened ash-ridden wreck. It has been reduced to mere carbon.

Oh shed of beauty, shed of dreams.

Rita and I solemnly picked through the wreckage, but the only surviving items that we could find were:

1) 3 × scythes
2) Spare hammer head (not of shark but of hammer)
3) Box of Feisil Powder (why didn't it burn? Just what is it?)
4) Trowel
5) 6 × empty cans of Pennyfeather's (NB: no need to talk to Tony)
6) Nail scissors
7) 1 × Pruning glove (i.e. only 1, as in not 1 pair but 1 glove)
8) 3 × marbles (they really are quite indestructible)
9) Tony's wretched paraffin heater

I then searched desperately for my little friends, Smithie, Binky and Alfredo, but when I came across their plastic pot, now melted down to the size of a thimble, I knew that I'd lost them forever.

It was a tragedy.

And so, hand in hand with Rita, I said a few quiet words for my fallen companions, and my fallen shed, and then walked slowly and forlornly back into the house.

Life, Dear Diary, will never be the same again.

Wednesday December 21st

Spent the day in mourning. Wore dark clothes – black shoes, navy socks (black ones burnt), black jumper, and dark white shirt. Sat in chair a lot, and didn't smile much.

As a further mark of respect, I forfeited various food items I would normally enjoy, i.e. toast, butter, jam, potatoes, chicken, eggs, ice cream etc., and instead got by on just a couple of buns, some cheese, a few sausages, a bit of lamb, some 'oven chips', and a packet of mini rolls.

I'm sure it's what Smithie, Binky and Alfredo (R.I.P.) would have wanted.

Thursday December 22nd

Tony threw another 'sickie' today (further complications with his 'clanartis gland') and came round to help me clear up the mess in the garden. He told me that everything between him and Susan was now 'back as it had been', although I wasn't too sure if he meant this as a good thing or a bad thing. I didn't ask either.

Afterwards we sat in the kitchen and had a couple of butter sandwiches (Rita bought butter again, as a 'get-well treat'). Tony said that it felt strange not being in the shed, and that he didn't feel it was 'quite right' to drink his Pennyfeather's inside the house (although I'm pretty sure I heard him opening a can in the bathroom a few minutes later).

In the evening, Rita and I put up a few Christmas decorations (tinsel along wainscoting, baubles on doorknobs etc.), then did a bumper crossword together.

Unfortunately, one of the clues was 'small freestanding garden structure' (4).

Went to bed early.

Friday December 23rd

Did some Christmas shopping this morning.

Presents purchased:

1) RITA:
   a) Mug emblazoned with the slogan 'World's Best Wife' (it's true – she is!)
   b) Roll of special calligrapher's vellum parchment paper (for next 'copying-out' project: the American Declaration of Independence document)
   c) Hairspray (she'd run out)
   d) Tub of cold cream (she'd also run out)
   e) 'Pineapple' earrings (not real pineapples, but earrings shaped like pineapples)
   f) 'Apricot earrings' (as above but with the word 'apricot' used instead of 'pineapple')
   g) Scarf with sparkly umbrella pattern

2) MOTHER:
   a) A voucher, which I made out of coloured paper, offering 'Free Driving Lessons from Mr Robin Cooper'
   b) Driving gloves
   c) Copy of Highway Code (large print)

3) TONY:
   a) Nothing!

4) MICHAEL
   a) A book all about the football player Gary Lineker (Couldn't find the one he asked for on 'Wayne Sleep', so hope this will do)

5) OLD MILLY (shhh! It's a secret!):
   a) A new tube of lipstick

Saturday December 24th – pre-Christmas Day/ Christmas Eve

Helped Rita with the preparements for tomorrow's Christmas lunch. We've invited Mother, as well as Linda and Ian (who I do hope are talking to me now). Laid the table, hoovered the house (I hate hoovering the house) and then dusted the curtains (just what is the point?).

Also bought a box of Christmas crackers, but (secretly) swapped the jokes inside for ones that I'd specially written. My jokes:

Joke no. 1:

What did the leopard say to the man with measles?
– 'You're lucky – at least you can change your spots!' (i.e. when the man recovers from his illness)

Joke no. 2:

What did the bolt of electricity say to the Queen?
– 'I'm sorry ma'am, but I'm in charge!'

Joke no. 3 (to be read after the last one):

What did the Queen then say to the bolt of electricity?
– 'Well, I charge you with treason!'

Joke no. 4 (to be read after that):

What did the bolt of electricity reply (to the joke before?)
– 'Oh no – I hope I don't get the electric chair!'

Joke no. 5:

What is glass made from?
– Sand, mainly.

NB – Joke no. 5 is more of a fact really, as I couldn't think of any more jokes.

I wish myself (Christmas) luck!

Sunday December 25th – Christmas Day

We wish you a merry Christmas,
We wish you a merry Christmas,
We wish you a merry Christmas,
And a Happy New Year!

Good tidying we bring (never understood that line),
For you and your friends,
We wish you a merry Christmas,
And a Happy New Year!!!!!!!!!!!!!!!!

Hoorah!!!!!

First of all, the most important thing – the presents:

From Rita:

a) 2 black socks (i.e. 1 × pair – to replace ones destroyed in fire)
b) Bumper book of crosswords (hooorah!)
c) New typewriter (had to promise I would only write a few letters next year)
d) A tangerine (family tradition)
e) A plum (also family tradition)
f) 3 × pairs of pants (stripy, but not a family tradition)
g) A quintin of kisses (i.e. 5!)
h) Best present of all . . . a brand new DIARY! Hoorah! Oh whatever lies in wait next year . . .?

Think Rita was pleased with what I got her, although she did say that the hairspray and the tube of cold cream felt a little like 'general household items'. Lucky I'd stopped myself from getting her that three-pack of bleach!

Linda and Ian were noticeably 'frosty' towards me at first, but after a few sherries all the 'ice' seemed to have broken (it's a shame it wasn't a white Christmas, Dear Diary, as I could have continued this fantastic theme of frozen water!).

Mother, however, was on excellent form, and graciously accepted my offer of driving lessons. Hoorah!

Other presents:

a) Video from Linda and Ian entitled 'The Possibilities of Taurus' (we don't have a video recorder)
b) Cheque from Mother for £8 (don't know why it didn't go up to £10 like my birthday cheque, but didn't say anything)

Unfortunately, my Christmas jokes didn't go down too well, as I think I'd laid the crackers out in the wrong order. Linda started by reading out my factual 'non-joke' about glass, which seemed to throw everyone a bit, and then Mother did my third joke about the bolt of electricity, which didn't make much sense without hearing the other two first. In the end, Rita made me fish the original jokes out of the bin.

Luckily, lunch was delicious. The turkey was perfect (not too dry, not too moist), and with heaps of roast potatoes (I had 10!). I also ate 9 Brussels sprouts, about 60 peas, lots of stuffing, 6 parsnips, and 14 mini sausages.

After lunch (oh – and Christmas pudding – 3 helpings), we watched the Queen's speech on television. Her Majesty was in yellow this year, and Mother nodded in agreement with everything she said. Then Ian and I played Orag, while Mother, Linda and Rita talked about handbags.

Fell asleep on couch for about an hour, then after dinner spoke to Michael on the phone. Must say he sounded a lot chirpier (he wished me a 'fab Christmas'!), although he did say that Simon was a bit upset as his friend, Jeremy, had just flown back to England. Anyway, Michael had bought him a bracelet to cheer him up, and apparently they were now dancing together again.

Fingers crossed – Michael is coming home next year. Rita and I already can't wait! I wonder if he's changed . . .?

Finished the evening watching Mother do the foxtrot, and then, when Ian sat on Rita's glasses, I helped Linda pick out the pieces of glass from his bottom.

And it was while I was applying the tweezers to his behind that I suddenly realized just how differently things could have turned out . . .

If it wasn't for Rita coming to my rescue on that fateful morning in the shed, I may never have seen Ian's bottom, or for that matter, any other bottom ever again.

Merry Christmas everyone!

Monday December 26th – post-Christmas Day/Boxing Day

Spent most of the day eating cold bits of turkey, and doing crosswords with Rita. I must say, turkey and word games do seem to go very well together. Perhaps it's something to do with the white meat and the white paper.

In the evening Tony called to wish us both a merry Christmas. He sounded rather merry! Anyway, he's invited us see a pantomime – 'Jack and the Beanstalk' – tomorrow night.

And guess what – Susan is coming too!

Tuesday December 27th – we go to a (Christmas) pantomime

After 5 years, Rita and I finally met Susan Sutton. And my, how things haven't changed . . .

She was just as how we remembered her: pink shoes, pink stockings, pink skirt, pink jumper, pink lipstick, pink face, but not particularly 'pink' mood (i.e. friendly).

But how things HAVE changed . . .

Tony and Susan couldn't keep their hands off each other during the pantomime!

To be honest, it didn't bother me that much, but I was worried that they were missing all the major plot points (Jack gets beans, growth of beanstalk, appearance of ogre etc.).

Anyway, when the show finished, Rita and I offered to take them both out for a meal, but Tony replied, 'Thank you but we really need to get back, for, well, you know . . .'

I tell you, Dear Diary, I didn't know where to look!

Thursday December 29th

If Christmas be the season of good tidings, then I received a very good tiding (as opposed to a very good 'hiding'!) today. In fact, I received two very good tidings:

(Very good) Tiding Number 1:

I was pouring myself a couple of bowls of cornflakes for break-fast, when I suddenly heard a very familiar 'squawk' coming from the garden. I got up and rushed to the window, and there, perched on our fence, staring – and squawking – right back at me were Smithie, Binky and Alfredo.

They were alive! They were physically alive!

It was a miracle! A miracle of wings, beaks, and squawks!

Even Rita agreed it was a miracle, although she did make me promise never to bring the birds back into the house again. (I sort of promised.) And then . . .

(Very good) Tiding Number 2:

Buller & Bleicher Schokolade GmbH
Lepziger Strasse 12
CH-8021
Zürich
Switzerland

December, ²¹th

Mr Robin Cooper
Brondesbury Villas
London
UNITED KINGDOM

Dear Mr Cooper,

Thank you very much for meeting with me on Monday November the 20th at 10:00.

I enjoyed discussing the product <<Aqua Choc>> with you, and was sorry that our meeting ended in such a manner. However I was content to hear that Herr Gunter Schwartz is now back in good health.

You may be interested to know, Mr Cooper, that I had the opportunity to try <<Aqua Choc>> after the meeting, and I liked it very much. I also revealed it to my work colleagues here in Buller & Bleicher Schockolade GmbH, and it met with great success. In fact, we were in agreement that it is a very individual and exciting product.

We would therefore like to discuss with you ways in developing <<Aqua Choc>> for the production in Switzerland, and with the possibility of international sales. We would also like to tell you some of our own ideas, for example, what we could do in the middle of the chocolate bar, and also regarding the general safety when eating.

The offices will now be closed until Friday, January the 6th of the next year, but I then look forward to speaking to you, and making <<Aqua Choc>> a great business success.

Have a wonderful Christmas festival and a healthy new year.

Yours sincerely,

Herr Ralf Buller
Direktor, Buller & Bleicher Schokolade GmbH

As soon as I'd read the letter (see above) I popped open a bottle of champagne (well, fizzy wine), and then Rita and I celebrated by dancing all around the house, until Rita got one of her ankle 'twinges' and we had to stop.

Surely now, the following rhyme (which I'm just about to invent) must be true . . .

Fame and fortune are but a certainty,
And we shall have butter for all eternity!

Hoorah!

Or as they say in German . . .

Oh, my German dictionary was destroyed in the fire.

Well, anyway, hoorah again!

HOORAH!!!!!!!!!!!!!!!!!!!!!!!!!!!!!!!

P.S. – One bit of bad news – our talking toilet is back. Have just flushed it, and could have sworn it called me a 'slovenly sloth'.

Friday December 30th

Tony let himself in extremely early this morning. He was sporting a fresh bruise just above his left eye. As we passed in the hallway he nodded at me, pointed to his forehead, muttered the words 'serving spoon', and then went straight into Michael's bedroom.

Poor Tony.

Had a look through my new diary this afternoon. I have to say, it was most exciting seeing all those blank pages, just waiting to be filled in. I wonder what will end up in it (apart from words of course).

Later, while Rita did a special Christmas dot-to-dot ('Santa's Dotto Grotto') in the living room, I looked back at my old list of

New Year's resolutions, to see just how well I've fared this year . . .

How well have I fared this year re: Robin Cooper's (Official) 10 New Year's resolutions:

1. **Start writing a diary** – Well, I've done 364/365ths of it so far – so not bad going!
2. **Stop writing so many letters** – Ditto (apart from the bit about the 364/365ths).
3. **Become a world-renowned (or at least locally-renowned) inventor** – Due to Aqua Choc, this is now a certainty. I award myself one point!
4. **Learn to whistle** – I'm sure I struck this one off the list last time.
5. **Tidy up shed** – I don't think I need to say anything here (although I am DEFINITELY going to buy a new shed next year, and I've already seen the model I want: the Heskith 124 Flat-Top. Hoorah!).
6. **Cut down on toffees (the eating of)** – This was just too difficult.
7. **Visit Mother more** – A record year for visits!
8. **Get Tony to stop using my shed as a drinking den (NB: URGENT)** – See point 5.
9. **Rectify employment situation** – Make way for Herr Cooper, co-director of Cooper, Sutton, Buller und Bleicher Schockolade GmbH! (Must find out what that last bit means.)
10. **Sort out Rita's wretched ankle problem FOR ONCE AND FOR ALL!** – This, I swear, will happen next year!

So – after eliminating points 4, 5, and 8 (due to general irrelevancies) – my final score this year comes to a total of 5 and 364/365ths out of 7.

In other words, I got 85.68% – out of a grand total of 100%.

Well done Cooper! Well done I!

Saturday December 31st

Landsberger Strasse 60
CH-8006
Zürich
SWITZERLAND

Sunday the December ^{25}st

My dear friendly Robin,

At first can I be wishing you a very fantastik Christmas festival to you and your Rita.

Once again it was so wonderful to be seeing you in Zürich but I am must to be apologizing for my eating error of your new chockolat in the meeting. I am sorries.

I am thinking you may remember the problem we had with the house handles. Do not be sad but now I have to tell you that we are having a new problem with the water lumpen.

My dear Robin, the water lumpen has been making our lifes in such difficults, that we are not in the happy. Yesterday we have even to be in the long room with the Spritzengemeiner.

Heidi thinks that the water lumpen may be tempory (short time) although she has a great problem in the bending in order to reach it. I am also having the problem, mainly with the Ubersprochen (is this a word in England?) but then again we would not no otherwise.

My dear Robin, I am sorry to be writing such troubles but I am sure you are understanding of the major difficultys with the water lumpen.

I send you my regardments and also does Heidi, and we are wishing you a happy and helpful new year.

Your ever friendly,

Gunter Schwartz

Günter

SP – Heidi is beginning a new jigsaw with the wine berries.

Hark! A new Swiss German enigma for us to unravel!

So, Rita and I wrote out the following list on the easy-wipe message board on the fridge.

Water lumpen (might be):

1) Water on the knee (?)
2) A hamster-related infection?
3) A condition that makes bending down to reach things impossible (back literally stuck to wall?)
4) A problem with Gunter's ***** (Rita didn't want to write any of this word down, just in case guests wandered into the kitchen)
5) Something that only affects Swiss Germans and no one else in the world

We think it's probably number 5, although Tony (who reluctantly went back home this afternoon) suggested it might be:

6) Water with lumps in.

Finally, with the house to ourselves again, Rita and I spent a lovely, quiet evening together on the sofa, sipping our fizzy wine and eating chocolates (Rita ate 2½, I ate 9½). Then, at midnight, we listened to the chimes of Big Ben on the radio, heralding the end of this year and the start of the new one.

Who knows what the next 12 months will have in store for the Coopers, but I have a feeling – just a feeling – that there are some very great things to come. Very, VERY great things.

And so, Dear Diary, as I sign off this final entry, I leave you with these four special words . . .

I wish myself luck!

Acknowledgements

Hearty thanks to the following (people) for all their help:

My parents, Jonny, Simon Trewin, Tom Bromley, Antonia Hodgson, Peter and Sarah (and 'Hebbo' little Sam), Caroline Hogg, Alex Morris, Sean Garrehy, Susan Moorse, Jeremy Dyson (thanks for the chat), Nira Park, Karen Beever and all at Big Talk (thanks for my little dwelling), and everyone at Momentum (thanks for the stamps and use of stapler).